Beloved Dissident

Laurel West

Beloved Dissident

Laurel West

LEDERER

Messianic Jewish Publishers
a division of
Lederer/Messianic Jewish Communications
Baltimore, Maryland

All characters in this book are fictitious, and any resemblances
to persons living or dead is purely coincidental.

05 04 03 02 01 00 99   7 6 5 4 3 2 1

ISBN 1-880226-76-6

Library of Congress Catalog Card Number: 99-70370

Messianic Jewish Publishers
a division of
Lederer/Messianic Jewish Communications
6204 Park Heights Avenue
Baltimore, Maryland 21215
(410) 358-6471

Distributed by
Lederer/Messianic Jewish Resources International
order line: (800) 410-7367
e-mail: MessJewCom@aol.com
Internet: http://www.MessianicJewish.net

Prologue

THE FIRELIGHT INTENSIFIED THE GLEAM in her short auburn hair, as they sat, face to face, on the floor in front of the couch. David's heart ached with longing, and he hated himself for it—especially now, after she had assaulted everything he believed in, betrayed their common heritage, and declared her love for another man. If only she wouldn't look at him that way, her sleepy green eyes a mockery of innocence.

He turned away, staring blankly into the flickering fire. How had it come to this? How was it possible, in less than six months, that he, a son of Israel who from his youth had studied the Scriptures and worshiped the God of his fathers, had become so enamored of this one who took so lightly the teachings of *Adonai*? If only he had kept their relationship on a professional level—as she, apparently, had succeeded in doing—the way it had begun. If only he hadn't given himself over to his dreams of her, hadn't gazed once too often into her soft, caring eyes, or read into her compassionate words a message of love that wasn't there...

Even now, although he knew better, he allowed his gaze to follow his heart, only to discover that Leah—this hard-won ally who now knew more about him than anyone else in the world—had fallen asleep, her head resting against the seat cushion of the couch. How dare she look so peaceful, he wondered, when she had just blown apart his very life? Gently, he lifted her and carried her to bed, determined to leave her there and to maintain his honor, even in this isolated cabin where the unexpected spring storm had stranded them for the night.

Honor. He almost laughed out loud at the thought. Where did this enigma of a woman stand on that?

As he drew the covers to her shoulders, he steeled himself against the warring waves of desire, hostility, and disappointment that coursed through him. Resolutely closing the bedroom door behind him, he returned to his spot on the floor in front of the fire. The realization that, even after her confession of betrayal, he loved her all the more, confused and angered him almost as much as her twisted interpretations from the sacred Book. Would he ever understand who she was—and if he did, would it change anything between them?

Chapter 1

"Nice? You call that nice? You said the same thing about Byron the *bore*."

Leah put down the pen and leaned against the straight back of her chair. Andy was standing at mid-room, her mouth still open, her sandy hair dripping rain over solid shoulders jacketed in red. "A doorway encounter changes my entire concept of man," she continued, "and you think he's...nice."

Leah envisioned Jonathan, probably just now getting back into his car. "He doesn't know I'm Jewish."

Andy stared. "Oh, right. With your family, worry." She unbuttoned the windbreaker and took it off.

"Andrea, I've been hurt before." And not just once, she thought. "If he calls, I'll tell him."

"*Leah Rachelle Beaumont*," Andy articulated airily with a not too bad French accent, "you inspire me."

How long had Andy known her, Leah thought. Eight months? Ten? They had lived in this apartment together all of September and for four months last spring, and still Andy did not comprehend what it meant to be Jewish, that it was in the blood and in the brain and in the bone. She could not allow a relationship to develop with any man without his understanding that. Besides, she was reminded twice a week from home that there were good reasons to wait, as Mama put it, for "the right Jewish boy." How many times did she have to explain it?

"There is one thing about you that isn't 150 percent honest, Beaumont," Andy groused. "Make that two—your name *and* your nose." She laid the jacket like a fan over the foot-end corner of her bed, and Leah saw mischief in the curve of her mouth.

Let it alone, Leah thought. She made a face at Andy, rose to look into the mirror above her dresser and frowned. The glow of summer, long days of working the Saddlebreds for Aunt Claire and Uncle Paddy, had become her complexion. She ran her fingertips through her casual "breezy" cut. The wavy auburn hair was close to blonde now, the eyes all the lighter for her tan. The preacher's son today had asked if she was named for the Leah of the Bible, and she had said it was not the first thing she told people. He understood—not just that, in conversation, she would avoid immediate reference to religious matters, but also that Leah of Haran had not been Jacob's first choice, or his selection at all, for he had fallen in love with her younger sister, Rachel. Although he was tricked into marrying both, and they and their maidservants mothered the twelve tribes of Israel, Rachel forever remained his true love. Leah could still see Jonathan's face as he looked at her and said he believed that delicate eyes were not the flaw but the forte of Jacob's Leah and that, emerald as her own were, he could look into them all day. "'For Leah was tender-eyed,'" he quoted as he touched her cheek, and his voice itself was tender and filled with wonder.

"Are my eyes green?" Leah asked unblinkingly of the mirror.

"Turn 'round," Andy responded to the reflection, then, peering at her, "With that dress. Is that what he told you—right out of that old love song?"

Leah teased her with a Cinderella sweep of the kelly dress, fluttering her eyelids, and Andy's laugh pitched high with delight. "You petites," she said, sprawling, stomach down, on her bed in anticipation of the story. "Guys are such pushovers. Did you know he'd be there?"

Leah shook her head and sat slowly on her own bed, details racing silently through her mind. Her mother had told her only that Aunt Paulette and Uncle Charles had invited them for dinner Sunday, along with the local pastor and his family. Leah, at home for the weekend, had been swept away; she couldn't tell them she needed both days to write. At Paulette's, she had sneaked glances as Papa spoke to Jonathan of construction and Uncle Charles, of railroading. Jon knew what to say and what to ask. Three years out of Bucknell, he might have followed his father into the ministry except that the good pastor had told him it was the toughest job in the world. More than once, when Leah peeked at him, she caught him looking back. Their eyes kept meeting at dinner, and afterward, he walked with her up the hill beyond the row houses. They sat in the grass and looked down on the valley. Her reticence must have frustrated him, but he was patient. She told him it was just that she had so much to do, so of course he asked if he might take her home.

Eleven-year-old Jeremy and Peter, nine, spying on them from the thicket, giggled when he took off his cardigan and put it over her shoulders to protect her from the first drops of rain, and Jon was not above tossing them a warning, addressing his brother, not hers. He led her down the hard and rutted path to say goodbye at the house and get her things from her parents' car. Then they drove over and among the low, forested mountains of central Pennsylvania in the rain.

What had Andy asked? Had she known he would be there? No, she hadn't known there was a six-one, honey-haired, hazel-eyed Jonathan Grante, or that as she hopped a ride from University Park to Brush Valley to see her folks Friday, he was driving from Harrisburg to Lewistown to see his. She leaned back on an elbow. "To Aunt Paulette, every week is a concert on its way to finale, a Sunday potpourri."

Andy nodded soberly. "Fate. How easily you could have missed each other."

Three times this year Andrea had married her off, as if landing a guy were the end-all. Leah moved too quickly to permit defense.

The pillow, making only a slight arc, caught Andy in the shoulder and face. The victim rolled to the wall, taking the weapon with her, and lay with it over her head, laughing. "Write your speech. He'll call."

Chapter 2

AT THE END OF THE HALLWAY, Leah opened the door and allowed a bent old man she called Mr. Brock to shuffle into the waiting room ahead of her. He found his coat, said he'd see her Friday, and left through the far door. "Leona?" she said to the young woman who was seated. Leona fastened one side of her long brown hair behind her ear, laid down *Seventeen*, and stepped toward the hall.

Most of the staff of the University's speech and hearing clinic had gone home tired at five. Leah would not finish her day until the group clinicians arrived for the evening session, and irksome as it was to at least one of her colleagues, she would breeze out the same way she had breezed in at one—cheerfully. As she opened the door wide for Leona and stood back against it, a swatch of blue caught her eye. A young man she did not recognize sat on the vinyl couch, the blue a singular wide stripe encircling his soft heather rugby shirt at the chest. He had pushed up the sleeves as if to free his forearms. His jeans might have been, at one time, as black as his hair.

The receptionist who handled intake work had left with the others, and Mr. Hurland, who had spent more than enough time observing sessions, had retreated to his office to catch up on his own work. There was no one but herself, Leah thought, to introduce a new client to procedure. He caught her look. "A-a-a-I'm...here t-t-t..." He rolled his eyes, and his hand began to drum on the arm of the couch. "Here t-t-to..." Leah had not yet worked with an adult stutterer, but she had covered the subject in class. She waited, knowing she must. His mouth opened, and he stated the obvious: "I stutter." Irritation creased his forehead, tensing his boyishly handsome face, and the thought struck Leah that it was unfair that a mouth so attractively formed should stutter.

5

She waited until his long-lashed brown eyes lifted toward her, then told him about the missing receptionist. She said if he was local—he nodded that he was—he could leave his number; she would see that he was called tomorrow.

He pulled a notebook from under two textbooks. "I'll wait," he said, his voice soft, his eyes downcast once again.

Leah wondered whether the surprise showed on her face. It didn't matter; he was writing in the notebook.

"It'll be an hour," she said gently. "Why don't you—"

"About 6:15, then," he stuttered without looking up.

She raised an eyebrow, unobserved, then followed the young woman out of the waiting room and closed the door.

In the therapy room she seated herself across from Leona and asked whether she would like to start with the sentences she had practiced at home.

The girl began. "The baby likes his blue bathtub," she intoned, a "hm" sounding in each "b." She articulated the sentence a second time, and on the third Leah held a finger under Leona's nose as if to stop a sneeze.

"Much better," she told her. She pulled a small, reflective metal paddle from a drawer and placed it under Leona's nostrils while the young woman repeated the sentence. Leah showed her the paddle and said her exercises were beginning to work. Leona smiled and adjusted her glasses.

"When you've mastered it," Leah told her, "there'll be no vapor at all." The girl watched, mouthing the words as Leah put the paddle to her own nose and repeated the sentence. "Now, let's try an S."

LEONA CONTINUED DOWN THE HALL as Leah reentered the waiting room. The young man was still there. He stood and she smiled, extending her hand as she said her name. He was not tall—five-eight, she guessed—but his hand felt large because it was calloused and his grip firm. He gave her the sheet of paper on which he had been writing. David Jordan Rothman, he had lettered, student at the University, from Lansdale. She scanned the sheet for functional information and saw the pattern: Four times, therapy; four times, temporary success. Hurland was highly capable as a speech pathologist, and considering the reputation of the faculty under whom she studied, she decided on optimism. "I think there's help for you here, David."

She took a chair near the couch, reseated him with a flick of her fingers, and asked him to tell her more about himself. His eyes moved to his hands. She waited, and he began slowly, trying to control the uncontrollable. He said he was from the Philadelphia area, a third-year business major, "mmmanagement, really—on the gymnastics team."

Severe disfluency, she thought, trouble with eye contact, maybe not so much trouble with the gymnastics team. The latter explained the way the rugby fit. Rothman. She had seen it on the electric board above the upper stands: Rothman, 9.60; Rothman, 9.50; Rothman, 9.80. Ben Epstein had taken her to several meets last year. Ben was always dragging her to sports events; he liked them. She asked David whether she remembered correctly that he had scored a perfect 10 on—what was it, the pommel horse?—in last year's international meet. "The one against..."

He gave her a sidewise glance, and a sensual incident flickered through her, taking her by surprise. *Why?* she wondered. She had only remarked to herself that he had a five o'clock shadow.

"Parallel bars," he said, correcting her poor recollection. "Against Japan."

Leah tried to override the still-present sensation with a demeanor of sheer professionalism. "I've seen you perform; you're consistent." She thought she saw the start of a smile, but it didn't develop, and he looked away. Repeated failure following therapy; remarkable success in this pastime. The case filed itself with her

research. Why could he master gymnastics and not communication? Try it open-ended. "What is it you like about gymnastics?"

David blinked slowly and fastened his eyes on the wall where
nothing hung. Working on composure, she thought, or an answer.
No, that wasn't it. More likely, he knew what she was doing and
was assessing her competence—or already mourning the lack of
it. He couldn't write her off this early, could he? If he didn't even
want to break the ice, why did he wait?

"David," she said searching for contact with his eyes, "I need
to know."

He drew in a breath and let it out. Using an aid called continuous phonation, he said he thought it was the discipline of it, the
challenge of perfecting the moves, the hard work. He looked at her
squarely for the first time.

"It fulfills you in those ways," she ventured.

He smiled and exhaled audibly through his nose, brought an
ankle to rest on his knee and held it there. "Whatever you say."
The look was not insolent; she did not know whether to read cooperation or a shutdown.

"You walked in here today hoping something," she said quietly.

He looked steadily at her, then fell silent while he studied his
shoe. He told her he'd had the best. The sentence flowed, and he
pushed into the next as if to get it out before his luck changed.
"You saw the list: three speech camps, New York. Every time I
thought I had it together, it came apart." Before the last statement was fully out it was, again, fact. His hand pattered the
pain of it on the arm of the couch and, with a gentle roll of his
head, he stuttered that he just wanted a shot on his own. He
looked at her. There they were again, those beautiful eyes—
deep brown and thick-lashed. How wrenching it must be, Leah
thought, to approach a young woman and know your first words
might be your last.

"What worked for you?" she asked.

"Reading. Alone or with s-someone."

"That's where we'll start," she said, rising. "Give us two weeks to get your records."

He picked up his books and stood. "Ms. Beaumont," he stuttered, then paused. "Leah," he said in a whisper he could trust. "You'll work with me?"

She had just said so. "It takes two weeks."

He shook his head. "Am I talking to my therapist?"

This was not procedure. It bypassed the office, ignored Hurland. "I'll see what I can..." Meat for her thesis; Hurland would see that. Besides, he needed her. Behind the bold blue stripe he wore, he was desperate, a little boy holding out his hand, one last time, for rescue.

She nodded, perplexed by her inability to rid herself of that disturbing inner sensation. "Two weeks."

THE KEY CLICKED IN THE LOCK, the knob turned, and Andy, in white shorts and sweatshirt, dumped a bag of gear and books into the apartment. Her face and thighs still glowing from the afternoon's exertion, she leaned the stick into the corner behind the door as she closed it, pulled her sweatshirt up over the mop of moist and separated hair, and dropped it to the floor. Leah was on the phone. Andy would go ahead and shower, talk to her later. Her tee-shirt clung to her back as she sat on the bed to unlace her cleats and kick them off. She pulled at her knee sock, brown with dampness at the heel and toe, till it slid from her calf. You never knew who was on the line with Leah. She didn't fluster with a guy; she didn't gab with a girl. Andy heard her say goodbye and looked up to see the receiver slide from an upturned hand into its cradle. She rested her fists on her knees and looked at Leah, waiting for her to speak.

"Business trip tomorrow. He wants next Saturday."

Satisfaction lit Andy's elfin face—she had called that shot. Pulling the tee-shirt out of the waistband of her shorts, she slipped it off over her head and walked into the bathroom. A hand on each side of the doorframe, she leaned back into the living-sleeping area to make two wet little clicking sounds with her tongue, then disappeared into the bath and closed the door.

Chapter 3

THE WIND WAS RUDE. It turned their cheeks and the lobes of their ears a clownish rose and blew into their mouths when they tried to speak. Jonathan pulled up his coat collar and, seeing that Leah had drawn one arm taut across her midsection, took her free hand in his glove and said, "Run." She clutched her jacket lapels at the throat and, watching only for curbs and icy puddles, ran, head down, beside him toward the coffee shop across the street from campus.

Warmth enveloped them as they stepped inside. The place was not yet crowded. At the counter, a man in a plaid shirt sipped from a hot cup and listened while his friend told him of siting a black she-bear and two cubs up 't the Barrens last June. A waitress, her red hair swept up into an explosion of ringlets, was filling two mugs with steaming chocolate from a machine. She placed them on a tray and, having shaken a can of topping, released from its nozzle a creamy spiral so generous that the sweet, dark liquid swelled over the brim and trickled down to the paper mat. The second white pyramid placed, she delivered the cups to two young women in the first booth and walked to where Leah and Jon had seated themselves at the far end of the shop. Greeting them with an overly friendly smile, she pandered, "Cold out there tonight, huh?"

"Windy," Jonathan agreed, then ordered without consulting Leah or the menu. "Two cheesecakes and two coffees, please."

The waitress gone, he took his gloves from the seat, folded them, and stuffed them into the pocket of his coat, hung on the booth hook. He reached across the table to take hold of all of Leah's fingers, then cupped her hands in the warmth of his.

"Now, little daughter of Abraham, I want to know all about your week."

It was not on the phone that she had told him; it was face to face—or rather, side by side and hand in hand—their first Saturday, a month ago, in Eisenhower Auditorium. She could still see him listening in absorption, only listening, until he squeezed her hand and kissed the back of it. The curtain went up, the show began, and the evening went on as if there had been no distraction, no serious matter. They had seen a professional production of *Gigi* that night, and the music, the color, the aura of proven and promising stars—or perhaps the happiness ever after—seemed to carry Jonathan throughout their time together. Yet when he left her at her door later that night, she had worried that he might have borne the evening out of duty. Holding the same hand as one would grasp a pistol, he had kissed her lightly on the cheek. It might have been goodbye.

But the phone had rung again on Monday, and he told her he'd be up to watch Paterno's Lions take on Notre Dame—two reserved seats if she'd like to join him. It had been a good day with Jon, the Saturday of that game. The crisp October air, the stadium crowd, the aroma of a renegade pipe burning that made her think of Uncle Paddy and good times. And the win. Jon had spent the whole day and, by the end of it, she was fairly sure that he was not a man of pretenses, and she liked being with him. Tonight, it was only a movie, but it had been fun. "You're the first to know," she said. "My proposal's been—"

"Approved!" he exclaimed with her. "Tell me."

She said she was trying to link emotional history to certain disorders, and to recovery. Everybody had a theory or a neurological study going, saying nothing was gained by confronting a client's past; she wanted to study enough cases to know. The waitress placed their desserts and set down two cups, which she filled from a bulbous carafe. "Enjoy," she instructed, smiling the smile, moving away. Jon pulled the napkin into his lap and said the cure would be worth her effort. For the client, it could mean a better chance for friendships, employment, promotions. He asked whether her caseload was her research. Leah allowed several faces to people her thoughts. Not exclusively, she told him, but every day, she saw problems that fit. He stirred his coffee, preferring her words. She slid the fork down into the cheesecake, cutting a small delta free. Not with Andy—not even with Suzanne, the indomitable confidante—did she discuss clinical cases. With family, perhaps, minus names.

"What do you do on a *mission de la finance?*" she asked. "Is it classified?"

His smile was disarming. He told her there were clients who didn't populate bank counters in person or even send a junior. "We parley in *their* cushioned conference rooms." She let him see she was impressed. So far, he told her, he had worked with Stan or Walt—execs out of New York, personal bankers to the *très riche.* Leah thought of her father: a building contractor and well enough off, he stood in line like everyone else. She, personally, didn't know anyone that wealthy. Jon described a man he had met last week in Philly. Department stores there, he said, and in Pittsburgh, New York, Atlanta, Chicago, Dallas, San Francisco, other major cities, several in Canada. Personal assets into eight figures—an empire.

Leah was holding her cup with her fingertips. "You advise him on investments."

"Not this time. He wants to borrow."

Her brows arched.

"For a store in Tel Aviv. Bad idea; inflation's wild over there. We're not finished talking about it." Two bantering young men and their dates took the booth across the aisle, but Jon never looked at them. "You and I are, though. I'm boring you."

"*No,*" Leah said with too much assurance.

"Let's talk about your family, may we?" He laughed. "That was not a pun; it would've been a bad one."

"*Mais oui, je suis d'accord avec toi,*" she said, laughing. "You know French."

"Too little." He looked into her eyes. "You have to be where it's spoken."

She smiled over the cup, sipped, and put it down. How long would she go on testing him? He was sincere. Besides, she had to be honest with herself: she wanted to see him again. "I'll be home weekend after next."

"Chart me a course through the wilderness; I'll find you. Bush Valley?"

"Brush. Brush Valley."

Chapter 4

TUGGING HER BOOK BAG to where she could rummage through it, Leah approached the door to her apartment. She was carrying two additional books and a binder on her left arm, and it had cramped. It was Monday, nearly dinnertime, and aromas of vegetables sizzling in soy sauce and lamb simmering with herbs piqued her hunger. She pictured, behind her own door, meat set to braising and potatoes ready to mash and butter. But no one was cooking there. She found the key and let herself in. Shifting the books again to the other arm, she backed against the door to close it and, her hand still on the knob, allowed herself a moment to remember the sweetness with which Jonathan had left her there Saturday night. He had kissed her briefly, gently on the mouth and then, with that same disarming smile, had turned and disappeared down the stairway.

The burden of the books made further reverie impossible. She let them down on her desk and moved the arm to work out the soreness. She had just entered the kitchen and unwrapped a package of chicken pieces when the phone rang. Leaning on the desk chair to answer and then pulling the seat to where she could sit on it, she replied, "Yes," and then was silent while the caller explained his reason for the call.

"I understand, David," she said when he was finished. "If you can tape every day until Monday, we'll take it from there." She replaced the receiver, glad she had taken the call herself; it was awful. The tension of making a call was bad enough without having to cancel an appointment—two appointments, in fact. She reprimanded herself for not wishing him well in the meet he mentioned, but she was not convinced he was telling the truth: an exhibition meet against the Soviet Union—one of the guys out with a sprain and now one sick—everyone practicing extra hours, in case Mac wasn't well enough by Saturday to pull it off. Was that the problem?

There had been the expected clinical progress for David Rothman in the nearly six weeks in which they had met, but transfer of his skills to the classroom had been less than encouraging. His phone conversation just now had fallen far short of the practice session he'd had only this morning. Had he tried to call someone with whom he was less comfortable, someone at the clinic desk, it would have been worse for him, if that were possible. Was the pattern repeating itself: learned proficiency crumbling into old habits outside the clinic? If so, why? Maybe it was just a temporary setback. Hadn't Hurland warned her there might be a change in the client's attitude at this point?

She rose from the chair, her mind out of gear, walked to the kitchen, and stood facing the sink. In the early weeks of David's therapy, she had spent a lot of time building his trust in her. She had talked with him about his feelings when he stuttered and about why, in his opinion, he was disfluent. She had read with him; she had stuttered with him so that he would be able to see and understand what he was doing, realize his facial expressions when his speech was blocked, identify behavior related to the stuttering—like the drumming hand—that was subconsciously meant to distract the listener. Her work had been painstaking. He had responded, and it had felt great.

But in the three most recent sessions, she and Hurland had decided the time was right to press him for greater commitment to goals, challenging ones. He had to have felt that pressure, and according to Hurland, he might experience some negative feelings toward her until he had internalized the goals, making them no longer hers but his. Maybe, she thought, that's where he is: he's had it with Leah Beaumont and her program, wants a week off. Maybe what he really wants is out. Next time they met, she would encourage him to talk about his fear, his discomfort. But it'll pass, she told herself, hoping she was right, hoping Hurland knew what he was talking about.

She tried to remember what she had been about to do. The chicken, yes. She pulled the wastebasket to the sink to receive the skin of the bird and, seeing that it was unlined, reached into the cupboard for a plastic garbage bag. The box was empty. Returning to the sleeping area of the efficiency she looked for something into which she could discard kitchen waste and, finding nothing useful in her own closet, sifted through the debris in the bottom of Andy's. There was a good-sized plastic bag with handles, which she opened and placed in the pail. Both hands were on faucets when she stopped and went back to the bag. Pulling it out, she looked again at the front of it. Rothman's. Of course, she thought, one more reason that the name had struck a familiar chord. She had shopped Rothman's in Pittsburgh two summers ago. Andy would have shopped handily at the Philadelphia store—by no means a savings for a Reading girl, but a justifiable treat: plush carpeting, glass-enclosed jewelry displays, expanses of label clothing. Leah could hear the paging bell, see the well-groomed salespeople, the spacious elevators, escalators, and lounges.

Coincidence, she thought. Must be lots of Rothmans. Why would this one send his son anywhere but to a private school?

She was tearing lettuce for the salad when Andy came home. The impish face appeared in the kitchen doorway saying, "Mmm-mmmm. Let the peons have fishsticks and pizza." Opening the oven a crack, she declared her nose never wrong: baked chicken, Idahoes, and corn. "Superb."

"Ready. Ask no more of the aging."

With supper over and the dishes defeated, something David said returned to Leah: "I've had the best." She looked up from her desk to find Andy engrossed in a book and asked anyway. Supposing she were a business magnate and could afford exclusive schools, why might she send her son to a state university?

Andy read to the period, looked up, and repeated the premise, then said, "Give the kid what he wants. Who?"

Leah was quiet a moment. "Rothman. The department store family."

"D. J. Rothman, the gymnast?" The link came too quickly; Leah made no response. Andy told her Rick knew him in high school. Gymnastics was his passion; that was why he was here. She said she had met him Friday night. "Stuck on himself. The jaw, that hair. I have this giant urge to touch his hair," she said with a distant look followed by one of bemusement, as if she herself was perplexed by the thought she had voiced.

"The David Rothman I know isn't stuck on himself," Leah said, shaking her head.

Andy looked at her sideways, one eye a slit. She said she and Sue, after a little hoops practice the other night, had talked to the guys for half an hour outside White Building, and he didn't give them the time of day.

"He's quiet."

"Cat's quiet. Rothman's a snob."

"You don't know him."

Andy's eyes rounded, but Leah offered no more. Andy said it was lucky he would come into the old man's money; he'd never make his millions in gymnastics. "Like me and field hockey. It's over at 23."

LEAH LAY AWAKE, STARING INTO THE DARK and trying to piece together the puzzle. Stuttering was a fairly common speech disorder in children. If ignored, it was usually outgrown before the child reached puberty or adolescence. But certain factors could prolong it. What kind of emotional patterns would David have developed, growing up a Rothman? What was "old man" Rothman like? Or David's mother? He had mentioned a brother named Martin. Were there other brothers, sisters?

Strange that Rothman and department store kept coming up— like a new word you heard three times in the next week. What if Rothman was the owner Jonathan mentioned who was building a store in Tel Aviv? What would that tell her? She saw herself in the kitchen earlier in the day, lifting the bag from the waste can, and began to feel the mummery of it. Leah, she thought, you are the definition of the schoolgirl playing Nancy Drew. She envisioned the page:

> *Carefully, Nancy replaced the clue in the garbage can. Now everything was dovetailing. David was Rothman's son, and Rothman had this harebrained idea about building a store in downtown Tel Aviv. Only one thing to uncover and Nancy could wrap and tie this case. She would call on every faculty she possessed as a sleuth to bare the answer to that question, and the question was this: So, what?*

The laugh escaped before she could cover it, and Leah looked to see if it had wakened Andy. Safe, she sighed and turned her face into the pillow. Her body relaxed, her mind ceased its striving with the day, and she gave herself over to sleep.

Chapter 5

THE TEMPERATURE OF THE CROWD and of the gym was high and climbing. Without thought for the considerable mechanics of it in her limited seating space, Leah slipped out of her sweater-vest and laid it across her lap. Her attention was riveted on a small blonde gymnast in a blue and white leotard who stood, hand upraised, on the approach path to the uneven bars. An instant on tiptoe and the little figure was propelled by churning legs toward the springboard. A bounce, a twist of body and, her torso arching and jackknifing over the lower bar, she grasped the upper with both hands, drew widespread feet together, swung upward and down into a series of moves the swiftness and intricacy of which held onlookers utterly quiet. A double giant swing on the upper bar, a layout somersault—Andy always added "flyaway"—and her legs flexed to absorb the landing. They straightened, the back arched, the arms reached up, and the hush was shattered with applause, cheers, and whistles, repeated a minute later when the judges' assistants turned mounted flipboards to display four scores: 9.50, 9.50, 9.60, 9.50. State was holding its own in the women's part of the double dual meet.

Leah smiled as Andy cuffed the air, grinning at the small blue energy who now waved to the crowd from a place between the apparatus and her seat with the team. Thumb and finger between her teeth, Andy whistled one more time and clapped until the applause died.

There was another breathless moment and the sound erupted again, this time in response to a USSR man's finish on the pommel horse. The meet was a two-ring circus; it always was when the men and women competed on the same night. But the PSU crowd was large, knowledgeable, and enthused. Never did a gymnast want for attention, on this night or any other.

Leah's eyes wandered back to the row of chairs where State's men's team was seated. She watched David. He was intent on a teammate who, ready to mount the pommel horse, awaited the judges' signal. Behind Leah someone said, "MacAteer? A virus." Someone else asked something and the reply came, "No, out of bed Tuesday." A third voice expressed disbelief and asked why the coach would put him on the roster tonight. "Because this and the floor ex are his strongest," said the one in the know.

So, David had been telling it straight. Evan MacAteer's performance in the floor exercise had not confirmed to Leah that he had been down with the flu: his score was third of the five maintained in the team score. But perhaps he could have done better. She asked, and Andy replied that under full steam he'd have won the event against most competition, including tonight's; he couldn't have gotten in many hours.

MacAteer returned a ready sign to the judges, then mounted the horse and swung into his routine with spirit but something less than strength. He worked the three areas, sweating, and the scissors that followed were strained. At the three-quarter point he broke but recovered without falling off. He brought the exercise to a close, looking relieved to have finished, and was applauded by fans who, remembering past performances, were eager to console. The scores were dismal: high sevens, low eights. He waved dutifully to the crowd and returned to the bench, where David greeted him with one hand clasping his and one on his elbow. They sat down together and other team members offered solace, a hand on the shoulder, a soft fist to the side of the knee.

"He won't make it to the next round," Andy said under her breath. Leah watched the next Lioness on the uneven bars and caught the end of the next CCCP man's pommel horse routine, but she found her gaze often on the bench with David. He had not done particularly well in the floor ex, Andy maintaining that he was a little too tall to excel in that event. Now he approached the pommel horse. There was matter-of-factness in the mount, vigor in his routine. Following MacAteer's as it did, the exercise looked to Leah all the more fluid. Two arrow-straight legs circled as one over each end of the horse, the flap, flap of chalked hands audible in the stands. His scissors, rhythmic and of superb height, drew quiet sounds from the crowd. He whirled with centrifugal energy over the horse and into the air and landed with a distinct *fop* of his feet on the mat. Arms upraised and head back, he smiled at the faraway ceiling and then, with a wave, acknowledged the roar.

He was almost to his seat before the scores went up—9.70, 9.60, 9.60, 9.70—and he turned to smile and wave again. His teammates offered hands and pats as he returned to the bench. He made no reply that Leah could discern, and although this was common for a gymnast coming off the apparatus, she tried to remember whether indeed she had seen him talk with anyone since the team had taken the floor.

Through the next four events—the rings, the vault, the parallel bars, and horizontal bar—she found herself studying, as much as his performance, David's interaction with teammates and coaches. He continued to do well, losing a fraction of a point here and there for an off-balance dismount or a small infringement on form, but without question, he was supplying his share of the score. His routine on the parallel bars especially pleased the spectators, and the 9.70, 9.80, 9.80, 9.80 scores indicated that the same could be said of the judges. Through the best moments of the evening David captured the fans with his virtuosity and something more, something that reached into the crowd, something that Leah couldn't identify by name but that she couldn't deny touched her as well. But as far as she could tell, he had not spoken a word.

The Lady Lions and the Russian women were warming up for their finale, the floor exercises, as the men's coaches finished checking the high bar for their last event. Andy laid a hand on Leah's arm while she raised the other to someone across the floor.

"Rick," she called in a clear voice that carried. The standing figure motioned a meeting and pointed to an exit ramp. Andy nodded and waved. "He'll want to go for a Coke, okay?"

"And Leah makes three. Thanks anyway."

"Nooo. Rob, Cat, probably Suzanne..." Realizing that the floor exercises had begun, she urged in a two-note whisper: "Le-ee..."

WHEN ANDY AND LEAH REACHED THE EXIT, Rick and Cat were waiting. Quiet Cat. Leah remembered Ben's telling her how he, Jerry Camden, got his name—from the way he moved on the ice. Cat captained the hockey team, but Leah wondered how; he was no leader. It was Rick who suggested a sticky-bun stop at the diner, but he wanted first to see D. J. State had turned in a decent performance despite the setbacks and the early date, the Soviet Union taking the meet 284.450 to 281.550; and David's high bar routine as a fill-in for MacAteer, although not his strong event, had been, Rick felt, a personal best. The women's team had also looked respectable against near-professional competition, and the elation of the evening had left its print on face after face as the fans poured into the corridor and past the waiting four.

It was a good half-hour later when David appeared under the stands. Rick and Cat met him, funneling their respect through handshakes and punches. The congratulations delivered, they asked him to join them for a sticky, and it seemed he would have until he caught sight of the women. He murmured an excuse, refused to change his mind and, with a wave to Leah and Andy, walked up the ramp to the front gate.

Leah was not surprised. He could have been uneasy about their client-clinician relationship and whether it might be uncomfortable or unprofessional for her to be with him in a social setting. Or he could have feared an encounter with unknown

variables: he did not know Andy well, or what turn her exuber-
ance might take. Yet Leah felt robbed of an opportunity to know
more about David Jordan Rothman—strictly on a professional level,
of course. She saw her own disappointment mirrored in Andy's
face but imagined that it was forgotten as Rick, returning, placed
his arm around her neck, pulled her to him once, then rested his
wrist on her shoulder and moved her and himself to the door.
Leah and Cat followed, and as they descended the steps from Rec
Hall, they saw only a few of the gym meet faithful and one lone
gymnast, bag in hand, walking home.

Chapter 6

"IT IS ALWAYS THE PARENT," Hurland empathized, folding his hands over the knitted tie. "Read my thesis," he said, nodding toward a compact, black volume on his bookshelf. Hurland himself, however, was the antithesis of compact. Had the white shirt stayed tucked, the stomach would have hidden his belt.

Leah was seated in front of his desk. Although William Hurland held a master's degree in speech communication, was a certified speech pathologist, and supervised several clinicians pursuing specialties in his field, he, too, was a graduate student, a doctoral candidate, and older than some. It had felt better to Leah from the beginning to call him Mr. Hurland and not Bill as certain others did. On the notepad in her lap she wrote something and circled it. The one that concerned her more, she said, was David Rothman. He looked over his glasses and recalled aloud that last Monday she was euphoric. She answered quickly that David knew the exercises from Day One. He understood his struggle behavior, and when he avoided a word or substituted, he was aware of it. They had started easy onset and it was like turning on a CALM button; in two weeks he was close to fluent. But last week he had told her that he couldn't transfer it to the classroom, that outside the clinic he was the same old D. J. Rothman.

"D. J.?"

"It rolls off. 'David' blocks."

"Come off it. He doesn't want it bad enough."

"He *does*."

"Look, he's young and bright; he could be one of the fortunate few who succeed—but every time he blows it, his chances slide." He tipped back in the swivel chair. "He's told us the factors we don't need to look at, and we've swallowed it—so has he. Are you hitting it off?"

"He's almost perfectly fluent with me now; but when he phoned—"

"There's no such thing. Perfectly fluent."

"I'm sorry. He called last week to cancel two appointments. It was so bad I thought he was quitting on me. How can he pull off three good calls in the morning and have a complete relapse by afternoon? Maybe we're pushing..."

Hurland leaned forward on the desk. His fingers formed a wedge. "Complete relapse?"

Leah blushed. She was not, she assured herself, abusing superlatives: It was as anguished a conversation as the first she'd had with David. "He wasn't calling the desk; he was talking to *me*."

Hurland's mouth puckered. "Hard for a conscientious kid to miss two sessions," he murmured, thumbing back a page in the book in front of him. "Still, to you or to the desk by now..." He pushed his glasses into place to scan the page, then tapped it with his pen point. "Step up encounters. Build bridges."

"Bridges?"

"You're a constant from the clinic. Be there for his next talk. And get some people into the clinic. Where are his friends?"

Leah was writing. "Teammates, a couple of football players, a hockey man. They talk; he gets away without it."

"You've seen him with them?"

"Not up close. He begged off."

Hurland jotted several lines. "Go to lunch with him again; talk friends, family. Open him up."

"Cafeterias make *me* nervous."

"A place with wait-staff, then. Have him order for both of you."

"Isn't that a little..." Leah paused, seeking a polite phrase, "...old fashioned?" That very behavior on Jonathan's part whenever they ate out was the only thing about him that irritated her.

"Do it. Get him ready in today's session." He looked at his watch. "I'll see you Wednesday."

Leah gathered her notes and stood. She said she *would* like to read his master's thesis. He pushed the chair left to where he could pull a copy from the shelf and, rising, handed it to her across the desk; he held on to it. "I know I don't need to remind you..." he said.

No? Leah thought. She waited.

"Whether David's down on you this week or not, he admires you, your capability, your willingness to invest time in him. Be sure he understands that this is therapy and nothing more. Give him your share of the tab ahead of time."

"Of course, Mr. Hurland." She couldn't believe this. He felt it necessary to caution her. She drew the book from his hand. "I guess you've thought of—everything."

"It happens. If I'm wrong, *you* explain the phone call."

She rearranged her notebooks. She knew she was naive in ways, but Hurland was too quick to plant flags on her every oversight. She had not considered the possibility that David was developing feelings for her, but on thinking about it, she was sure Hurland was wrong. She resolved to forgive him—he was only looking out for David's wellbeing, and hers. As for her competence, by semester's end she would prove that. She punctuated the vow with a quick nod and a smile that she told herself was genuine. "Thank you, Bill. I'll take care of it."

Chapter 7

DAVID OPENED THE ENTRANCE DOOR FOR LEAH, and she allowed him the inner door as well. She had agreed to go along with Hurland's tactic, and she might as well play her part in its entirety. Where did it leave David in his own mind, she wondered, to publicly act the chauvinist, the relic? He understood that this was not a date, and so far, he had behaved like nothing but a good sport about the project. She admonished herself for fretting over details. Her job was simply to use this situation to understand the client's makeup in order to help him conquer his disfluency. On at least two counts now she had guessed wrong about David and what he was thinking anyway. He had not invented Evan MacAteer's illness; he had to miss those sessions. And this morning he had assured her that her challenges to harder goals did not upset him; there was no trace of anger.

She slipped out of her coat and allowed him to hang it on the rack. The hostess showed them to a table with a view of the street, and as Leah took her seat, David adjusted the chair so adroitly, it occurred to her that he must have expected him to fumble. He sat opposite her, smiled, and picked up the menu. Trying not to fixate on his smile, she decided to stop assuming. She commented on the small bouquet on the table, said she had always liked mums and, receiving no more than the smile, perused the menu for something light.

The waitress brought water and asked whether they were ready to order. "Nnnot quite," David answered, dismissing her. He asked Leah what she would like. The meatless quiche sounded good, she said, with a spinach salad and tea. The more courses, the more practice, she thought; tomato juice, she told him, would be

28

nice. There was a lapse, and she realized she had not mentioned the meet; there was much in it that was positive.

"Everyone was aware that we were up against next year's Soviet Olympians Saturday night," she said. "You did a marvelous job."

"Thank you," he said, contemplating the place mat. Then, remembering it was against the rules to avoid eyes, he looked at her and said it again.

Order pad in hand, the waitress reappeared and asked Leah if she was ready. David's hand, which had been relaxed on the menu, began a rapid tap-tap-tap. He stuttered deplorably on "Two tomato juices, please" and, having gained the attention of the waitress, began to phonate slowly, continuously, as he had learned to do: "Thevegetableqquicheformyffriend, withthespinachmmushroomsalad...andhottea." The woman looked bewildered, and the thought recurred instantly to Leah that it was Hurland's dumb idea to have David play the spokesperson for them both. On the other hand, she could have ordered something easier to say. But they were not here for "easy." The objective was to overcome difficulty.

David ordered a Reuben and coffee for himself; his hand continued its tap-tap. Leah wanted to hold it down. Terribly unprofessional, she told herself.

When the waitress left, the hand stopped and David, seemingly unaware of its disobedience until now, stroked his water goblet and fastened two fingers around its stem. Leah wondered whether he was accustomed to offering thanks to God for the provision of food and if so whether, under these conditions, he would forego gratitude; she would not blame him. She did not wait as she had at the cafeteria for his evaluation of the encounter. "Much better. What needs help?"

"The hand," he said, and she winked. He said he was glad she was high on him today, because he had made a fool of himself again in class Friday. "You'd have denied you ever knew me."

She knew the look; it meant, You wouldn't have, would you? She gave him a funny little twist of a smile. "Tell me about it?"

Same story, he told her. How many times had she and he gone over that paper? He knew, he'd cut sessions. Ride a slippery slope, and you go downhill. "Some of the guys had..." His eye contact had been constant; suddenly it was gone.

"Had..." she repeated.

He looked into her eyes. At length he picked up where he'd left off. "...all they could do to stifle it. On the hardest blocks, of course, and then I'd freeze."

No immunity from ignorance and cruelty, Leah thought, even in the university classroom. "Pointing at you is their cover. We'll work right till class on the next one. And I'll be there."

He looked surprised. His mouth curved at the corners. "Bring your wand."

The juice and then their platters arrived, and the waitress asked whether there would be anything else. David said, "No, thank you," forgetting to look at her. He moved the salt and pepper toward Leah and sliced the first bite of his sandwich with knife and fork, preoccupied. Leah offered a fleet and silent thanks for the meal, then started with what she knew.

"You're close to your father, you say. He must have worked at that."

He chewed the bite and the thought, then said his father was a generous man. They had probably had less time together than he remembered, but when he was with him, he, David, was Number One. "He'd explain things to me, you know—always explaining things. And everywhere we went, people knew him."

"Satisfied customers."

"More than that. Schools, hospitals, institutions. Like I said, a generous man."

"Oh," Leah said, but it was not a reply. She was looking at her salad.

"What?"

"Uh, this...dressing." She moved a small bit of golden and brown meat with her fork. "But it-it's...all right. N-n-no, don't, really..."

"Why, Ms. Beaumont, ease your onset." She thought she saw him suppress a grin even as he raised his hand to summon the waitress. When she presented herself he stuttered, "This dressing..." He stopped and resumed with prolonged sounds, his hand moving in spasms. "Could we have a salad with a different dressing, please?"

"I'm sorry," Leah added, addressing both David and the waitress. "I should have specified...I mean, often, a spinach salad..." She was distracted by a sound, unlike the prior tapping on the menu, a drumming on the table.

"Don't worry—" David stuttered.

"It *is* described on the menu, Miss," the waitress interrupted, "but it's no trouble. What kind?"

To keep himself the intercessor, David repeated the question. He stuttered it badly, his hand metering the distress of having to keep up in rapid conversation. The waitress was now absorbed in the drumming and Leah, reacting, slipped her palm beneath David's, enfolding with her fingers, using the weight of her hand. "Just vinegar and oil," she said to him.

"Vinegar and oil," David stuttered to the waitress.

"Sure," she said, taking Leah's salad.

Leah returned her attention to David and, realizing that her hand remained in his, retrieved it. He grinned. "That was to calm me down?" Her cheeks flushed, and she imagined Jonathan in disbelief, Hurland in a cloud of gloom.

"I didn't mean..." she began. Words came to mind, but she could not choose the right ones.

"You were asking about my father," David proffered.

"Yes," Leah answered quickly, relieved at the change of subject. Her knees bumped each other under the table and she felt nine years old. "I...just marvel at the way he was able to build that bond with you...while he was...so involved in the business."

"So was Mom—involved. Still is. Always on the go."

Leah's own mother came suddenly to her consciousness. Keeping the books evenings for Beaumont Homes was often the reason Mama had given for not permitting Leah and the boys to return to the living room after bedtime, and it usually worked. Yet she had never thought of her mother as employed until, when Leah was eighteen, the family business took on a fulltime bookkeeper, and Miriam Beaumont accepted a position at the university.

Why, Leah asked herself, did she always assess people by comparing them with members of her family, as if they were the standard? Were they? She tore her thoughts away and put them back on track. In a clinical session, David had mentioned a brother. "Martin is how much older—four years?" she asked.

"Five. More than Mrs. Morganthal, Martin was in charge." He chuckled and said old Mrs. Morganthal would plunk them down at the table and say *Eat, eat*, then pull her chair as close as her roundness would allow and show them how. "Didn't believe in chit chat either. Marty and I called her"—he dropped his voice to a bass—"The Morgue."

Leah laughed. "Then you and Martin got along?"

He indicated a so-so and said a few times he could've done well enough without Martin. "Sometimes he'd get on me, and nothing I could say or do made any difference."

"Teased?"

"Used to call me M-Machine Gun D-D-Davit—with a *t*."

Leah wondered whether the stutter was his own or a re-creation of Martin's teasing. He had been running his thumb around the rim of his coffee cup, his eyes resting there. He looked at her.

"How old were you?"

"I don't know. Martin's always been Martin. But he looked out for me." He guessed her thoughts and said he'd heard it before— that it could have started there.

"Supposing it did. You seem to hold no grudge."

"*He* didn't know what he was doing. Are you kidding? He wouldn't have hurt me on purpose. Isn't that the crux of it? You go from where you are."

A sitter who never talked to him or rewarded his talking to her, Leah thought. A brother who called him a stutterer before he was one and nailed him every time he groped for a word. And parents who were, to a great extent, absent. Yet he seemed to hold a warm affection for them all and to exonerate them. Had his counseling been that effective? She would need time to think this through.

The waitress, delivering the new salad, refilled David's cup, offered Leah more hot water, and was gone. They ate in silence for a moment, then Leah, attempting to pick up the conversation, said maybe soon the family would be better known for its gymnast than for its entrepreneurs or philanthropists. His laugh denied it. David Rothman, he said, was already known by the Jewish community far and wide for the longest bar mitzvah in the history of the synagogue. She smiled with him, feeling the barb. Good that he could laugh, she told him; it would get him through the valleys. Some day, he'd beat this, and then the joke would be on everybody else. She tried to impress the surety of it upon him with her eyes, and suddenly it was she who sought relief from his gaze in something lifeless—a saucer, a spoon—as her cheeks again burned with color.

The waitress stopped to ask about dessert, and Leah was grateful for the interruption. She shook her head to David; he declined for both of them with fair fluency, his attention on holding his hands still under the table. The waitress left the check, and he returned her pleasantry with little trouble. Leah smiled her approval and, taking her handbag, prepared to rise. They could assess the hour objectively on the walk back to campus, she thought, but for now, she would encourage him. She said that by January his new clinician wouldn't believe he'd ever had a problem. She moved her chair back an inch and waited for David, also still seated, to leave the tip and pocket his wallet. Suddenly he looked at her, astonished. "New clinician?" He reached across the table for her forearm. "What...what d'you mean?"

She glanced at the patrons around them. His voice had been too loud, and he continued to hold her by the arm; his grip was firm. *No one has told him,* she thought, *and who but I should have?* She put down the bag and leaned toward him. "New semester, new clinician. You don't become dependent."

His look was pained, and he did not let go. He stuttered that it didn't make sense; he had thought it was important to build trust. She looked at his hand, then at him. Nonplussed, he released her. "Is there any w-way?" She shook her head and said he would be fine, and it wouldn't be because of her, or the next clinician, or the next. He'd beat it himself. He was silent for a moment. When he spoke, the stutter bloomed. "As a friend," he asked, "couldn't you work with me on any part of this? On my presentations for class?" She did not answer. "I'll work with the new person, too," he told her. "I'll never be dependent, never. But I have confidence in you." His voice dropped to the whisper: "As a friend."

He had already, in the past hour if not before, drained her of energy and self-esteem. What more did he need from her? *And how does he relate to his friends?* she heard Hurland ask. She conjured her answer: *I wouldn't know; I never was one.*

She looked at David, hearing again the tortured, stumbling words: *as a friend, never dependent.* She took a long, quiet breath. "As a friend."

He smiled, and the crease on his forehead softened. He picked up the check and came around behind her to pull back the chair. She preceded him to the lobby, frowning inwardly, refusing to grade herself on clinical skills for this day. *Time will tell,* she thought. *Time and whatever this boy is made of.*

Chapter 8

THE SNOW FELL IN GREAT, FLAT FLAKES that lighted, one upon the other, until the lawn and road were blanketed in white. The evergreens that lined the Beaumont property sagged beneath the pillows laid upon them, and still the crystals drifted down by billions from a silver sky. It was the season's first snowfall of measure, and Leah, forgetting that she had thought the same last year and once in every year before, was certain this one was the most beautiful she would ever see.

It felt good to be home. Leah, in short skirt, black tights, and an oversized sweater, sat in the bay window seat, looking out. This had been a favorite place through the winters of her childhood, some fifty panes separating her from the cold while framing, each within itself, a landscape worthy of remembrance. Her mind's eye still could see, lined up on cushions of red velvet, a crowd of dolls and bumptious dogs and bears, placed by her hands that they might know this perfect spot with her.

She had tried not to feel worried through the morning, through lunch, that Jonathan was driving the Seven Mountains today. Now, sitting at the window, she offered again a prayer for him, reminding herself that faith leaves worry with God. But she wished his car in view there near the Gottlieb farm, where a depression in the whiteness marked the ribbon of road. No Amish would be out in this; there would be time enough for sleighing when it stopped and chores were done. Leah checked the road again, thankful that Jon's last twenty miles, at least, would be over flatter ground, from Potter's Mills through Centre Hall and east into the Valley.

She held her mug of cider in both hands to warm them, then exchanged it for a portrait from the table nearest her. The woman in the frame wore her hair swept back into a large, soft bun; her eyes were resolute yet peaceful, her nose Grecian, her mouth tender, perhaps naturally so, perhaps through the photographer's touch. Leah felt a drawing, as if the woman waited willingly to hear a feeling shared, to clarify it just by having listened. But she had never known her grandmother. "*Grand-père*," she said without looking up.

The frail man on the couch woke with a start. "Uh! *Quoi? Quoi.*"

She apologized, continuing softly in French. "We can talk later."

"I wasn't sleeping," he replied in a sleepy rasp. "What is it?"

She sat down beside him, the portrait in her hand. She said she felt so...cheated...for never having known her. Sometimes the window seat, she said, used to be her grandma's lap; but it was just pretend.

He sat up slowly and, awkwardly, not fully awake, laid his hand on the back of her head. He touched the portrait. "Your grandmother was just as beautiful inside. She would have loved to hold you, as she did with your papa. Such love she had for Antoine and my girls. Such love—" He stopped to fight the catch in his throat. "For me."

She gave him time, then stole into his thoughts. "Was her hair the color of mine?"

He stroked her hair and, winding a strand loosely about his thumb, looked at her. "Darker, yet with the glint of red. Eyes. Yours are her father's. Her strength is in your eyes."

He turned the portrait toward himself, and for a moment, Leah thought he had forgotten she was beside him. "She was a brave woman," she said.

C'est vrai, he said; she could have married him, Pierre Beaumont, earlier for safety. Not until France was liberated did she say yes, for love.

Leah placed the next piece; she knew the picture well. "Your family gave her haven during the occupation."

He said Josephine knew they would risk what they must to

protect her and the boy. Her father and his, Pierre's, since cavalry days, had been as brothers. "It was my father who helped her inquire into the whereabouts of her husband when he disappeared."

Until now, Leah could have told the tale herself, and although Grandfather never seemed to notice which part of the story he had told before and which he had not, she felt his confidence in her readiness to bear it on a more mature level now as he continued.

"A brilliant man, Bernard Hausmann," Pierre said. "From Munich he came to Paris to study, met Josephine there and stayed. His reputation in physics was international by the time he was twenty-eight. How proud Josephine was to see her husband off on the train to Berlin to lecture at the Institute. Had she known she would never see him again..."

"*A cause de la guerre,*" Leah offered.

"Because God let out the leash on the devil," he amended. "After weeks of uncertainty and endless inquiry by Josephine and by my father, Jean-Baptiste Beaumont, on her behalf, she came to the shop holding the child by the hand and showed my father and me the letter informing her of Bernard's 'accidental' death. We took them in to live with us that day, your grandmama and Antoine. It would be months before we knew about the camps."

The camps. Leah knew about the camps. Mama had told her when she was twelve how Grandfather Hausmann had probably died. "It must have taken a long time for her soul to mend," she said softly.

"From such a thing, some never mend; God must cover the wound with love. This God did for my Josephine, and she learned to live, to sing again. I could not think what my life would have been without her, without my Paulette—and Claire."

"You were wonderful to Papa. He considers himself your son."

"Antoine *is* my son," Pierre chortled, thumbing his chest. "The papers say so, and I say so." A bony finger poked her knee. "And you are my granddaughter. Never forget. You are the granddaughter of Pierre Beaumont."

She placed a tender kiss above the hollow of his cheek, and the portrait slid to the couch between them; she took it up and bound it to herself. Today, she confided, still in French, a friend would be coming for dinner.

"The lover of football? Miss Sebring? She who watched the television with squeals and shouts."

"Did you not like Andy?"

"But yes. Such joy in living. A lively girl."

It had been the Pitt game, Rick at defensive back. But Grandpa had little use for sports. "Today, it's not Andy...." A car turned into the driveway; her heart jumped. She slipped into her shoes, put the picture on the table, took the mug, and straightened the newspapers in the rack on her way to the kitchen.

"Someone to inspect, *hein*? Must I be put away?"

"The son of Aunt Paulette's pastor," she called back loudly. "Don't you go anywhere." She intended no games with the ringing bell; she was happy for Jon's safe arrival, and by the door thrown wide, he knew it. He kissed her face hard, then catching sight of Grandpa Pierre, once again softly on the side the old man could not see, and she took him into the living room, still in his coat. He released her hand to greet the old man, who had risen and was saying something in French. He repeated the welcome in English and Jonathan, thanking him, gave his coat to Leah and obeyed Grandfather's direction to sit down. For questioning, Jon thought. When ten minutes had elapsed, however, and Grandfather Beaumont's subject remained the lack of craftsmanship in modern cabinetmaking as compared with the days when he had been engaged in the trade in France, and how he had, through the years, impressed upon Leah's father the need for skill, care, and time duly applied to the art of building, whether carpentry or cabinetry, an internal debate commenced inside Jonathan as to whether this was a good sign or bad. Grandfather was holding forth upon the hours he had invested in Antoine's apprenticeship and the resultant quality of the homes that his son now built, when Antoine himself appeared to renew his acquaintance with "young Jonathan," remembering that they had enjoyed a pleasant hour over dinner at Paulette's. Miriam Beaumont joined them in the living room for only a few minutes before returning to the kitchen. Leah had thought her greeting passably genial but knew her mother capable of much more warmth. She offered to set the table for her, and having done so, said she would be back soon to help with the sauces. She excused Jonathan and herself from the company of the men to give him time with her in the family room before he faced scrutiny at dinner.

She had just sat beside him on the couch downstairs when they heard a scratching sound, and an unclassifiable little dog with silky brown hair bounded from an adjacent room, tail and hindquarters moving side to side. He did not claw or jump but positioned himself before them on his haunches and pawed the air. Rewarded with affection, he requested it again and again in the same way until Leah, no longer thinking it winsome, said firmly, "*Chocolat, ça suffit. Couche-toi.*" The silken swab dropped, snout to the floor, and with doleful eyes between his paws, remained there.

"Your *dog* is bilingual?" Jonathan spurted.

Leah laughed and said no, he spoke no English. It fell suddenly upon her, the scope of what Jon would need to assimilate. She placed the first block for him. Grandpa walked every day with Chocolat, so he responded best to French. She scratched the dog's ears, sent him back to the room, and rose from the couch. A photograph had served her well an hour ago; she walked past the piano to a small cloth-covered table beside the patio door and, taking from it a family portrait, returned to Jonathan. She sat close to him to point out people he already knew—Papa, Mama, Peter— and to his question about the latter, responded, "Reading in his room." She indicated the door of Chocolat's entrance and exit. Then, pointing to one of the two people remaining, she told Jon that Bernie was married and had a little girl; the other was Matt, who would, in two years, be an architectural engineer.

"Matthew?" Jonathan asked. She told him he was quick to say it was Mattathias. Jon said her father must be pleased to have a son able to take over the business. Two could, if they wanted to, Leah said, but Bernie had gone south.

"Mattathias. That must've been good for a bruise or two in school," Jon said.

The idea that the name invited bullying was amusing to Leah. "Mattie loves his name, always has. He played Maccabee till it was part of him; nobody intimidated Matt." She thought of him at six, brandishing that tattered cardboard sword.

"Played what?"

Block Two. How many more blocks would he have to lift into place before the evening ended? The Maccabees, she told him, were freedom fighters; their tactics were still studied at military academies. Jon nodded. There was no life in his eyes, but he was listening, so she told him the story: The Syrian-Greek emperor Antiochus IV had, more than two thousand years ago, filled the temple in Jerusalem with idols and ordered the Jews to abandon their faith in one living God or die. An elder named Mattathias called on the Jews to revolt, and Judah, one of his five sons, organized the volunteers into an army. "They became known as the Maccabees, taking the name—"

Jon shook his head, holding in a laugh, and said, "Mattathias Maccabee. I'm sorry, I keep seeing bagpipes and a kilt."

Leah obliged with a smile and "You're teasing."

Jon swallowed his smile and reached for her hand. "Yeah, I was. Really, I'm sorry."

She backed up to Judah the Hammer, explained that Maccabee—Hammer—was not his father's family name but, rather, a nickname well earned, and made Jon pledge to listen closely. She gave him detail and color: When the Jews recovered Jerusalem, there was celebration in the streets. They cleansed and purified the temple and it became again a house of worship to God. "You know the legend?"

"Legend."

She told him how they found one jar of holy oil, enough to keep the "eternal light" before the Ark of the Covenant burning for one day. Miraculously, it burned for eight, day and night. By then, the priests had prepared more oil, so the light could remain lit from that time on. "It's that miracle, and the rededication of the temple, that we're celebrating."

"Hanukkah." He said it as one would look down on a moving ocean from a plane and say, *tsunami*. Had he not known? She knew when it was Christmas. She asked whether he had seen the menorah on the mantelpiece. He nodded and, now quite serious, added for points, "The candelabrum with eight branches—for the eight days and nights."

Give him two. This evening would open new vistas to him; she wondered if he knew it. She asked him to listen to the words of her favorite hymn after dinner when they sang, taught him to say it—*Ma'oz Tsur*—and tried to see herself through his eyes as he pronounced it. A call came from the kitchen, and she moved in response to her name, asking Jon whether he would rejoin her father and grandfather, or come to the kitchen with her. The bedroom door opened, and Peter asked what Ma wanted. He recognized Jonathan and tossed him a noncommittal greeting. Leah assured him that it was she who had been summoned, not he, and Jonathan snatched the opportunity to talk a few minutes about sports or whatever interested Peter, here, downstairs. As she climbed the steps, Leah thought it a judicious choice: he had gone several rounds already without the sounding of the bell. And, maybe, so had she.

Chapter 9

THERE WAS GOOD REASON to compliment Miriam Beaumont on her culinary art. She had herbed and broiled a tray of thick salmon steaks and laden the table with colorful and savory vegetables, hot and cold, which caused Jonathan, when he saw them, sudden famish. Antoine gave thanks to God, and Peter, as he passed dishes to Jon, enthused over the prospect of potato latkes the next day, as well as his willingness to demonstrate the way to top them just right with sour cream and applesauce. Jonathan had his first bite in his mouth when Antoine and Pierre, both, applauded the cook verbally, lavishly. It was left to him only to agree, which he did in chorus with Leah and Peter. He resolved to be on his toes in the future, and by strict attention to what was said, he did manage to make intelligent observations, turn his phrases with sensitivity, and ask two or three polite questions. From the exchange, he learned that the elder Mr. Beaumont—Pierre—was, by early background, Roman Catholic, the son of a French cavalryman, Jean-Baptiste Beaumont; that he had been privileged to fashion furnishings for the finer homes of Paris from his suburban shop; and that, a bachelor until his late thirties, he had then married a young widow not of his own faith, a Jewish woman with a small child, and emigrated to America. Jonathan gathered from tone and glance that the *boy* became the father of Leah and her brothers. Their mother, Miriam Beaumont, he deduced, had come from a Jewish family longer established in America, one from which had come at least one rabbi—it had not been clear whether the reference was to her father or her brother; she had been "well brought up" and was now active in community affairs and as an administrator on campus. Leah and Mattathias, it seemed, had chosen to attend

Penn State, not only for its excellence in their respective fields but for pragmatic reasons, not the least of which was Mother's sizeable discount.

"One becomes well off by being careful of pennies," Grandfather Beaumont confided regarding this subject, "and one remains well off in exactly the same way."

Had Jonathan not been keenly aware of his circumstances, he might have appropriated entirely the flow of amity at dinner. As Leah's suitor, he sensed with not a little relief a beneficent acceptance on the part of the men; even Peter had sounded the tocsin for him, downstairs, on the matter of gifts. It was primarily, perhaps only, Leah's mother who was requiring him to prove himself further, and he feared that anything short of Abrahamic blood would not suffice. That he was in a state of relative ease as the family moved to the living room was interesting to him in view of his position across from Miriam. At some time during the telling of the Hanukkah story, the lighting of the candles, the prayers and songs, he began to enjoy the happening outright, to feel almost a part. Peter, who had soberly received the kindled *shamash* from his father's hand and lit seven of the candles, now sat on the floor spinning a cellophane *dreydel* with the delight of a child about to collect a small fortune in chocolate Hanukkah money from his grandfather, in whose care it rested. Leah, seated beside Jon on the couch, whispered that she would like to talk to him privately after the family exchanged gifts, and he guessed that she, suspecting he had brought nothing for her, was providing a way out.

They had not yet begun the exchange when the doorbell rang several times running and someone barged through the door with a *Happy Hanukkah*, open arms, and a laugh that declared the party begun. The Beaumonts confirmed it, Peter throwing himself bodily at the young man while the others, all but *Grand-père*, made their way to welcome him. There was an unintelligible interchange of which Jon, rising slowly, caught parts:

"...thought you couldn't come tonight..."

"...knew I could study the rest Sunday night, and how could I not be here?"

"...you brought Dessa..."

"...didn't even see her there behind him."

Jonathan stood a few feet from the gathering, where he could see Leah's hands enfolding those of a small, dark-haired young woman who was entering the house. He noticed that her mother greeted the girl in the same way. And then Leah turned to him and, indicating the young man, said, "Jonathan, my 'little brother' Matt."

"Mattathias Beaumont," little brother said, plunging his hand into Jonathan's. He stood nearly a foot taller than Leah, easily Jon's 6' 1", a crown of very dark brown ringlets adding further to his height. Leah's eyes were nearly shut with the pleasure of having foretold the way that Matt would present himself. Catching Jonathan's glance at her, Mattathias took him in more carefully.

"Jonathan Grante," Jon offered. He looked at the young woman who was, with the help of Matt's left hand, removing her coat.

"Dessa, this is Jonathan Grante," Matt said warily, "...Dessa Levin." Dessa offered her hand, and the banalities over, she and Mattathias moved to fuss over Grandfather, who had struggled to his feet. The group melted once more into a holiday scene, but now there was laughter and, Jon thought, light in Miriam's eyes. He noticed as the gifts were exchanged that Matt—although he, with something akin to the presence of a magician, brought forth small offerings for everyone else—gave nothing to Dessa. A private time for them later too, he guessed.

And then a little package was handed him, marked only *Jonathan*. He tried to read faces, but on each was the same half-smile that said, "Open it." He removed the wrap and lifted the lid. Banded fast against the satin lining was a pocket pen— sleek, black, unengraved. He moved his eyes from face to face, saying thank you and receiving more half-smiles. A movement of Leah's head indicated Mrs. Beaumont, and he repeated the words to her without satisfaction that her expression was any more than had been offered him before, nor more than would have been tendered any guest.

Leah allowed a little time and then said quietly that she and Jonathan would be downstairs. She asked Matt if he'd be staying and, assured that he and Dessa would, descended to the family room with Jon. At mid-room she turned and kissed him gently on the mouth. It had not been an easy day, she said; he had done well. Admiration, he wondered, or sympathy? He returned her kiss with warmth, then reached inside his jacket and pulled out a slender box wrapped in stripes of green, gold, white, and red. He enjoyed the surprise; he would tell her afterward. They sat on the couch while she pulled the wrap away. In the box lay a necklace, four fragile chains of gold. She looked at him with widened eyes, unsmiling. "Jonathan," she said, which meant too soon, too much.

"I can, and I wanted to," he told her. He kissed her well, until she ended it, then, taking the necklace from the box, he clasped it about her neck.

"It's beautiful," she said, a strand laced through her fingers.

"*You're* beautiful," he said, kissing her softly, briefly. "I didn't buy it for today."

"Jon..."

He felt clumsy. That he had bought it this morning was purely Providence. He would have to go about this more carefully. He held her face as if to look inside her. "Forgive me?"

She took his hands. "By tomorrow night, you'll know us all, we'll all know you..."

"I shouldn't stay. Your mom—"

"...likes you," Leah interrupted. "Mama rarely cooks on the Sabbath, but only on the day before. What she did, she did for you. Besides," she said, turning him gravely toward the window and the ever falling snow, "you're stuck." He saw her smile then and felt his own begin. He held her, breathed the essence of some wildflower in her hair and knew tomorrow would be good, whatever happened. She squeezed his hand, then walked into a guestroom and returned. The gift was wrapped in blue, printed with golden menorahs. He opened it reverently, thinking it, by size and shape, perhaps a Jewish Bible. It was, instead, *Wanderings: Chaim Potok's History of the Jews*. Well chosen; she had recognized his need. He thanked her with a solemn kiss. He wouldn't have a gift for her tomorrow, he said, feeling wretched.

"You will," she said. "You'll have stayed the day." She tugged his hand. "Come upstairs. We'll talk to Matt and Dessa a while. I'll bet the rest have gone to bed."

To bed, he thought, and if he'd known no Jesus... He followed her upstairs, to Matt and Dessa.

Chapter 10

Leah pushed away the covers and swung her feet down to the floor. Sleep would not come while conversations replayed in her mind. She slipped a satiny robe over pj's of the same and walked to the window. Snow lay like a moonlit cloud on the sweeping valley and on the distant hills, tranquil, content at last; it granted to her nightclothes luminescence—benediction, pale aquamarine. She thought she could see movement through the trees within the hedgerow—deer, perhaps, braving drifts to nibble sapling bark. Specks, she thought, they and I in the cosmos. So little change would snuff out all of life. But *Adonai El Shaddai* never sleeps.

Her door was open. There came a quiet rapping, almost too light to be heard. A low voice spoke her name. "Still up?" it asked.

"Come in," she said to Matt. "You've tucked in Dessa?"

Next door, he told her as he sat down on her bed. "I bade milady goodnight at her chamber door—not too long after you sent Jon to the dungeon," he said, his grin catching moonlight as he glanced at Leah's clock. It was a little past 2:00 A.M. "Peter and the *goy* in their own cells. They'll do fine." He kicked off his loafers and slid back on the bed. "All right, tell Mattie. Did your coach turn into a pumpkin at midnight?"

She tried to recall when he had first become her counselor, encourager, and friend, this person who had so infuriated her as they grew up. It had happened both gradually and suddenly; neither could have charted how or when. She slipped between the sheets and sat cross-legged. She guessed she didn't know, she said, how to like a guy so much the way he was, yet give to him the world in which she lived. She told him her impressions from the start with Jonathan. Matt listened, questioned further, and reflected what he heard. He told her she should stay her course, make no decisions yet. From what he saw, he thought Jon was all right. Then he turned the subject to her schooling.

She said her coursework would be finished before the month was up; research was fascinating, and her cases added grist. There was one, though, that was more than she could figure. She outlined the Rothman file without his name and told Matt of the luncheon she'd had three days ago, the one she felt she had not handled well. He listened, sometimes nodding, sometimes asking more. She finished, and he sat up, grim, and gave it back to her: She herself had set up this luncheon—even paid her way. Knowing the guy's Achilles, she had ordered a tongue-twister; let him sweat. Next, the meal's not kosher; send it back. Leah laughed a little, not sure where Matt was going. Sexy waitress shows up, he said; hold the guy's hand. Waitress leaves; it didn't count. Leah balled the sheet beneath her chin to squash a squeal, but Matt pursued: Promise him the world, then say you're leaving. Tear his clutching hand away; be strong. "Don't you see?" Matt cautioned gravely. "He's out to make you look bad. Axe it. Now. Get...rid...of...him."

Leah was holding both hands to her face, tears of laughter wetting her palms. She toppled backward squealing that it wasn't like that. "But it was," she groaned. "Oh, Matt, I even winked." Her fists squeezed both her temples to force away chagrin; it spurted out again, an eddy of cleansing laughter, and washed her where it would till it was done. In foam and ripples, she lay limp and beaten, and then Matt, smiling, pulled her to himself. His mouth at her ear, he rocked her and said it would be all right. She took in a breath, held it, then let it out slowly. "There's one more thing, Matt. My supervisor thinks this kid really does have feelings for me. I can't let that happen, and I don't *want it to.* Seriously—what am I doing wrong?"

Matt shook his head and held her away from him to look into her pleading eyes. "I know you, Leah. You're not one to intentionally lead a guy on. You don't even think on that level. You just wear your caring nature on your sleeve, that's all. But don't try to be somebody you're not. When the time comes, you'll know what to say." He kissed her face. "Happy Hanukkah."

"Good night, Matt," she said, wiping tears with the flat of her hand, tired. "I hope you're right."

HER FOOT WAS COLD. In her dream, she heard Matt call. And then her foot grew warm, and she knew it was her dad. She was a girl of four in a yellow sunsuit, legs splayed in the grass beneath the willow at the old place, playing house. Her foot was in her father's hands, like a fledgling fallen from the nest. She felt the pat-pat and waited for the upsetting when he would tickle, roll, and sweep her from under the tree, toss her high over his head, spin her 'round and 'round till she was dizzy and he stopped. "Again, Papa," she would plead, her head still reeling.

"No more now," he would say, cradling her in his arms. "Tomorrow..."

"...Good morning, Princess." Antoine held her foot in his lap, rubbing his warmth into it with both hands, and Leah awakened. It was his second greeting.

"Good morning," she said, sitting up. She pulled her feet together and, kneeling on the quilt, pressed a kiss onto his cheek. "Happy Hanukkah, Papa. Did my laughing waken you last night?"

"How else would we know Matt was home?" Antoine asked.

"He helped me with some things," Leah said, pulling the robe from off the footboard, slipping into its sleeves. She had not talked with her father alone since the night before last, when she'd felt him out about Jon. She covered her feet with the robe, her shoulders relaxed, and she turned to the thought that still troubled her mind. "It's hard to know why a person fails, why he keeps failing. I have this case..." He took her hand in both of his and patted it.

She told him she was scared. "It's someone's life."

"God doesn't fail, and you're of him."

"But it's so exasperating. Pray, Papa, while I'm gone."

"As for Jonathan," he said as he pulled her gently to the edge of the bed and tapped her temple, "let your mama see inside. Talk to her."

She kissed him and took her toiletry bag to the door. "Did I say 'Pray'?"

Chapter 11

Broad campus walkways were cleared of the new-fall, but there still lay between the banks of the narrower lanes an inch or two of trodden snow. Most 8:00 A.M. classes were still in session, but David's had been dismissed on completion of his final presentation on this last day of the semester. Their feet made crunching sounds as he and Leah walked back up to Moore Building. She was speaking with her hands. "I'm talking *overall*. You were coming across with confidence the first two-thirds, then you tripped. What was it? 'Potential...'"

"'...for economic aggrandizement,'" he supplied.

"'Aggrandizement,' yes—and you tuned to the block. People stumble. Why fix on the stone?"

"I've never seen you all ablaze. It's terrifying."

"Be serious."

"When *you* are," he said, smiling. "Tell me how great I was, except this, except that. What am I supposed to believe?"

She stopped and placed her hands on his arms below the shoulders as if she would shake him. Looking into his eyes as fiercely as she was able, she pronounced each word for his future recall. "You asked me to be your friend. A friend doesn't tell someone just what he wants to hear. I'm telling you the truth as I see it. I will always tell you the truth as I see it. Is that clear?"

He was looking down at her through those lashes. She felt his bicep move as he shifted his books from right to left, and her motherly posturing seemed instantly absurd. He shook her hand solemnly, fighting the grin. "I will hold you to it till the day I die." And then the lightsomeness was gone. "You're the reason I made two-thirds. You know that."

He frustrated her, he made her day; he was inscrutable, he was transparent; he was impenetrable, he was wide open. And in a few days he would be someone else's nemesis. She reclaimed her hand and turned again into the walkway; he fell into step beside her. What were his plans for next semester, she wanted to know. Maybe Shakespeare, he told her, one eyebrow raised. She allowed him a little smile and said an international entrepreneur ought to be well-rounded.

"I-In the intellectual s-s-s-sense," he added. They were both aware of the lapse into disfluency.

"David," she said, slowing her pace, "to manage a chain—is that what you *really want*?"

Twice they saw their breath on the frosted air before them; then, watching the path as they walked, he said, "Choices aren't for Rothmans."

The impact of his words could be seen in Leah's face; she felt it through her frame. So, Hurland, right again. Small wonder he didn't "want it bad enough." What went with recovery of fluency was not only overwhelming, it was not what he wanted to do with his life. Denial of his true feelings now tacitly admitted, though, there was little cause to be angry with David; look for domineering parents, Hurland had said. It had never entered Leah's mind to ask her parents what they intended she become; happiness and fulfillment were their wish for her, of course, and for her brothers, too. Indignation welled. They had moved a dozen steps before she laid a hand on David's arm and stopped. "Your father expects you to follow in his footsteps, no questions asked?"

"He's asked."

She could only look at him. Talk about telling a person what he wanted to hear. She began to walk again, unnerved. "What would you do," she asked, "if you were free to choose?"

"Ah, well, now. I'd be...a...peacetime paratrooper. The man who discovered and delivered the...cancer vaccine. The guy who carried the AIDS meds to the last hut in the Congo...or... What's the matter? You don't believe me?"

She walked, her eyes on the path. She felt his hand on one shoulder. It slid behind her collar and he appeared in front of her, cajoling with a crooked smile. "Come on. You know what they say about us Jewish boys. We're businessmen. Born to it. Certain fields—we just excel..." Untaken, she would have moved forward, but he did not allow it. He closed his eyes an instant then looked away; his jaw set and when he turned again to her, there was no smile. "I c-can't walk out on him. He needs me *now*. MMMMartin's got his hands full, d-depending on incompetents when I-I-I c-c-c-I c-c-can do this f-for D-D-D..." He took two steps backward and smashed his hand flat on the bark of a tree. He retrieved it a fist, applied it firmly to the trunk and stared. A woman walking toward them tried to appear unseeing as she veered into a higher path.

Leah clenched her hands inside her pockets. When he turned, his eyes met hers, and more than she had ever wanted to be somebody's friend, she wanted to be David's. She moved her head in the direction they had been going, and he walked toward her. She did not wait for the apology, but it came as she laced her arm comfortingly through his and they continued toward the clinic. So low that only he could hear, she said, "You know he loves you. Couldn't you help him see you might not be the one?"

"No. No. When spring semester's over, I'll be going to Israel with him to plant a store. That was his 'Happy Hanukkah' to me."

"Wait, here she is." Andy handed Leah the phone and added, "Jonathan."

Leah greeted him warmly, shouldering the receiver to work her way out of the jacket. Yes, it did, she told him, and Dad had put it on the door for her. "A masterstroke, Jonnie. She sees the

symbolism, asked me if you knew my father is also of Judah."
Andy pictured a brass knocker on Miriam Beaumont's front door,
a lion's head with a ring through its mouth, and doodled it in her
notebook. Leah told Jon she thought it would be a good time—
nothing going on at her house. She twisted and untwisted the phone
cord for another ten minutes before she hung up and Andy could
ask questions.

"Giving it his all, isn't he?" Andy ventured.

"Off with a roar."

"So...why are you looking like a motherless lamb?"

Leah sat on the bed. "My turn in the den, I guess."

"Semester break?"

Leah nodded. "With the Grantes."

"Mm. Rick's asked me home with him for Christmas too, but
since I didn't see my folks over Thanksgiving, he's coming my way."

"My life should be so simple," Leah said flatly.

"Save it. Mom's dating. Who knows what I'll find."

Andy was right; she was not the one with whom Leah would
want to trade places. How and when do parents who love each
other decide to love no longer? Leah tried to imagine her own mom
and dad splitting up, or Bernie and Roseanne. No, the pledge of
faithfulness would overpower the rub. It was beginning to look
like lifetime love for Matt and Dessa, too. She thought of Grandpa
sitting on the couch, gazing at the photo of his Josephine. Maybe
there was something about faithfulness that people caught or
learned from family.

Jonathan. Good looks aside, he was intelligent, responsible,
sensitive—especially since Hanukkah—persevering, tender, committed. She saw things happening in Jon that made her sure he
would not abandon her; she would survive the lion's den. And
there were more reasons than that for getting her chin up. Her
casework was coming along. Today, she had touched the core of
David Rothman's trauma, and that had lifted her as much as anything. Indeed, as much as anything.

Chapter 12

THE LEATHER WAS SUPPLE AND SOFT. Leah buttoned the coat, belted it, pulled up the hood, smoothed one lapel under the other. She stood before the mirror on the back of the apartment door and turned around. Elegant. She needed this coat, and Jon could afford it. No. She needed *a* coat, and Jon was stretching for this one. Why couldn't she have been born the seventh of April or the seventh of June? She slipped out of the sleeves and ran a hand over the lining, then hung the coat in her closet beside her everyday jacket and her old all-weather coat. She was not at all sure she could allow herself to keep it.

Classes were back in session as of today. It was heady no longer to feel the returned student, as such. Now there was only clinical work and the thesis to finish. She heaved the red suitcase onto the bed and unpacked the laundered clothes. She had emptied all but the cosmetic bag when Andy came in grumbling about her first two classes as if they had never parted. With a tissue, Leah dusted from the mirrored tray on her dresser the patterns left by perfumes and lipsticks earlier removed. When the last of the toiletries was again in place, she sat on Andy's bed, still listening. "So, how'd the visit to Jonathan's go?" Andy asked, her voice a little tight.

"How long have you got?"

"Lee, can we talk?" Andy swiped at her lower lip in a distracted way, and Leah sensed that by "talk" she meant about something other than what she had mentioned. She pulled her feet onto the bed and Andy sat next to her. "It's Rick." The lip quivered again; she bit it to make it behave, but now there was no voice.

"Your mom doesn't like him?" Leah asked carefully.

"My mom..." Andy said, frowning. She left the thought unspoken, swallowed, and plunged in. "Rick made love to me two nights before Christmas—in my own room. How could he do that?" she crabbed, fighting tears. If she expected support, it did not come in Leah's look. "I know," Andy responded to her silence, "if I didn't want it, why'd I let him?" She poked the corner of her eye with a thumb and told Leah they were just looking at her high school yearbooks. Her mom was at a party with "that bozo." Snatching a tissue, she said, "Rick really got into the basketball pictures of me, thought they were great, kissed me a couple of times. Somehow before we knew it..." She grimaced, and her voice squeaked, "I thought it would be different. What's this garbage about ecstasy? It hurt—it ruined Christmas." She picked up a book, sent it flying to the wall, and yelled, "I hate him." Hoarse sobs came with the tears.

Leah laid an arm across her shoulders and touched her head to Andy's. "Your timing was off, that's all," she said.

"Aw, no, don't give me that crap about wait till you're married. I love Rick." The sobs kept coming.

"Listen to you," Leah said, sitting up. "You hate him, you love him, you're mad 'cause it hurt. It's his fault you didn't wait; you don't care that you didn't wait. It shouldn't have happened at home. How many sides of your mouth can you talk out of?"

Andy's eyes shut, and tears squeezed from under the lids. "We went to Dad's Christmas. I couldn't even look at him. What if I'm pregnant?"

"How soon will you know?"

"If I'm lucky, twelve days."

"Assuming you're not—pregnant, that is—you still have a problem: You can face it now...or later when it's snowballed."

Andy blew hard. "You mean that it was wrong? Come off it. People *live* with each other."

"You've got a conscience, and you've had psych. How's Rick?"

Andy fiddled with the tissues she held, turning them over and over. "Not himself. He had to be back to campus two days later to fly out with the team for the bowl game. I think he'd have left early, anyway, because I wasn't myself, either. He came over last night when he got back, and I didn't even want to see him. But he must be hurting, too. That third quarter, his mind was anywhere but on—"

"You love him?"

She took her time, nodded, a smile playing on the corners of her mouth. "I don't hate him."

"Then split the blame—fifty-fifty. And back up."

"I'll call him."

Leah was due at the clinic by one. She said if Rick, for any reason, couldn't come over tonight, she'd take in a movie with Andy. "Deal?"

"Deal." Andy accepted the hug with heavy arms, then Leah pulled her jacket from the closet and slipped into it. At the door, she turned to survey the figure on the bed. Andy nodded, forcing a smile, and signaled her out the door. She closed it gently behind her, but part of her stayed. She hoped no one at the clinic today would further drain her emotions, her reserves being so low that the air in the hallway was stifling. As she exited the building into the crispness of the January day, she pledged to herself that she would not, in any circumstance, give away the beauty and the holiness of her own wedding night. The man to whom she would give herself would be the man, and only the man, who had slid the band onto her finger.

CARL PFENSTER WAS LEAH'S SECOND STROKE CASE. She looked forward to working with him, knowing that because his recovery had begun so quickly, he would make good progress. The interview had proceeded pleasantly, and she continued to chat with him as they walked back down the hall to the waiting room. When she opened the door, David Rothman was heading for it from the other side.

He brightened when he saw her, and she asked about his break. "Same as always," came the non-answer. With a tentative smile, she mentioned the lit course he had hoped to take, and he asked if she had a minute. She had five. They sat on the couch, and he told her of a course he'd heard about and got: an introduction to the history, literature, and religion of ancient Israel; a couple of presentations required. "Shades of Rabbi Feingold and hacking my way through Hebrew. Help me?"

She was pleased to see him upbeat; she said, "Sure. You're in a group session, I see."

"Two clinicians. What did you tell them, anyway?" He was on his feet smiling, saying he'd call, raising a hand with a book in it, and the door swung shut after him.

"Joelle?" Leah said to the little girl who was winding her way between the pieces of wooden play equipment, her hand on one and then the other. None seemed right. She looked at her mother, seated nearby, and walked to where she could grasp her hand as the woman rose to follow Leah.

Chapter 13

Suzanne was waiting at the appointed corner, her shoulders hunched against the wind, her blonde hair whipping about her face, skewing into tangles. Leah hastened her steps. She was not late, but she could see by the rose of Suzanne's face that she had been out longer than the few minutes it had taken Leah to walk from the clinic. It was the twelfth of March, a Monday, and the sidewalks were wet with melted snow, the shrunken mounds to each side flecked with grit. Most students had gone home on spring break; Suzanne had stayed to spend some time with Rob, whose family lived in town. She and Leah exchanged a quiet "Hi" and moved heeled boots in concert toward the brick apartment building down the street. "Why hasn't she told me?" Suzanne asked. "How is she?"

"Lonely. Says she's on the outside." She thought of Andy during those first hard weeks when she had begun to suspect there was no turning back. The early pregnancy test, the day it colored positive, had brought on retching, without physiological cause, for the next ten hours. Leah had tried to provide a shoulder for her through the myriad moods of those next days—the despair, the *if only's*, the irritability; then gradually, increasingly, acceptance and determination to see it through, to decide direction. Leah had let her research slide to give Andy all the time she needed to talk out feelings. She had tried to make up a little of it while Rick and Andy were working things out in the apartment; she would stack up her notebooks and head for the library, or work in an empty room at the clinic.

Ultimately Rick suggested, for the sake of Andy's state of mind, that the sooner they were married, the better. Never once had either brought up the possibility of eliminating the baby from the matrix, and Leah had let them know in subtle ways that she was certain that when he or she arrived, they would be glad for it. On a Friday, Leah and Cat stood witness to a quiet wedding in Mrs. Sebring 's Reading apartment. It was clear Cat also grieved; a joyless spirit hung over the day. Ordinarily, Andy was outgoing and Rick, to say the least, gregarious; celebrating with a crowd of friends and relatives from far-flung towns would have been more to their liking. But Andy had said no. She wore a simple suit, and there followed after the ceremony a modest meal in her mother's dining room. Leah and Cat—Jerry—headed back to school soon afterward; Rick and Andy honeymooned the weekend in the Poconos.

Twice prior to today, Leah had visited the newlyweds' apartment. On the latter occasion she had found Andy's feelings mixed on married life. Yes, she loved Rick; yes, he had been sensitive to her needs, as she had tried to be to his. Her schoolwork wasn't getting what it needed—too much to do—but she'd pull it off. A couple of shows a week on TV, then hit the books till twelve. Who needed to go out? But the worst part, Andy said, was being lonely in a crowd, a fish in a jar in the ocean. The ring, the baby—something cut her off. No one related to her in the same way that they had before, or at least, it felt that way to her. That was the night Leah had gone home and phoned Suzanne.

The two of them climbed the steps to the door, and Suzanne said that if Leah would be staying in town in June, she'd be glad to give up the dorm for half-rent on the efficiency Leah and Andy had shared; she was sure she could get work. They found their way to the ground floor apartment numbered 14. Someone had made, or heated, a coffeecake.

The door opened with Andy's "Come in, come in," and they entered to the whistle of a kettle. She took their jackets and showed them to a small table in the kitchen where she had set three places. They sat to eat the cake she cut and drink the tea she poured, and the conversation soon was easy, peppered with bursts of laughter as they brought forth scenes, events, and people from the last three years. They had been there nearly an hour when Suzanne absently carved a second, smaller piece of cake and, lifting it from the pan, belatedly asked whether she might; her slender fingers, nails polished petal pink, held the morsel in mid-air.

"Have my share too," Andy said, her plate still clean from the cupboard.

"Morning sick?" Leah asked.

"The term is not descriptive."

Suzanne hesitated.

"Eat," Andy ordered. "Leah?" she said, cutting a fresh slice.

It was going on five when they rose to leave. Andy said she'd miss them after May and, good grief, she'd be an elephant by then. Suzanne assured her they'd all be in tents for graduation.

"Not quite all," Leah said, reminding them that neither her clinical competency certificate nor her thesis would be done, and probably not for two more semesters. "Where will Rick be working?" she asked.

"Anywhere but here," Andy said, propping her chin on a hand.

"The six of us should get together while we can," Suzanne said. "How about Wednesday night? Would Jon come up?"

"I won't be here," Leah answered. "Why not Saturday?"

Andy gave Suzanne a knowing look. "She's going to his place."

"Johnstown," Leah amended.

"With your folks," Andy offered.

"With a friend. Sue, you remember riding with me as far as Uncle Paddy's hunting cabin last fall. Perfect place to concentrate."

"On what?" Sue asked.

"A talk for class."

"You don't *have* class," Andy said.

"He does."

"He?" Andy glanced at Sue and back to Leah.

"Now wait," Leah said, leaning back in her chair, "it's strictly academic." There was an awkward silence. "Well," Leah said, trying to pull her voice back down, "let's let this spouse cook for her man." She carried her cup to the sink. "So much to do over break; we're not home free."

THEY PARTED AT THE SAME CORNER where they had met, and Leah walked on, alone with her thoughts. Maybe it was unnecessary to remove herself and David from the scene, but she remembered too well the frustrations of trying to work with him on the Pentateuch at the HUB, where there was privacy for little more than editing the talk for flow. Practice on delivery had to be confined to an unused clinic room, and the sterility of the place was a trial of which she'd had enough by seven o'clock. Uncle Paddy's hunting lodge was ideal. They would have all the time they needed, no interruptions, one whole day.

Wednesday would be good because David would be back Tuesday night from Mac's. He had gone home with Evan to bone up at his Turners' Club for Saturday's gym meet, and by midweek, he had said, he would welcome a day's break. At the farm, he would have a chance to meet some easy-to-talk-to strangers in Aunt Claire and Uncle Paddy, to learn a little about riding since he never had before, to get a grip on the project in the still of the mountains. And she could talk with him further about his future; that alone would justify the trip.

Ironic that Andy—Sue too, she thought—reacted the way she did to the mention of a friend. Granted, she had never said anything to either of them about her pact with David, but surely they both knew she was seeing only Jon. As for the allure of a mountain retreat, she had thought they knew her better than to wonder. When reputation is important, one is careful even of appearances. Did they not know that where she came from, Father as head of the household set the standards; the standards were behind the times, and Mama was, if anything, more behind the times than he.

Except for a year or so in high school when she had felt an anachronism, Leah had never minded. Too many of her acquaintances were already illustrations of remorse bred out of so-called freedom. Her freedom was the kind God gave—the freedom of a heart in subjection to order, a heart at peace.

She turned into the entrance of her building reasoning that Andy was too close to her own regret to remember: Leah had the straightest arm in town. She walked the hall to 22 and stood before her door. Leah, she thought, staring, you are debating the wrong issue. They know as well as anyone your principles are sound, but here's the fact: Peace from God is not a plastic anchor; it is as rocklike as is needed for the ship. Yet for weeks, yours has been moving in the water. You need a quiet sail with David. You know why.

Chapter 14

It was Wednesday afternoon, 4:20 by the clock on the desk. David leaned heavily toward the window frame, his weight coming to bear, through a locked-straight arm, on the heel of his hand riveted there. His head rested on the arm as he looked at the floor, and he held the receiver to his ear as if he would rather have not. It was a long time before he spoke, and when he did, the stutter was bad. "A very nice girl, Mother, that's what kind...and with her aunt and uncle.... The cabin's tomorrow.... No, overnighting at the *house*.... Farrell." He listened again, annoyed that he, at twenty-one, could be having this conversation. If only he had not retained the propensity to stutter his worst with family, he thought, he would have had better command of this pattern by now. Would he ever be of age to her? "You're not hearing me, Ma. It's therapy.... A course on the *Tenach*.... She doesn't have to know it; she listens.... To get a hold on the talk.... Ma... Yeah, well, Ma, I've gotta go. Trust me."

He hung up the phone and pulled on a suede jacket, thinking as he snapped the waistband that it would do well for riding. He slid the Book and notebook from the desk, picked up the fresher gym bag, the one he had packed, and walked from the dorm to the old Peugeot in the lot. Having tossed his things into the trunk, he kicked the snow from under the fenders, got in, and started the engine. The immediate response, the quiet hum still, after seven months' calling it his, made him smile. He would not let the memory of that first drive taint his feelings toward this car. It was on Martin's insistence that they passed by on the berm. Couldn't miss his flight, he said. They made Newark on time, all right, and the wreckage was cleared when David got back. It was the next day, when he read about the old man, that he knew how rotten he felt. Evidently no one else had stopped, either, not till it was too late. Maybe he could have made the difference. God help him, he would not make that mistake again.

Leah was standing next to a small red bag when he stopped in front of her building. Ready and traveling light; he liked that. He put the bag in back and, with Leah beside him, pulled out. Today, he would ask the questions; she would answer. There were four Farrells, he discovered. Mike, seventeen, and Danny, in eighth grade, would be overnighting with the horse club, there being no school tomorrow. "Uncle Paddy" and "Aunt Claire," who had for a number of years bred Quarter Horses, were now investing time and money in the Saddlebred, for which there was an expanding market. While she was growing up, Leah had helped at the farm with whatever tasks she was ready to do—including some of the training—receiving room and board for the summer, plus a small wage for her work. Concerning her close family, David learned she had a brother still at home, one on campus, one in heavy equipment in Florida. She liked music, lots of kinds, played piano; she made her clothes when she had time; and she loved to swim. Always, David had found her easy to talk to, but now, with the clinical relationship ended, she seemed to share herself without the old precautions. When they reached the rural area north of Johnstown and she suggested he slow down near the entrance to the farm, he was half disappointed; he wanted more. At the house there would be relatives and at the cabin, work to be done.

The old sign at the mouth of the dirt road was freshly painted; below a silhouetted prancing horse it read, *Spring Hill Farm, P. D. and C. J. Farrell.* The road was long, bordered on both sides by young maples not yet in bud. Behind these stretched white fencing whose crisscrossed boards appeared to spiral where there was a dearth of trees. A small wooden sign on the side of the straightaway warned: *Think dust—Slow down.* Nearer the house, the trees were tall, and the house itself gave the appearance that it had stood in its place a hundred years. Leah asked David to drive past it, pointing out the graveled area in front of a long white barn, and he pulled off, braking for a mottled kitten bounding toward the grass.

A slight woman in her forties appeared in the gaping doorway of the barn. She wore jeans and a blouse once indigo; her hair, tied back, was red. She put down a bucket and walked to the car, where Leah introduced her as Aunt Claire. Her greeting was spoken with a note of surprise, and as David returned it, he was, himself, surprised at his fluency. He just might like being here.

Claire asked if he wanted to see the stock while she finished the watering. They followed her into the long, well-manicured barn, breathing air dense with aromas of hay and creosote. The bearer of the water bucket was dwarfed by each animal in turn as she commanded him or her to move back in the stall and let her in. She described the attributes, good and ill, of each by name in the first three stalls, speaking alternately to David and to the horse, and then fell more to working than to talking. She filled the pails one by one, coming back each time to a hose that reached so far and never farther. Leah showed David the next five animals which, according to the plaques above their stalls, were Cherokee Lance, Stetson Rose, Pal O' Mine, Winchester, and Danny Boy's Dinah. At the last, she picked up another bucket and began to fill it for the horses on the other side. David carried his share until the job was done. He marveled at the number, and Claire, pulling free a forkful of hay and laughing, said Paddy and Frank—whom he assumed to be a hired hand—were doing the other barn.

They carried their bags to the house in late twilight. The glow from the kitchen promised warmth and relief from the hunger they felt. Claire showed them to their rooms and, in minutes, called from the foot of the stairs that their plates were on the table, hot from the oven. Having poured three coffees, she sat with them while they ate.

A starless evening had fallen when P. D. Farrell came through the anteroom. He was a man formidable of build and ruddy of face, his black sideburns peppered with gray. "What's this? English is back," he teased Leah. "*Now* we'll show that stallion." Leah laughed, remembering the first time she had sat an English saddle and regaled Paddy on the "zillion ways" she liked it better than the Western. From her place at the table, she introduced David.

"G-glad to know you, sir," David offered, rising. "Q-quite an operation you have here." His hand, extended, was engulfed in Paddy Farrell's while Paddy grinned a thank you. The larger hand shook David well, then set him free again to sit before his plate.

"Just don't get thinkin' it's glorious, son," Paddy added with a mischievous look at David. "What I do all day, if the truth be known, is shov—"

"Paddy, have some coffee," Claire said urgently.

His eyes a-twinkle, he leaned to kiss her head. "A beer when I'm cleaned up."

After dinner, Claire nudged David with fingertips and "shushes" toward the living room, where he was to wait for Leah, Paddy, and herself. The Farrells' home was neither lavish nor meticulously kept, but large and filled with overstuffed chairs and couches, a hodgepodge of Early American furnishings, antique and simulated, and on nearly every flat surface there stood or hung trophies, natural and manmade. An old corner cupboard held not china, but statuettes and cups of every size, ornate and designating excellence in conformation or performance, the tribute of horse show panels in and out of state. Above the mantel in the living room hung the largest buck's head David had ever seen, its overgrown rack surely the cause of its demise. In both living and dining areas he saw the work of taxidermists: a quail here, a ring-neck there. And pictures of fine horses, alone and in groupings, decorated the walls.

Paddy sauntered in holding half a glass of beer and, pointing to some of his favorites, talked to David about Quarter Horses and the breed called the American Saddle Horse, of which the Farrells owned five and fourteen, respectively. Three brood mares had foaled already this spring, and six more would do so by the end of May, Paddy said, so if the weather cooperated, it promised to be "a good year, with boarders, grain and hay sales, and all." Claire entered the room offering to show David, before he left, the Saddlebreds, the mounts that appeared in the photos and paintings with long manes and flowing tails, their riders, if shown, in full regalia—saddle suit, low boot, hat, and crop. He thus far, she told him, had seen only the Quarter Horses and boarded stock.

The more David heard about equitation and equestrian matters, the more he realized he did not know. He determined that his inexperience would not sully the ride the next day. Leah had never laughed at him; why would she start tomorrow?

It was 9:40 when the Farrells declared they had been up too late and would have to say goodnight. Claire said she was glad the weather had been dry all week, seeing as the trails were mucky enough from the spring melt, without rain. Paddy wished them a good ride and asked Leah to see whether he had left his meerschaum at the cabin. David tried to pull from his memory a definition for "meerschaum" but could not. Maybe it was a type of rifle or coat or cap. He thanked them for dinner, and they climbed the stairs to who knew what safari-like trappings among which to sleep. David celebrated the unexpected time to talk with Leah only to discover it was not to be. Five-thirty was a blink away, she told him, pulling him from the soft, old couch. She led the way upstairs and left him at her doorway, disappearing inside with a promise to waken him when her alarm rang.

He strolled the hall wondering who first started day at night—an overzealous farmer or a dimwitted horse. He amused himself awhile with the relics in his room. A portrait—probably reproduced from a daguerrotype—sepia in color and greatly enlarged to hang over the fireplace, had caught his attention earlier, and now he took time to survey it from mid-room. In a V-shaped configuration two uniformed men sat astride sleek, perhaps bay, mounts. They posed not with arrogance but with dignity, or noblesse oblige, for this occasion upon which their demeanor would be forever captured by the photographer's lens—judging by their dress, a good many years ago. Each pinned his plumed parade helmet beneath a bent arm the hand of which held, laced through gloved fingers, double reins. The left hand of each man rested on the hilt of a sheathed sword. The scabbard of the rider on the right was visible; it extended to the flank of his horse, behind his boot.

The cavalrymen made a handsome set. David studied their faces. He was drawn to that of the soldier on the right, something about his appearance a fascination. What a striking man he was, the light irises so unlikely with his black hair, the bearing so kind, so kingly.

He moved to the desk near the fireplace to pick up a color photo of two boys, also mounted—the sons, he guessed, of Paddy and Claire. The garb was the formal riding habit; the horses each wore a ribbon on the bridle—one red, one blue. Having replaced the picture, David sat on the edge of the sleigh bed—much too soft—and examined his boots. Low, made for dress, but they would do. He pulled them off. He wasn't tired; he was ready to go tonight. How was he supposed to shut off the adrenaline long enough to sleep? He pulled off his shirt and pants and exchanged them for pajama bottoms—a favor he granted on visits—took his toothbrush and headed for the bath. Returning, he turned down the billowy quilt and slid between the sheets, taking with him his notes for the next day's work. Six minutes passed before his eyes grew heavy. He tugged the lamp chain, sighed, and sank into the down.

Chapter 15

THE HOUSE WAS QUIET except for the clink of steel on steel in the kitchen. When David came down, Leah was filling two plates with scrambled eggs. She was wearing deep brown jeans over boots that tapered to the toe. A jacket of like material dressed the back of a chair; its piping was the color of butter, the color of her blouse. She moved dexterously, placing two biscuits on each plate and the remaining basketful on the table set with cream, jellies, a juice decanter, and a well-used, steaming carafe. She asked him if he'd slept well—he had—and, sitting down, waited for him to take his place.

He poured coffee for her and for himself, picked up a biscuit and, seeing the jam was nearer her, was about to request it when he noticed she sat motionless. Her hands rested on either side of her setting, palms up. She tipped her head back and, as if God were perched on the ceiling light, thanked him softly for his kind provision, including the morning. They ate and talked, and both were good.

She led him to the upper barn where, he assumed, they would find their mounts. But when Leah had taken two halters and two lead ropes from the wall, they went out the other side to enter a fenced pasture into which, she explained, Uncle Paddy had already turned out their horses; to ready them for the ride, he had fed them at five.

"These are..." Quarter Horses, he thought, completing his guess in private.

She said, indicating the sorrel at mid-pasture, that the mare was a Quarter Horse; the gelding, she told him, nodding toward the lean chestnut against the far fence, was a cross. Timberjack, she called him. The horse raised his head and cocked his ears. Slinging the halters over her shoulder, she asked David to wait at the gate. He watched her walk the considerable distance to the mare, offer something from her pocket, halter her, and attach the shank of the lead. She led her part of the way to the gelding and let go of the rope. The sorrel stood still while she approached Timberjack, now walking to receive the offering in her hand. While he ate, she spoke to him softly, slipped the halter over his head, patted his neck, and moved her hand stroke by stroke toward his withers and back. She offered him another chunk of whatever it was—carrot?—and turned him a little. David was no longer able to see her. From his place at the gate, it seemed she attached the lead then abandoned the horse. When he next saw her, her mid-section was against the dark back, then a leg swung over to straddle it. She leaned down to retrieve the gelding's lead rope, then rode to the mare at a jog. David gave her a 9.8 and a smile; she had done it sans springboard. He watched her pick up the mare's rope and ride to the gate with her in tow.

Dismounting, she handed him the sorrel's lead and guided Jack by his halter to the tack room. "This is Claire's penny dog," she said over her shoulder. "You've got Dinah. She was broken in Colorado, and Danny's taught her everything he knows."

Leah tied their mounts between the building and separate posts. She handed David a brush and told him to be particular about the saddle area. When the thick winter coats were smooth and the manes and tails knotless, she took him into the tack room, striding through the area where show and equitation saddles hung close to one another on wide, pipe-like protrusions from the wall and over two central railings. They walked to the end of the building, which David guessed had been, at one time, a milk house. Lifting a hand-tooled saddle and two striped blankets from the railing, Leah said they would ride Western today. She carried the tack over both arms toward the back wall, where she selected a second saddle. He'd feel secure in this, she told him, but he wasn't to go hanging onto the pommel. As she made her way back to the door and outside, he heard her say something about his seat, good hands, and wanting to elope. No. Depending on his seat and whether he had good hands, she'd said, they might want to try a lope. He followed her, carrying his saddle, laughing to himself. He told her she was riding with a guy who knew "three g-gears— g-giddap, clip-clop, and whoa." She let her saddle nose into the grass while she blanketed the horses. Her face was summer and health this morning. Maybe it was the presence of dawn light, or the absence of makeup—she was as fresh as the new day.

"No one's going to rush you," she answered. "And forget those words; I don't think you'll need any." He felt the tension dissipate. Did she always know what to say?

To David's surprise, the lope was the most comfortable of the gaits he had tried so far. Except for the exhilaration that came with the wind in his face and the meadow passing under him, he was not much less secure on Dinah than he would have been on an over-sized rocking horse. He noted that Leah rode down in the saddle, at one with Timberjack. He shouted to her as they rode that he wanted to borrow her glue. She slowed to a walk, and he did the same while she explained again how to move with the back of the horse. Balance, he had, she told him; practice would improve his seat. In his discreet opinion, hers needed no improvement; neither did the way she moved. All morning, he mused, she had talked to him on one level, and he had heard her on another. Her inno-cence, her grace, a certain sensuousness, innate, had him one moment immersed in light fantasy about her, the next chiding him-self, and through all, trying to look skillful on a beast five times his mass. Holding the reins in one hand, he moved Dinah out using his weight and the pressure of his knees and calves, as he had been shown to do; he put her into an easy lope. This time he had it. There was no slap at all on the saddle, no jolting of his back, and the stirrups didn't move; he was, in fact, no longer dependent on them. Bobbing as if over a child's drawing of gentle waves, he sailed at one with Dinah on the meadow. A new measure of competence filled him and, with it, a celebration of this day with Leah.

They slowed to a walk to ascend another section of wooded trail, he following behind her. He was able to hear her if she turned from time to time to face him, which she did if either had a thought to share. When there had been game to observe in the lowlands, she had simply pointed it out for his enjoyment: the doe, a coon at the base of a brook-side birch, a groundhog in the brush. Now, although they were not at any great altitude, they saw no forest life. About 400 feet from the top of the ridge, they entered a clearing where stood a good-sized lodge fashioned of seasoned whole timber. Leah dismounted on a patch of barren ground. As David reined in too and swung his leg down, her horse backed into Dinah, who skittered. His left foot still in the stirrup, David hopped after the mare, grabbing for mane and the cantle. Behind him he heard Leah say, "Whoa. Drop your reins—she ground ties." He let the reins fall, and Dinah froze. Carefully he separated his boot from the stirrup. The legs he stood on belonged to someone else, a sailor maybe.

He was glad to be there. He was hungry. Leah had gone around to the back of the cabin and now reappeared carrying two halters, one of which she handed to him. She unsaddled Timberjack and turned him into the small corral, the fourth side of which was the northwest end of the lodge. David asked no questions; he unsaddled and led Dinah through the gate, envisioning himself on a couch, with Leah bringing food. He watched the mare sway lazily among the meager tufts of grass and choose the lushest cropping for herself. When he walked back to the cabin, Leah was not there. From somewhere down the hill, she called that there was another bucket on the porch. He picked it up and followed the voice a hundred yards or more down to the spring. They filled both pails to nearly full and climbed, with care, the path up to the lodge. His legs had never felt like this before, not even after too long on the mats; they were not yet his own. Leah placed one pail outside the fence and said they'd save the second for the cabin. She pulled a hoof pick from her pocket and showed him how to scrape the clods and pebbles from Dinah's frogs and shoes. She looked on with approval while he worked, till finally, he let the last clean hoof slide from his cradling knees. They rubbed the horses down from ear to tail and smeared foul-smelling ointment from a can on hairless spots. Leah put the lid back on and took everything to a bin next to the cabin. She rubbed the residue from her hands on one of the old terries, tossed it to him, and brought the watering bucket to where the horses could reach it. "Quarter of nine," she said. "To work."

He looked at her in disbelief, searching for a smile held back. As she stepped onto the porch, she turned and looked at him, he thought, in a way she had not before. The smile was there, small but warm, and it spoke mercy: "Let's eat."

Chapter 16

THE LODGE, INSIDE—ALTHOUGH ROUGH-HEWN—was not, as he had expected, stark. Neither was it like the house. Someone had arranged silk day lilies, daisies, and snapdragons over the fireplace and on the large, round kitchen table. Counters and a propane stove, aged to an ecru, were wiped to a shine. The furniture in the sitting room was maple, cushioned; and afghans lay folded or spread where color belonged. David opened windows to let in sun and air while Leah washed and carried the basin outside. Returning, she offered it empty to him and unrolled the blanketed supplies: dehydrated soup, more biscuits, cold turkey, cheese, some packets, a couple of apples, a globule of something that looked like a baseball in a plastic bag. Sourdough, she told him; they would be hungry again by two. She placed it in the sun on the dry sink and said soup would be on in twenty minutes.

He explored the place, amused at the presence even here of an ancient, gnat-bitten stuffed grouse. There in its guardianship was a sleek, white tobacco pipe. Paddy's, he guessed—both. On a hassock near the wide front window lay some sketchpads and pencils. The ridges opposite the lodge would make, he could see, an interesting background in watercolor or oils. Maybe the sketcher, whoever it was, painted too. He went outside to take in the building from all sides and found the rear half not living area for the hunter at all, but for the mount. Well swept, orderly. Whoever kept the stable probably kept the cabin, as well. Bales of hay and straw were stacked in separate pyramids. Several cartons of oats and corn, sealed shut, were ranked against one wall. He picked up a smaller container that rattled: pellets—vitamins. Everything a body equine could desire. Overhead, two meat hooks hung from a

75

rafter, awaiting the hunters' kill, and outside, tire tracks ran through puddles, leaves, and mud, and made a road that dropped into the woods. He walked the grounds until he found the structure needed, then walked back toward wafted coffee, broth, and biscuits.

The soup, although he had never had Cup-a-Soup so early, tasted good, and three servings with six biscuits was enough. There was fruit and cheese to follow, and he hoped that by the time he had finished, he would not be too satisfied and doze-prone to work. Leah cleaned up quickly, suggesting that he run through his paper once alone. She went outside, came back smelling of sweet hay, and joined him on the maple couch, where he had laid his notes and little Book.

He said, not complaining, that the course had taken more time than the rest combined. She knew, she said. Taking the comment as sympathetic, he added that he had read several of the prophets in the past three weeks; it seemed clear that the theme was, again and again, the stubbornness of the Children of Israel. He was beginning to think disobedience the major theme of the Bible: Adam's day, Noah's day, Moses' day, through the judges, the kings, to the exile. "Page after page, we let God down."

"Page after page and year after year."

He stopped shuffling papers.

"We still do," she said, retreating a little, "...let him down."

"No one denies the sad lack of principle in the world," he said carefully, "but, specifically, I meant the Chosen People."

"Yes."

He had never been offended by her before. Misunderstanding, surely. "You agree, the Jewish People let God down?"

"He told us to bring the world to him," she said. "We've done everything but."

Again, she had said "we." The image of Leah thanking God for breakfast and brunch took on new meaning and set his mind to questioning. "You're not Jewish..." he began tentatively.

"I'm not?" she said, enjoying the moment.

"Beaumont?"

"What is it about France that troubles you?" Her eyes were alight; again, behind them, she was laughing. Joy spurted up inside him seeking a wide, shining pool. A *yid*. She was a *yid*. She was saying that she had never met anyone with a deeper knowledge of God than her papa: he still talked of the Six-Day War with all the relish of a man who had seen the Lord, through Barak, destroy the Canaanites. He maintained, she said, that God's promises were often fulfilled more than once and that during that week in 1967, the Lord again made certain that Israel had *few* enough men to assure the glory of the victory to himself and not to numbers. Like Barak's warriors, each was empowered to fight as ten. David raised his eyebrows and looked overly impressed. Leah laughed, threw out her hands and said, "God told Joshua one would chase a *thousand*." She took his Bible from the couch cushion and opened it. "Right here," she insisted, but he did not look.

"You believe his promises are fulfilled more than once?" he asked.

"It's happened."

"And his threats? Twice, we've lost the Land."

"Never again."

He wanted to believe it. She flipped pages to the prophet Amos, where she showed him God had promised that following their dispersion throughout the world and his regathering of them to Israel, the Chosen would never be uprooted again. "Furthermore," she said, "he promises to raise up the fallen tabernacle of David and give Israel all the nations called by his name."

David sank down into the couch and propped a boot on a worn footstool. He chuckled inwardly at his mother's warning that Leah would not know the *Tenach*. Had she had this course? "Who else is called by his name?" he asked. "We're the Chosen."

Leah did not answer immediately. "Chosen for what?" she asked.

"To...be favored by God," David ventured.

"To be proven," Leah amended. "To be rubbed to a gleam by the nations 'Joshua left when he died'—Judges, chapter two. To lead the world, by our reflected light, to God."

"Wait. Is that what you're looking for? To be tumbled like an agate by everybody in the world? I'm not. No Jew I know—"

"God promises peace to anyone who does what he requires, what he expects."

"What more can he expect than the patience of the Jewish people through centuries of persecution?" He took his Bible back, leafed to where he had marked those tantalizing words of God to Jeremiah, and read to her:

And I will gather the remnant of my flock out of all the coun-
tries whither I have driven them, and will bring them back to
their folds; and they shall be fruitful and increase. And I will
set up shepherds over them who shall feed them: and they
shall fear no more, nor be dismayed, neither shall they be
lacking, saith the Lord.

"God's acting on that promise now," he said, feeling in better control of the conversation. "He'll put an end to persecution, and to terrorism, too, you'll see." Silently, he wondered how many centuries it would take.

Leah played with the cording on her cushion. "But first, we have to stop denying God," she said softly.

That her words perturbed him was evident to them both. "Who de-denies God? I-I-I-I don't. You d-d-don't." In stumbling, stuttering half-phrases, he told her she knew as well as he that the Jewish people were the most philanthropic race on the face of the earth and the least understood. Smacked in the face for their astuteness, no matter the country, they were maligned, hounded, used, and cast away, yet they struck back only in self-defense, and until the State of Israel came into its own, too often they would forego even that. They devoted their lives to the good of humankind in every field of endeavor, he told her, color rising in his face. "Who denies G-God?"

Again, she did not answer him at once. Then came the soft voice, feeling its way as if in a place of darkness. "People in high places. People in the street."

He was not in darkness, his mind retorted. She could leave her soft voice in the same place where lay her opinion. "And as for Israel's leadership," he continued aloud, "you know better than to find fault with those God himself has placed in authority."

"He upbraids them."

"God is GOD."

"A Joshua—a David—wouldn't hedge over the truth."

He stared at her. "What do you want?"

"God is right," she said into his eyes. "We are a stiff-necked people."

"We win," he whispered.

"For the sake of his *name*," she said, taking up the Book.

"Are you finished?"

She touched his arm, and he thought he felt her hand tremble. She gave him his Bible, open to his place. "Two sentences more."

He stared at her then took the Book. It read:

Behold, the days come, saith the Lord, that I will raise unto David a righteous sprout, and he shall reign as king and prosper, and shall execute judgment and justice in the earth. In his days Judah shall be saved, and Israel shall dwell safely; and this is his name whereby he shall be called, The Lord is our righteousness.

When he looked up, he saw tenderness in her eyes. "The Messiah," she said, "is peace. And we've rejected him."

His eyes widened. "Rejected? You... Don't tell me you think..."

"I know. Yeshua—Jesus—is the Messiah of Israel."

Revulsion stabbed his abdomen. How could she shatter his

joy? How could she? He wanted to shake her, spank her, knock the poison out of her. He wanted to leave. "Excuse me," he said with meaning he wished her not to miss. "I'm taking a walk." As he stepped off the side of the porch, the screen door banged twice behind him. How could she do this to him all in one day?

Chapter 17

FROM A FLAT ROCK NEAR THE CREST OF THE HILL, David looked down on the valley. The climb had only made him hotter. It was the irony of the thing. Why had there been no great obstacle when she was Leah Beaumont of the *goyim*—the non-Jews? He thought of Janna, and his mother's coolness the evening he brought her to the house. There had been no unseemly reaction to Margot or to Ellen, the difference being, of course, that Janna was not "one of us." Martin had known better than to bring home the wrong girl, ever. Why had he, D. J., always thought Gentile girls attractive? Hadn't he always known it was dangerous? If Leah, from the beginning, had been dangerous, now she was worse—a deception. A girl of the Covenant who bowed to Jesus, to three gods. The air was cold and moving; it—or was it the thought?—made him shiver. How does a person come to believe a lemon is an orange, he thought, or more unlikely, a plum? Someone's fed it to her with sugar. He kicked a small stone over the ledge and watched it bounce four times before he lost sight of it. He was certain that Leah was flying in the face of God, and it hurt him as if she were an errant sister—no, much worse. He scanned the forest below. The farm, he was sure, lay somewhere northeast of the lodge, the corner of whose roof he could see through the trees. There, where the treetops formed a V, would be the gully cut by the stream. He could walk back by the creek-side trail to the car. That would make his point. Or he could take the dirt road; it no doubt joined the highway one side or the other of Spring Hill. Wouldn't his leaving tell her clearly where he stood?

A lemon, a plum. Leah had to be smarter than that. Who had sold this to her? Her hand had trembled when she told him, so she had anticipated his reaction, feared it. Would his walking out jolt her, free her? A tremor stole across his shoulders, shot down and up his back at once. Would she even miss him? How much did she care? How much did *he* care?

He looked a long time at the horizon. It formed, thought upon thought, as he sat on the rock: the knowledge, the fact, that he was not willing to let her go. His stomach lightened, almost fluttered. The task lay before him. If he needed Rabbi Feingold's help, he'd get it; he would go to whatever lengths he must.

The sun had gone behind a bank of clouds, and the sky was darkening. He heard thunder, not close but long, and the wind that had hardly tousled his hair minutes ago now rippled his shirt through his open jacket. He rose from the ledge and made his way through low brush toward the trail. He had reentered the woods when the clouds burst. The rain pattered on the dead leaves that still clung to the oaks, then pelted the forest floor. He ran, his feet hitting the path in quick lightings, sliding in the mulch as the trail became wetter. He hadn't thought the lodge so far away.

When at last he broke into the clearing, he could see Leah trying in vain to herd the horses toward the corral gate nearest the entrance to the stable. He saw her opt instead to catch Timberjack, who evaded her twice. She managed on the third try to grasp a handful of soaked mane and one ear, then, pulling on his halter, she led him toward the stable door. The mare followed, her muzzle to one side then the other of the chestnut's croup. David took the quick route, over the fence on the support of a hand and straight to Dinah's halter. Reassuring her, he walked her into the stable. He did not speak to Leah when she saw him but gave her a gentle smile and went about his work, rubbing Dinah's coat dry with a towel from the wall hook. When the horses were stalled, David and Leah entered the lodge through the connecting door.

LEAH WASHED, then ran the clean terry over her hair. "Dry clothes in there," she said softly. He entered the bedroom. A patchwork quilt covered the double bed; matching tosses, eyelet trimmed, were propped upon the pillows, and a great, thick brown coverlet lay over the footboard of bronze. The bedside table held an oil lamp and a well-fingered paperback. There were two dressers, one cluttered with a man's toiletries, one with a woman's cosmetics. He opened the closet doors. Clothes, indeed. Flannel shirts, jeans—too large—wide belts, a hunting vest, a red-and-black checked coat; and to the left, blouses, slacks, loungewear, size five. It appeared that Paddy's hunting partner was chiefly Claire. He chose the smallest of P. D. Farrell's shirts, a blue plaid, and jeans; his own belt would do to hold them up. Shirttails nearly to the knees, back and front, made a moppet of him, but at least the cinched waist was covered. He returned to the living area, and Leah, without expression, passed him on her way into the room.

He hung his wet clothes on the mantelpiece and, with wood from the porch, started a fire. Leah had lit the stove and put water on to heat; the kettle was whistling when she returned. She was tying the belt of a blue velvet robe trimmed with satin lapels and cuffs. "Better jeans too big than too small," she said quietly. She made two cups of tea and sat at the table. He sat down near her and studied her while he stirred sugar into the brew. Holding her teacup fast to the table, she did not look at him. At length he said, "Why?"

She turned to him, the pale eyes placid, the voice, when it came, melancholy, he thought, perhaps tired. She said she had heard about him all her life. "The time came to decide: Messiah, or liar."

"All your life," David said.

She told him about an adoptive grandfather, a devout Catholic, and a "believing" grandmother, an observant Jew—contradictory terms, he thought, if he understood her meaning. She said her father had accepted Yeshua's claim at age twelve, six years after the decision of his mother.

"So it came through your father—and his stepfather," David said, ladling, behind a stolid face, a portion of anger over the image of a repulsive old man.

Leah kept a tight hold on her teacup and told the wall that her mother, nee Miriam Eppelman, had, in her late teens, also "come to Yeshua" and "by the grace of God" later persuaded her older brother Joseph, an ordained rabbi, to believe as well. Their parents, because of it, disowned them both, and Grandfather Eppelman had died just three years ago without forgiving either one. David supposed Leah had been reared Christian then, Catholic, and said so, the words strange in his ears.

"I did not choose Catholicism. I chose Yeshua."

"Not Catholic, not Jewish..."

She turned to him, kindled. "I am a Messianic Jew."

"Leah," he whispered, "you worship a convicted insurrectionist, executed two thousand years ago. How can you call yourself any kind of Jew?"

She looked at him long, then pushed back the chair, walked to the bedroom, and returned with the worn little paperback book, leafing through it. The cover read *Le Livre: Nouveau Testament*. She sat down, absorbed in her search, and having discovered the place, said, "The words of Rabbi Yeshua to the learned teachers of the Law: *You scrutinize—*"

"French?" David asked, tipping the book toward himself.

"Yes," she said, distracted.

"Read it to me."

She looked at him.

"Please."

"*Vous examinez les Ecritures, car vous croyez qu'elles vous donnent la vie éternelle. Or, c'est justement de moi qu'elles parlent!*" She looked up to gauge his reaction.

He smiled. "Read."

She had read to the end of the passage when he reached to expose the title page and, seeing her name on it, said, "You speak it at home?"

"Sometimes. *Et tu?*" He shook his head, enjoyed her surprise, and accepted a chastening smile. She reopened the book to the quote.

> *"You examine the Scriptures, for you believe that they give you eternal life. But it is precisely of me that they speak. And despite that, you do not want to come to me so that I can give you this eternal life!*
>
> *"It matters little to me whether you approve of me or not, for I know very well that the love of God is not in you. I know it, for I have approached you representing my Father, and you have refused to welcome me . . .*
>
> *"However, it is not I who will accuse you of it before the Father, it will be Moses. Moses, in the laws upon which you base your hope of going to heaven. For you have refused to believe Moses. He has spoken of me in his work, but you refuse to believe him, thus refusing to believe in me."*

No longer did the bow of her mouth charm him. "He claims he's in the Torah," David said, revolted.

"Everywhere Messiah's foretold: humble servant, conquering king."

He wanted to laugh. "Conquering king?"

"When he comes back."

"From *what? Death?*"

"*That* he's done."

"So rumor has it," he said, sensing the width of the quagmire into which, to extend her his help, he had stepped. He felt the touch of her hand on his arm.

"Would you die for a rumor?" she asked.

Only if I were unspeakably gullible, he mused without answering.

"Thousands died for believing Yeshua had returned from death," she said.

"Thousands died *rather* than believe it," he told her, laying a hand on her wrist. "There's history," he said, "and there's *legend*." Her skin was soft and warm, her cuff silken along the side of his hand. The turn of this day made him ache. He had wanted to know her—but not this...not this.

She was saying there was a difference between believing what you had seen and rejecting what you had not seen. "I'll pray for you," she said, her hand over his, "and I'll show him to you in your Bible." He felt a boil begin.

"You'll p-pray for me?" he said, retrieving his hand, not trying too hard to deny the affront; let her know. "I'll pray for you, t-too."

Damn the stuttering. Damn the open book it made of you. And now this. A droplet of spittle had sailed through the air to light on her face. She brought her hand, fingers folded, against the wet speck on her cheek and leaned on it. "The prayers of a friend never hurt," she said, attempting a nonchalance her voice could not carry. It was an obvious attempt to diffuse his anger, but what made him want to smile was the fact that she would cover for him with the hand. Gently, he pulled it away, moving his thumb over her fingers. He touched the cheek, the fleck that was no longer there and, allowing a small and silent laugh, told her he was sorry. He saw color come back to her face, the line of her mouth change; she moved to place her forehead, in relief, against his. Again, this time for his impatience, he said he was sorry and turned her tenderly to his purpose. She was whispering that she didn't mean to upset him. He kissed her mouth, felt her yield to it, accept it, return it. He brushed his lips against hers and kissed her a second time. Suddenly she drew away saying no, saying there was someone else.

Okay—that's it, he thought. It came out acrid, and there was no help for it: "Can *he* fathom what you are?"

Her eyes filled, and her voice quavered, "He's trying. He's Gentile...and *he's trying*."

She rose, opened up the sourdough and separated it into two sections. She pulled a cookie tin from under the dry sink, floured it, and drubbed one globule thoroughly on it, then commenced the flattening of the other while wiping, from time to time, the corners of her eyes with the back of her hand. She made no sound. If there is a just God in heaven, David thought, why did he arm women with tears? He sighed, walked to her, and turned her to himself. He held her and kissed her hair, glad that she could not see him smile at the fragrance of sweet hay. "Truce. Let me help."

Chapter 18

David stood at the window watching icy rain dash itself into the dirt. They couldn't go back in this. They both knew it, and that was what had kept talk at dinner, in spite of their efforts, so functional: there was no laughing and forgetting it and going home. He tended the fire, then sat on the edge of the couch watching the flames pop and roar and try to escape their confines. She was beside him, and he did not know when she had sat down. She laid her head back and said he couldn't afford this; his talk wasn't ready, and he'd be missing practice for the meet. He waved it away and searched for light talk—summers, vacations at the Cape; with these they could fill the time. When they had talked awhile, Leah told him more directly that she was sorry he had not been able, once, to go through his paper aloud, and maybe he could....

He said he still had more than a week and turned the subject back to their mutual interest in water sports and wondered silently if there were not a topic better suited to keeping him awake. There was, but she was not the one to ask. Yet, he was fascinated by what he had seen, and if he were ever again to broach the subject, why not there? He stood on the precipice of this conclusion when she rose from the couch with an apology for her sleepiness, saying he must be tired, too. She offered him the bedroom; she would take the sleeping bag in front of the fire. He insisted on the reverse, and she, having looked in on the horses, left him to himself.

Paddy came into the anteroom stamping, slamming, wet, and thirsty. He used the jack to pull off his boots and, entering the kitchen, snatched the towel from the handle of the refrigerator door to wipe his face and hair. Claire was peering out the window toward the road. "They're not coming home."

"Tomorrow noon," Paddy reminded her, running the towel over his neck.

"Not the boys. Leah and—what's his name."

"Would you? No footing, no light. Miserable sleet."

"Two miles by the road...." Her face was drawn.

"Claire."

"You could take the truck...."

"The road is muck, and no, I could not." Seeing her pain, he added, "They're twenty-one."

Her eyes widened and she breathed a long, incredulous sound. Pacing between the sink and the table, she moaned, "Last time she brought a Susan." Suzanne, Paddy thought, remembering the oval face, the perfect teeth. Disfluent, Leah had told her on the phone, Claire grumbled, and she got this picture in her mind.... "Did you look at him?" she demanded, leaving no time for Paddy's answer. "Did you *look at him*?"

He unbuttoned his shirt. He had come near breaking his knee on the Peugeot in the dark ten minutes ago, cursed David roundly, and then remarked to himself that the kid couldn't be all that reprehensible—he'd come here with Leah. "He's got good taste."

"You're not helping me," Claire said, yanking the terry out of his hand. She peeled the shirt off him and toweled his arms and said her sister-in-law would have her drawn and quartered.

"Two kids in love," Paddy told her. "What better place than the lodge?" He slipped his arm about her and, pressing her to his wet undershirt, began to sway. "Patter of rain, crackling fire. It was all we—"

She pulled away, lashing him with his name. "What am I going to do?"

"Nothing, my dear. Not a thing." Twelve hours ago they had left. What made her think the night more tempting than the day?

He said he hoped Leah would not forget to feed the horses and bolt the stable door. Claire threw him the towel, called him impossible, and returned to the window. She clenched the curtain. On second thought, he said, low, he really didn't think she would. Claire did not hear or respond. He took a can from the refrigerator and left her squinting at shadows in the night, talking to someone she rarely addressed and whom, in truth, she did not address now: "God, spare me the wrath of Miriam."

DAVID BROUGHT THREE LOGS from the porch and, having placed a couple of them on the fire, rid himself of Paddy's pants and shirt, spread the bag on the hearth rug, and slid into it. He felt spent, but sleep did not come. When the hypnotism of the fire failed, he tried counting rafters, then stones in the chimney. The question remained, a slatted fence between him and rest. He pulled the Book from the couch and opened it to the wrong place, to the page where Leah had first laid it open under his nose. *Chase a thousand* caught his eye. He read:

> *One man of you shall chase a thousand: for the Lord your God, he it is that fighteth for you, as he hath promised you. Take good heed therefore unto yourselves, that ye love the Lord your God. Else if ye do in any wise go back and cleave unto the remnant of these nations, even these that remain among you, and shall make marriages with them, and go in unto them, and they to you: Know for a certainty that the Lord your God will no more drive out any of these nations from before you; but they shall be snares and traps unto you . . .*

That one, he would be happy to go over with Leah—with regard to her Gentile love. He tried to picture him. Blue eyes? Straight blond hair? Even on the chest. Not amusing. He shut out the image and flipped to Isaiah...thirty-two...four. He read it again, then twice more, wishing he understood, trying. No light came. Slowly he pulled the zipper of the bag down, climbed out, took his own jeans, now dry, from the mantel, and pulled them on. He walked to the door of Leah's room, rapped and, when it swung open a little, asked whether she was awake. She was, he told himself, she just hadn't heard him; he asked again. There was a murmur, sleepy, faint. In the firelight, he saw the velvet robe flung over the footboard. From among the pillows at the other end, Leah raised herself on one elbow, a beige strap and one shoulder all that braved the air above the brown comforter.

"I don't know how to ask you this," he began, wishing at once he had started differently. "There's a verse I-I-I want to understand." Fluency fled. "You know how you can read something once," he stuttered, "even twice, and still the meaning...evades you."

"Mmm. I'll be out."

He was cold. He returned to the fire and pulled an afghan from the couch for an Indian wrap. He added a log and, turning, found her, in the blue robe, seated on the floor against the couch. He pulled the bag across their legs and, taking his Bible from it, read, of necessity, with continuous phonation:

> *The heart also of the rash shall understand knowledge, and the tongue of the stammerers shall be ready to speak plainly.*

He told her he was usually fine with her, fine with the guys in the therapy group and the clinicians. He had done a little better in class the last two times, when she had worked with him. But there were times—on the phone, with his family, with people older than himself or in authority, or when the pressure was on—he thought he was getting worse. Worse. Holding out the Book, he asked her what she made of it. She did not take it. She looked instead into the fire, and when she turned to him her eyes were wet. It referred to Messiah, she told him, to a time of healing, when the Chosen would be sensitized to him, recognize him, speak of him. Only then would he return to reign over the nations from David's throne. And at the end of his thousand-year reign, there would be a new and eternal Jerusalem, heaven on earth.

He picked up a fallen wood chip and tossed it to the fire. She touched him and said she believed with all her being it was so; she couldn't say when, but even now, there were healings in his name. He stared at the flames. "What would I need to do?"

"You *know* what..."

"It's your Messiah," he said, his eyes set.

She looked at him, unblinking. "Hand me your Bible."

"Mine?"

"Yours, *Monsieur*. Is it the Word of God?" She opened the Book to the first verse and showed him God's name. She said here, and in more places than not, in the Hebrew it was plural—*Elohim*. See, in the next verse, the Spirit of God moving upon the face of the waters, she said—an expression for *Elohim* himself and a mode of his being, was it not? She flipped to the *Shema*, and asked David to read it. The game was begun; yes, he could play. He did not look at the Book but gave her the words in Hebrew. *Echad*, she repeated, that's what it said "the Lord, their God, the Lord" was: plurality in unity—like the temple's golden lamp stand, several in one. Like water, revealed as vapor, revealed as ice: God, revealed as Spirit, revealed as Son. They wandered through the Scriptures—he thought, looking for the Son—but she showed him only that he had not loved his God with all his heart as the *Shema* told him to do, nor had he kept the Law. *Chatah*, the falling short, she said—that's why he needed mercy; so did she. The psalmist, quoting God, declared none good— not one. And only blood atones.

"Yom Kippur..." he began.

"Blood alone," she said, laying Leviticus in his lap. "By the Law, you, I, everyone must die." He made no reply; his God for- gave. What happened to love?

She painted him, David, bound, on an altar, soon to die. Then God looked down in mercy on his helplessness, she said; he loved him so much, so very much, that just as he did for Isaac, bound, whose death he had also required—just as he knew from the beginning he would—he sent the spotless ram, the Messiah, an expression of himself, to die in David's place. She looked into the fire and asked if he could comprehend what that meant for Yeshua: suffocating slowly as he hung, pushing in agony against the spikes to gain a breath. The lash, she said, had minced his back, the soldiers had beaten him blue; his strength was all but gone before they ever nailed him there. A crown of thorns jammed onto his head matted his hair with blood that seeped into his eyes and through what once was beard; his body glistened red with oozing life. Perfect life. A life at one with God. The reason only he could pay the price, yet live. Death could never claim him, much less hell. Her eyes were distant, soft. Yeshua hung dying, she said, naked... humiliated...exhausted—his mother before him in anguish so deep, there were no words to tell it. And people laughed. He must have wanted to shriek a curse on his tormentors, to unleash his Father's wrath, his army of angels. He must have wanted...to come down; but he had chosen. And now his Father, by whose power he had lived and loved and faced this hour, turned away because his perfect Son was covered with the filth of all the world, unfit for holy eyes to see. Yeshua bore it—as he promised—to the death, and into hell. A spasm moved her mouth, and David waited. It was then, she told him, that God tore the long veil of the temple from top to bottom. No further sacrifice, no other priest was needed to intercede for them, for the reality which they had for so long symbolized by the sacrifice of animals had come to them in the person of their Messiah. And soon, she said, God allowed the temple and Jerusalem to be razed because so many of his own despised his gift. She laid a warm, soft hand on David's cheek and asked him not to be deceived. "David, he's forgiveness. He is Love." He covered her hand with his own and brought it down to rest between them. She told him of a passage he should read before he slept. She laid her arm on the couch, her head against it, and opened his Bible. With the tip of her forefinger on Isaiah fifty-two, thirteen, she said, "Here is your Messiah." Her eyes were relaxed now, calm. He took his Book from her and read silently. He knew this passage; it went on through the next chapter, and he remembered asking Rabbi Feingold about it. He was a boy again, twelve.

"Who is this man who was so badly treated?" he had asked.

"It is symbolic, the 'he,'" the rabbi had told him. "It is the Jewish people, and it is prophetic. It foretells the Inquisition, the pogroms, the holocaust."

David read from the rabbi's perspective, intending to read the whole a second time with Leah's claim in mind: that this was the Messiah, who had come to live perfectly before God and to die for his people, for everyone who would receive him. Instead, he found the two points of view sparring with each other as he read, as he examined every word.

> Behold, *my servant shall prosper, he shall be exalted and extolled, and be very high. As many were astonished at thee; his visage was marred more than any man, and his form more than the sons of men: So shall he sprinkle many nations; the kings shall shut their mouths at him: for that which had not been told them shall they see; and that which they had not heard shall they consider.*
>
> *Who would have believed our report? and to whom is the arm of the Lord revealed? For he grew up before him as a tender plant, and as a root out of a dry ground: he had no form nor comeliness; and when we see him, there is no beauty that we should desire him. He was despised and rejected of men; a man of sorrows, and acquainted with grief: and as one from whom men hide their face he was despised, and we esteemed him not.*
>
> *Surely he hath borne griefs inflicted by us, and suffered sorrows we have caused: yet we did esteem him stricken, smitten of*

God, and afflicted. But he was wounded for our transgressions, bruised through our iniquities: the chastisement of our peace was upon him, and with his wounds we were healed. All we like sheep have gone astray; we have turned every one to his own way; and the Lord hath caused the iniquity of us all to fall upon him.

He was oppressed, and he was afflicted, yet he opened not his mouth: as a lamb which is brought to the slaughter, and as a sheep before her shearers is dumb, so he opened not his mouth. He was taken away from rule and from judgment; and his life who shall recount? for he was cut off out of the land of the living; through the transgressions of my people was he stricken. And one made his grave among the wicked, and his tomb among the rich; although he had done no violence, neither was any deceit in his mouth.

But it pleased the Lord to bruise him; he hath put him to grief: if his soul shall consider it a recompense for guilt, he shall see his seed, he shall prolong his days, and the pleasure of the Lord shall prosper in his hand. He shall see of the travail of his soul, and shall be satisfied: by his knowledge shall my servant justify the righteous before many, and he shall bear their iniquities. Therefore will I divide him a portion with the great, and he shall divide the spoil with the strong; because he hath laid open his soul unto death, and was numbered with transgressors; and he took off the sin of many, and made intercession for the transgressors.

At last, he laid the Book on his lap and looked into the flickering fire. Who was right? The rabbi, or the little *yid* who belonged to somebody else? Was this the Jewish "everyman" who "took off the sin of many," or was it the promised Messiah? He turned to Leah, having no idea what he wanted to say. Her sleepy eyes and the firelight gleaming on her hair silenced him. How was it that one woman should have such power over him, to kiss him then tell him she belonged to another, to thrill his heart by proclaiming herself a Jew then crush him with her declaration of faith in a dead "Messiah"?

Gazing back into the fire, he ached with the agony of his inward battle—the teachings of a lifetime, the tender words from Leah's lips. If only she weren't so beautiful....

When he turned his eyes to her again, she was asleep, her face tranquil in the firelight. Lovely woman, artless child...strong-minded, fragile...extremely knowledgeable or cruelly misinformed—whatever she was, his feelings entangled him with her, and deep as it might be, this abyss near which she stood, he would not back away like a frightened animal; he would not back away.

He pulled off the afghan, pushed back the sleeping bag, and knelt beside her. With her head on his shoulder, her hand limp against his chest, he stood and carried her to the bedroom. Gently, he lowered her to the sheet and covered her. No one would believe this night, he thought. Not Claire, not Paddy, not anyone. He could scarcely believe it himself, as a myriad of emotions raged within. He touched her hair, leaned to kiss her once, and left her in her slumber.

Closing the bedroom door behind him and returning to the fire, he sat on the rumpled bag. If Leah was right—if Yeshua was the Messiah and, as the passage said, "with his wounds we were healed"—then the healing of his stuttering could prove it. And if the stuttering was not healed—miraculously and completely—in the name of Yeshua, then he, David, would gain an even better win: Leah would have to admit her "Messiah" was a fraud.

He closed the Book and laid it on the couch, pulled the sleeping bag up over his jeans and zipped it. Tomorrow would be another day.

Chapter 19

THE NICKER WAS DEEP. David was only half wakened by it when a thud reverberated on the stable wall, followed by another. He heard hooves circling, the guttural nicker, and a third thud. Five-fifty by his watch. The fire was out, and his neck and shoulders were cold. Something fell with a clatter at the front of the lodge, and he separated the bag from himself to get to the window. His eyes strained in the half-light, then widened. "What's the rule for bear on your porch," he said under his breath.

"Wait," Leah said, suddenly there, peering over his shoulder, "and don't cook."

The black scavenger lumbered pigeon-toed from the far end of the porch to the near and passed their window, leaving split wood, like fallen Lincoln Logs, scattered behind him—or her. Another thud sounded, and Leah moved to quiet the horses and barricade the stable. "They'll have the stalls kicked out," she said.

David caught her arm. "I can probably handle that," he said with a friendly edge. He pulled on his shirt and boots and disappeared through the door that opened into the back of the stable.

With the lodge and stable doors secured, they breakfasted on leftover bread, cheese, and juice. Afterward, as she tucked her uncle's white clay pipe into her jacket pocket and snapped the flap over it, Leah asked whether David would like, for a change, to ride Timberjack. They put the lodge in order, gathered their things, and took their time saddling up in the stable. The morning was chilly and clear as they took the road down the mountain, riding the grassy mid-strip, changing gaits when it was natural to do so. David matched Leah pace for pace, and in the meadow when she leaned into a canter, then a gallop, he squeezed Jack with his knees

97

and leaned, as well. When they had descended to the flat, he contended that the half-breed could take the quarter-miler in her own race.

"You're on," Leah said with a grin.

They broke together and remained so in spite of David's devices. He bent low over the withers, aware that although Leah's Dinah was bred for speed in the short race, Jack had stride—he swallowed the road in the manner of a Thoroughbred—and David, letting the stirrups carry him, reveled in the pure shirt-flapping thrill of the ride. At about the quarter-mile, he reined back and declared himself the winner. Leah, gradually slowing to a walk, laughed and said he was three lengths short of the finish, but she would accept it because she, at that point, had beat him by a nose. They argued lustily, the horses at an ears-atwitch amble, and when they were done, nothing had been decided except that they could, at least to this degree, talk and laugh again. David considered teasing Leah lightly about their night together but decided not to risk it. He couldn't tell her, either, that he shared her worry that he had not rehearsed his presentation aloud with her so much as once. What he chose to talk about was the probable whereabouts of the bear. The warmth in Leah's eyes as she responded sent a surge of reassurance through him and, on its heels, a series of mental pictures of the two of them face to face, at worst and best, over the past two days.

The lane up to the house was a pleasant patchwork of shade and late morning sun. When they dismounted beside the tack room, David needed no instruction. He rubbed down and fed Jack while Leah did Dinah, and afterward, they entered the house to find Claire preparing lunch for the boys. She offered the same to Leah and David, her voice strained.

As David passed through the living room on his way upstairs to wash, Paddy, in his lounging chair, lowered the morning paper. He removed the pipe from the corner of his mouth and said, "A drink with me, David? A beer then?"

"Thanks, b-but we're just g-g-going to have lunch."

"How'd it go?"

"Fine, sir. T-t-two fine horses there."

"And your talk?"

"Talk? Oh. We—we w-worked on it. W-we—worked. If you'll excuse me..." Why did he have to sound incriminated? Doggedly, he added, "Leahhasyourmeerschaum. Finepipe. Finepipe. Finegirl, Leah." As he climbed the stairs, he sensed that Paddy did not return to his paper.

Lunchtime was peppered with talk of the Horse Club and Michael and Daniel's overnight eight miles east of Spring Hill. Claire suggested the boys show David the Saddle Horses when they finished lunch, but he asked whether he might first have an hour to sleep, to ensure alertness on the drive back. Claire, her face more pallid than he had remembered it, replied, "Of course," and Leah stayed to chat while he reclaimed Danny's bedroom, already evidencing the return of a fourteen-year-old. He flopped gratefully on the too-soft bed.

It was well over two hours later when he awoke, roused by Mike's voice at the doorway. He thanked him and sat on the edge of the bed, trying to get his bearings. There were the cavalrymen over the mantel, the two handsome cavaliers. His gaze was drawn again to the eyes of the one on the right. He stood and moved nearer the portrait. There was courage, almost tangible, in those kingly eyes. He had looked into them before, somewhere. The sun, offering the room its mid-afternoon gold to be kept for the night, was reflected off something on the base of the portrait's wooden frame. David walked to the mantelpiece. A shining brass plate in the shape of a scroll attached to the frame read: *Jean-Baptiste Beaumont — 1881 — Israel Katzar*. What had Leah said about an adoptive grandfather—Pierre, wasn't it? Perhaps Jean-Baptiste, on the left, was her great grandfather, but not by blood. He would ask on the way home. Right now, though, the boys were waiting to show him the class stock.

❦

"YOU WERE RIGHT," David said, his eyes on the country road. "I liked Paddy." He remembered the goodbye. There had been no restraint of friendliness over imagined transgressions. He glanced at Leah. Her profile was outlined against the tinted window in the late afternoon light.

"Everybody does," she said, watching the fields of fallow ground go by.

Their minds were anything but passive, but they had driven for nearly half an hour before either spoke again. As he turned onto the major highway that would take them all the way back to University Park, David said he wanted to go with her, sometime soon, to a service. She nodded pensively and asked if he had ever been in a church. He told her he had gone with Rob to pick up Suzanne after a dinner. That was the one, she said, her church; Suzanne and she had met there three years ago when Sue was a freshman.

"And Rick's wife?"

Leah's laugh was hollow. "God, to Andy, is the great spoiler." He smiled. Leah was quiet, and when she looked at him again, her eyes shone softly in the fading light. "It's been a roller coaster, these two days," she said. "But we know each other better now."

How should he read her? She had declared herself someone else's, yet there was much in what she said and did that made him want to take her hand, that made him think she wanted him to. He could not help hoping, thinking, knowing she was going to be all right. And then she wouldn't need whoever it was; she would be right with God—and with him. He felt his smile return.

She asked whether he could muster any excitement over going to Israel in the spring. He said it might be the longest, hottest eight weeks of his life, but he planned to see some sights when the store was off his mind. His dad, he told her, had asked Rabbi Feingold to go along. Still in good health, he'd be their guide; he'd been there several times.

"Write me. I've always wanted to go. More than anywhere."

"Not Italy, Spain—Greece?"

She shook her head. "Israel." It was the voice of a little girl dreaming.

"I'll send post cards. The desert...Dead Sea...wilderness..."

"Sun...on the Sea of Galilee...orchards...gardens in the Negev...the Jordan...olive trees..."

"Okay, okay," he said, exultant inside. He'd send a card for each. Where there was contact, there was communication.

Leah did not respond. The light had ebbed, and he could not see her face; she slept against the window. He moved his hand to cover hers and held on carefully as if to keep her from slipping away. "I'll write."

Chapter 20

Excitement and anxiety, the tide and backwash of every sport, were the undulating moods of the evening. The six perched like birds on a fence at the top of the extra stands on the gymnasium floor, Jonathan next to Leah, Andy and Rick to his right, Suzanne and Rob to her left. Dinner at Rick and Andy's had been simple but convivial. Leah had brought the salad and a dessert, the latter to be enjoyed after the meet.

Partly because he wanted to and partly for the sheer comfort of turning toward her in the cramped space allotted, Jonathan had placed an arm around Leah's waist for the early rounds of the meet. Now the heat prohibited it. The gym was packed with much the same knowledgeable and expectant crowd that had attended all season. Many had shortened their getaways out of town, to accommodate the inconvenient date of this meet. Their appreciation of the standings of all four teams was emotional, and the temperature of the place was climbing toward eighty.

UCLA had been tough through the first four events in the men's meet and now held a 1.5-point lead. In the women's meet against Louisiana State, PSU's Lady Lions were ahead by a healthy 5.60 and riding high on more than an hour of peak performance. Leah watched David as he waited for the assistant coach to straighten the mats on one side of the parallel bars. He had scored a 9.40 in the floor exercise—a .5 improvement over the last time she had seen him perform, just prior to the opening of the season—and he had pulled off a shining 9.80 on the pommel horse to take that event. Those socres, Rob had told her, were David's season bests for floor and horse. She found herself pondering whether David's adventures in horsemanship two days ago might have lent something to tonight. It could easily have been otherwise: had he over-worked muscles unaccustomed to it, there could have been, even now, ache enough to shave the edge off his performance. She remembered no telltale grimace as he demonstrated his strength and control on the rings, nothing but the resolute expression of a gymnast in mastery over mind and body. In the round that followed, he had executed flawlessly—twice—his selected vault, confirming that any stiffness he might have had was gone. She imagined him vaulting over the forbearing Timberjack with the same tuck, twist, and opening, and a smile came to her.

He had picked up the trail skills quickly. She had not intended a gallop on the first outing, but because of the bear, she had thought it wise not only to give him the right horse for the long race, but also to show him how to survive a panicked run. Had they chanced to come between a mother and her cub on the trail, the she-bear almost surely would have charged, and David would have had to cope. But if Leah's nudging him to new levels of skill was beyond his expectations that morning, his challenge on the flat was certainly a surprise to her. With difficulty she had held Dinah back so as not to provoke Jack to let himself out for the distance, and the sawing on Dinah's mouth had pained rider more than mare. It had been Dinah's first loss ever on the short race with Jack. Leah wondered if horses sulked or pined over injustice. Let it be; she was willing to chance a wild ride for David in an emergency, but only then.

No one had to spot him anything here, on his ground. She had just seen him match his personal high on rings and better it in the vault, taking the latter event. He was "on" tonight. He buried his hands now in the shallow dish of powdered chalk, rubbed away the excess and shook out his arm and shoulder muscles, pacing a length comparable to the bars, a few feet from them. When the judges were ready, he was, too, and signaled so.

The mount was unique, Leah thought, ingenious, a fitting introduction to the sequence of moves that now robbed the little blonde Lioness on the balance beam of her share of spectators.

His swings were high and steady, his handstands precise, unmoving, the exercise, for all its intricacy, smooth, flowing. The routine, to Leah, seemed long for such an arduous pattern of moves. She sensed the dismount's imminence, and—there it was, immaculate.

The bars reverberated back to stillness. David, in the place where he had alighted, stood with arms raised overhead, a roar of adulation in his ears. He broke the formal stance to turn to the crowd and wave, to turn to the opposite side and then the far ends of the stands, waving, smiling, yielding finally to continuing applause with the winner's fist raised once and then recalled.

The small company of friends were on their feet with the rest of the fans, clapping, whistling, and cheering, and the applause had not yet died when the judges raised the scores: There was a ten. The pitch rose and then swelled around the oval of stands as the second score became visible—ten. Activity on the floor stopped. The wave of noise followed the turning of the third and fourth placards—ten, ten—and the din engulfed them; for the second time in as many seasons, he had swept the judges, all four—ten.

Andy ceased her frenzy only long enough to hug Rick fiercely, and Rob held Suzanne, too, and then reclaimed his joyful duty as a friend—to applaud, to whistle, to shout. Tears stood in Leah's eyes as she watched David; her hands met much too softly to make sound. She remembered that their conversation once had turned to this—the work it took by day, by hour, to hone this routine to the *ne plus ultra*, to capture the moment of triumph. What he had invested years to attain last season he had done this time in months. Some day, she thought, he'll conquer all of himself; please, God, let it be soon.

She felt someone's eyes upon her and, blinking away the cloud, saw Jonathan smiling happily, putting his arms around her to hold her close. Early in the evening, before Rick had explained it, he had sensed the favoritism of the group and entered in. Leah slipped her arms about him, held him tightly to her, and felt something convulse within her throat and carve a hurt. The noise was dying, and they sat again together. The next UCLA man was up. While he chalked his hands, Leah watched an LSU girl mount the balance beam. Her heart went out to both. What must they feel, performing in the wake of perfection—or as close to it as people ever come? Her eyes came back to David, seated on the bench, still the focus of no small amount of attention. He handled it so well. The place, Leah thought as she looked at faces, borrowed something from him; happiness pervaded the stands, its chatter subdued only by the discipline of the crowd. She returned to Jonathan. He was absorbed in the routine of the young woman on the beam. His hand rested on his knee, and Leah, in spite of the heat, laced her fingers through his and forced her attention to the beam. He squeezed her hand and, when the exercise was completed, asked if she would like a drink. She said she would wait till they got back to Andy's, thanks. When he returned, the men were preparing for the horizontal bar and the women for the floor exercise. He gave soft drinks to Rick, Rob, and Andy, and handed his own to Leah. UCLA held a scant 0.25 lead in the men's competition, and LSU was now trailing by only 3.85 in the women's. The season wrap was not yet sealed, but it had already been worth seeing; the gauntlet was down, not just for tonight, but with a burning eye on the coming NCAA championships. The women's floor exercises, set to music, began, to be alternated with the men's high bar routines—a good thing, Suzanne remarked, since she could not have decided which to watch; each was a finale.

State opened the bar event with what the sportswriters would, the next day, call a siliconed performance by Waslo that brought the team scores to a dead heat; the next two State men, they would say, matched sterling to sterling only to see themselves slip under again by 0.05 and then return to even scores.

When David next came off the bench, it was to fill the fourth slot in the rotation. A patter of applause began to swell, a measure of respect and of encouragement—a measure, too, of expectation. Leah wished she could know how it affected his composure, his concentration. She looked from fan to fan across the gym, wanting to hush the clapping and buzzing so that David could think. And then the bar was in his grasp, his body swinging up into contact with it, and the event, for him, was under way.

Leah knew this much: if well executed, this exercise could keep a State win viable, perhaps even give David the edge over MacAteer and a UCLA man for all-around honors. Breathing shallowly, she watched him release his left hand to cross over the right, swing over the bar, turn, swing over again, then again, releasing to fly straddling overtop. The bar as the vortex of his circles was drawn into a moving arc. 'Round and 'round he swung, now attached, now free-flying, now in a one-handed giant swing that brought quiet vocal sounds from an audience who knew better. The bar sagged repeatedly until Leah wished for the dismount, and Andy reached to hold Rick's hand. It was Rick's hope that "the kid from Lansdale" would finish with a punch that would send the Bruins home smarting. He did. David left the bar with a clean double layout flyaway, landing with bent knees. He straightened without so much as a small step forward, and the crowd vented elation on all sides of him. He acknowledged the tribute with an easy smile and stiffened arm that said "I practiced it all year for you" and returned to his seat. The scores were posted: 9.80, 9.70, and twice more, 9.80, and the fans, whose zeal never ended ahead of the meet, cheered with abandon.

It was another fifteen minutes until the night's efforts were completed and translated to board scores. But those in the stands who had kept score sheets were messengers of the news as it unfolded: Rothman's high bar routine brought the team score for the first time into the lead by 0.15. The final two bar men—Villela and MacAteer—maintained it against polished UCLA performers and in fact tacked on another 0.10 between them. No State bar score had fallen under 9.40, so that even the one that was dropped was respectable. The meet was awarded to the Lions 287.20 to 286.95 in the men's competition and 183.75 to 181.05 in the women's.

David, having taken the men's total point scoring, stood on the highest of the three platforms, holding his award, MacAteer on one side and an L. A. man on the other. He appeared to Leah, as he did no doubt to many in the crowd, the epitome of wholesome American athletics, and she pitied Aunt Claire for the feelings that had seeped from her on Friday afternoon while he lay sleeping. If there was such a thing as blatant innuendo, Claire's conversation as she sat with Leah at the kitchen table had been filled with it. Leah had always believed her closeness to her aunt precluded misunderstanding, but nothing she could say assuaged Claire's fear. Fear, it seemed, not for Leah but that she, Claire, as the two-day guardian had failed, and that reprisals would come. Failed whom, Leah wondered; reprisals from whom? Mama? Papa? For what? A sadness came over her for her father's sister. Such want of trust was its own burden, its own punishment; how laboriously one must hurl the kernels of peace into the wind to keep the chaff. If only Claire knew David, Leah thought, as she was beginning to know him....

The applause died, and Leah felt Jon's arm around her shoulders at the same time that she heard Rick say, "Let's wait here till the crowd clears, then we'll meet him under the stands." They sat among the thinning throng and talked for twenty minutes before Jon excused himself. He had not yet returned when Rob suggested that they would miss D. J. if they did not move to the corridor, and so the five made their way toward David, to reinforce the hero image, to weave their joy through his. Their timing was right, and he received their plaudits, Leah thought, in a more relaxed way than he had on that first night she had seen him congratulated. She did not know whether he had come to this point gradually or all at once, tonight, because she had not seen him in this setting since the meet with the Soviets. Andy, who had by now hosted David several times at the apartment, hugged him without hesitation, commending his night's work with *"Great job!"* Leah waited for Rick and Rob to stop their arm pummeling and rehashing before she moved toward him, telling herself a hug was appropriate. But he did not return the embrace with so much as the cordiality he had accorded Andy, much less the warmth offered at the lodge. His arm, circling her waist, did not engage; he hardly touched her. She stepped back to look into his eyes and found them fastened on something behind her. Turning, she saw Jonathan at her shoulder, smiling at David, and her sudden bent was to insert space, much space between them. She could not sort fact from feeling while they stood facing each other on either side.

Too late she realized she had abrogated her social responsibility, and Rick had picked it up. Jon and D. J. now knew each other by name and had clasped hands declaring themselves glad. Andy invited David to join them at the apartment, tempting him with the fact that Leah had made a "wicked dessert." But he declined, saying he had just been over the night before and would see Rick again on Tuesday. His short speech was only mildly disfluent, so slowly did he deliver it; "thanks, anyway" tripped, but it seemed a natural thing. He picked up his bag and walked away. The scene—his departure from the group—was repeating itself, and Leah felt the tearing. She glanced at Andy with an expression that moved her to try again. Leah watched her stop him partway up the ramp, saw his look, heard him say firmly but with a stutter, "I'm sorry. I can't." He touched Andy's arm, thanked her again, and continued up the hall.

Relief tried to mingle with empathy in Leah. Then the emptiness she supposed filled David became the overrider, and she wished there were something of the night for him. What kind of friends were they, to celebrate his excellence while he went home to nothing? Then she remembered. She would see him tomorrow, first thing. That helped, if only a little. She turned to Jon and tried to think of something festive to say. He threaded her arm through his and held her hand. His gentle eyes twinkled as, with an exaggerated French accent, he asked, "What kind of surprise, Mademoiselle, 'ave you created for us tonight?"

Chapter 21

SUNDAY DAWNED CLEAR AND MILD. At 9:00 A.M. David appeared at Leah's door in a steel gray suit tailored for him personally, an understated tie, and shoes shined to a mirror finish by his own hand. She met him in a matched skirt and blouse, blazer, and heels. They drove through town making smalltalk until she told him that last night's victory party without the victor was a bit inane.

"You understood," he said, meeting her eyes.

She looked elsewhere, in front of her, and said he would be in her thoughts next week, and in her prayers. He tried to untangle the feelings that rushed at him, then forced them into suspension to look at her with pure inquiry. "The championships," she said.

The curve of his smile made a smirk. "You think no one's praying for Nebraska?"

"I'm not talking *win*."

"Thanks."

"I'm talking glorifying the God of Israel."

He slowed the car.

"As you did last night," she added.

"I glorified God," he said, not stating but asking.

" . . . who gave you your talent."

"Who'd Mac glorify?"

"I don't know Mac."

He looked too long away from the road and had to correct the steering. His eyes fixed on the red light ahead and he saw again the bane of Jonathan Grante at her shoulder, smiling, unknowing.

Saturday night, the meet had injected a pleasant fatigue into his system, a quiet mirth into his soul and, over all, without explicable cause, a longing for Leah more compelling than he, until then, had known. He had not expected to see her as he left the locker room. All season he had looked for her, and she had not been there. When he saw her last night, tucked away behind Rob, Rick, and Andy, his heartbeat had quickened. How had he known as she came nearer that the brown-haired man descending the ramp was the one who had claimed her, who *understood* her? The one for whom she had stated her preference.

"You've worked so hard," Leah's voice came over his thoughts, so in earnest that he wanted to hear it again. "Invest it for God, David. Use it for him." He could not think what to say. He wanted to hold her, very hard. There was silence, long and awkward. He found the church without her help and pulled into the lot.

As they entered the building, people who knew Leah greeted and smiled at them both, and David wondered whether they would be so quick about it if they knew he was from the other camp. They found Suzanne in the sanctuary and joined her. She introduced them to the people next to her, a couple from New Delhi in graduate study at the University, and then there was only the organ music. David scanned the worshipers. To the right and down two rows sat a professor he'd had in a sophomore math course and, two women and two little girls away, the mechanic, the one with the limp and the Lee Marvin face, who had worked on his Peugeot. In the fourth pew from the front— no, couldn't be. Yes, it was—Mel Greenburg, seated next to Ben... What was his name? They had met, somewhere. Why were he and Mel here? Trying not to stare, he picked up a red book from the rack in front of him. He opened it to find it was the Old and New Testaments bound together. Doubtful that these people, like Leah, were familiar with the Jewish Scriptures, he scanned Jeremiah to see whether the King James Version read at all like his own.

> *Therefore, behold, the days come, saith the Lord, that it shall no more be said, The Lord liveth, that brought up the children of Israel out of the land of Egypt;*

> But, The Lord liveth, that brought up the children of Israel
> from the land of the north, and from all the lands whither he
> had driven them: and I will bring them again into their land that
> I gave unto their fathers. Behold, I will send for many fishers,
> saith the Lord, and they shall fish them; and after will I send for
> many hunters, and they shall hunt them from every mountain,
> and from every hill, and out of the holes of the rocks.

He recalled the passage from his own Bible. Curious, David
thought, that God should fish for and then hunt his people. He
flipped to the New Testament, to a page from which his name
leapt. The text told of a blind man who called Jesus "son of David"
and asked him to restore his sight. He did it, the passage read,
right on the spot. So there it was—exactly the kind of thing he had
come here to test. The music ceased, and he looked up to see a
young man in a dark blue suit standing in the pulpit. David recognized the words the man read, about God speaking peace to his
people, about mercy and truth meeting together and righteousness and peace kissing each other; they were from a Psalm. And
then the people stood to sing:

> Ride on, ride on in majesty!
> Hark! All the tribes hosanna cry;
> O Savior meek, pursue Thy road
> With palms and scattered garments strowed...

David never stuttered when he sang, but today he chose to
listen; and in that singular song, he experienced the gamut of feelings that would assail him throughout the hour: self-conscious-
ness, encirclement; curiosity, surprise; defense, anger; fight-or-
flight boldness, resolve.

> Ride on, ride on in majesty!
> In lowly pomp ride on to die;

Bow Thy meek head to mortal pain;
Then take, O God, Thy power and reign!

God? They actually did call him God. Even Leah had not pre-pared him for that direct and immediate an assault on his sensi-bilities. The battle cry had sounded; David pulled on his armor, and out of the corner of his eye, he saw Leah glance his way.

A baritone stepped to the podium and sang a strange song. It was titled "The Holy City," and in it the supposed Messiah was, by implication, welcomed, hailed, rejected, hung, resurrected, and declared king. Preposterous, David thought; yet, against his will, it stirred him, and he wrestled with it until he came to the realiza-tion that what he felt was a longing for the day when the City would indeed open its gates and sing "hosanna" to the king, for he did believe in a coming Messiah. Samuel Feingold was one of those rabbis who still held to the messianic interpretation of Scripture, and he had taught David well. But now the young pastor was in the pulpit again, reading from the New Testament:

> *On the next day much people that were come to the feast, when they heard that Jesus was coming to Jerusalem,*
> *Took branches of palm trees, and went forth to meet him, and cried, Hosanna: Blessed is the King of Israel that cometh in the name of the Lord.*
> *And Jesus, when he had found a young ass, sat thereon; as it is written,*
> *Fear not, daughter of Sion: behold, thy King cometh, sitting on an ass's colt.*
> *These things understood not his disciples at the first: but when Jesus was glorified, then remembered they that these things were written of him, and that they had done these things unto him.*
> *The people therefore that was with him when he called Lazarus out of his grave, and raised him from the dead, bare record.*

For this cause the people also met him, for that they heard that he had done this miracle.

The Pharisees therefore said among themselves, Perceive ye how ye prevail nothing? behold, the world is gone after him.

An offering was taken and a prayer prayed; then a white-haired minister, sturdy and of medium height, rose. The message he gave detailed "the miraculous aspects" of the triumphal entry of Jesus into Jerusalem on that day preceding the Passover, "the timing, to the day, in precise fulfillment of prophecy," the progress of "the first coming of Israel's servant-king toward its consummate purpose—his death and resurrection," and "the preparation of our hearts to respond to him, now, while the door to grace stands open." It left David wondering if someone had told the man that he and Mel and Ben would be in the sanctuary today. The references to Israel, Jerusalem, Old Testament prophecy, and Jewish customs surrounding Passover aroused suspicion in him to the point that, pending some sorting out, he shelved the idea of putting Yeshua to the test. He heard nothing of the rest of the service. When it ended, he wanted only sunlight, openness, escape. But he was surrounded by people—elders, deacons, parishioners—who insisted, one after the other, on snaring his hand and asking questions until, excusing himself from Leah, he made his way to the doorway where Mel and Ben were talking. He felt the drowning man at last able to stand in shallower water, to gasp. He rejoined Leah minutes later just outside the door. Having guided her gently, directly into the car, he steered the vehicle carefully among the people milling at the side of the building, and pulled away into the street. They drove in silence until she asked what he thought. He had no words to tell her.

As a little girl, Leah said with a tentative smile, she had thought the greatest miracle of Palm Sunday was that Jesus sat on the unbroken colt of an ass and wasn't thrown for a loop. David turned onto the quieter route to campus. He wanted to look at her. "Lee...come with me to JCC Friday night, to synagogue."

She said nothing, then, "Are you going home for Passover?"

"I'll be with friends, here."

"I won't be in town Friday. If you didn't have plans Tuesday, you could come to my house for the Seder. Suzanne and my Aunt Paulette and Uncle Charles—"

"You celebrate the Passover?"

"Of course."

He saw that the question hurt and mumbled an apology. The morning, the mystifying woman in his car had clarified only two things: the more he was with Leah, the more confused became his perception of her; and the more confounded he felt, the more he recognized his need to be totally, indefatigably, immutably Jewish. On that base, he knew he was safe. And to that base of safety he vowed he would draw her. Love would come, he knew it; it was first a matter of identity, his and hers. He would use his time with the Greenburgs Tuesday to stockpile the armory, sharpen his aim. This morning's invitation to a Messianic Jewish home could not have come at a more advantageous time. He pulled the car up to her building and deposited her there without thought of lunch together. His plan was in motion. "I'll see you next Monday, a week from tomorrow," he said, revving the engine.

"Monday," she said with no gesture of goodbye. He pulled out of the lot, leaving uncertainty behind. Now it could be found only in Leah's eyes.

Chapter 22

At 6:45 on Friday evening, David drove past the familiar street that led to the synagogue. Continuing to the intersection, he turned onto an artery that pulsed with traffic headed toward the edge of town and beyond. Funny, he thought; if Leah had been around, she might have had to drag him kicking. Gone, she provided the perfect circumstance for a test unaffected by her nearness, or for that matter, by the physical proximity of Suzanne or Mel. Suzanne had left with Rob for his grandmother's this morning; Mel, although not the same Mel he had known a year ago, was under the *yarmulke* tonight. It puzzled him, this walking in and out of synagogue at will, but he hoped Ben would be over there, too.

He pulled into the church lot and walked to the door aware that his appearance in this place might be taken as a sign of interest on his part, especially since he was unaccompanied. He passed through the people in the narthex, looking at no one. At the entrance to the sanctuary, someone handed him a printed program. He stood a moment in the doorway. Ben Epstein was already seated in the sixth row, a young woman to his left and Art and Esther Greenburg to his right. David had no desire to sit with them, particularly after Tuesday's Seder. It had been a distortion of the ceremony he knew, unchanged in form but explained to him in terms of "Yeshua the Messiah's" presence in nearly every part of it. He felt remiss before God, as if he had not celebrated it at all but had been shanghaied instead into some unreal world where scenes were shrunken or stretched, torn away from the old traditions and tossed to him in pieces to be sewn back together, if he could find a way.

But he had learned much from Mel and his parents about the situation in which he now found himself. He knew now how strong and deeply ingrained were Leah's beliefs; they had pulled Ben over the wall months after she had broken off the dating relationship and in spite of his parents' grief. Little wonder he had gravitated toward the Greenburgs as surrogate family. David looked at the young woman seated next to Ben now. Gentile, he guessed, and it figured. So much in a name. The Epsteins must have skipped the chapter on the Benjamite War to think that their son, so named, would ever claim a choice daughter of Israel.

He picked a seat about a third of the way down the side aisle beside a man who looked to be in his fifties, gave him a fleeting smile, and sat waiting for the service to begin. Near the podium, a cellist was playing a mournful melody, called by the program "O Sacred Head Now Wounded." When she finished, the pews were full, and after a few moments, a procession of silent people in somber colors made its way to the front of the church and into the choir loft. A strange opening, David thought, unlike that of the Sunday before. Faces were serious; no music sounded; the congregation was utterly quiet.

The young pastor rose and asked the people also to stand as he read from Psalm 118, something about how "the stone which the builders rejected" had "become the chief cornerstone."

A tall man in a brown suit came to the pulpit and led the congregation in singing a hymn called "There Is a Green Hill Far Away," and afterward the young pastor returned to seat the people for his reading of a passage from Isaiah 53—the same chapter, David was certain, that Leah had handed him that rainy night at the lodge. Did they have no other text? They stood again, and a voice was heard saying:

My God, my God, why have you forsaken me? and are so far from my cry and from the words of my distress?

David recognized the tenor of the words: King David's writings, Psalm 22. The program called for the people to read certain parts and, obediently, they began. David knew he could trust his voice in a reading, and since it was a psalm, he saw no harm in it; defaulting, in fact, would call attention to himself. Who had more right to the ancient Scriptures, anyway? He read with the people:

> *All who see me laugh me to scorn; they curl their lips and wag their heads saying, "He trusted in the Lord; let him deliver him; let him rescue him, if he delights in him."*

The reading continued, describing a man encircled by enemies, pleading with God for help. The disembodied voice read:

> *I am poured out like water; all my bones are out of joint; my heart within my breast is melting wax.*

Out of joint? David thought. He reread the line as the people around him took up their part:

> *My mouth is dried out like a potsherd; my tongue sticks to the roof of my mouth; and you have laid me in the dust of the grave.*

David tried to read quickly what they had just read, but the bodiless voice forged ahead:

> *Packs of dogs close me in, and gangs of evildoers circle around me; they pierce my hands and my feet; I can count all my bones.*

It was time for the people to read, but David could not read aloud and study the passage at the same time. What was it the voice had just said? "They pierce my hands and my feet"? David of old seemed to be describing his own death and his feelings as he experienced it—death by torture at the hands of his enemies.

Pierced hands and feet, bones out of joint. Was that how he died? Wait. Of course...

The people read on doggedly:

They stare and gloat over me; they divide my garments among them; they cast lots for my clothing.

Now he saw it: the psalm, lifted out of its historical context, was being used tonight to depict a crucifixion. And not just any one—*the* crucifixion. Didn't the people who put together this program realize that crucifixion was conceived by the Romans centuries after this psalm was written? The psalmist, the David of history, could not be referring to it here. This described a very personal experience of the warrior-king, an ordeal undergone in his lifetime. He tried to recall it. When did this happen? He could picture only a wizened, white-haired David on his bed in a palatial sleeping chamber, the beautiful young Abishag lending her warmth to his bones as he lay dying of old age.

The reading ended, the people, who had been standing for the entire time, sat down, and David allowed his questioning process to founder as he watched four men step out of the choir. They sang something called "Alas, and Did My Saviour Bleed," and David tried not to be obvious in looking about him. Faces were rapt; there were no children anywhere to peek over the back of the pew or drop a bottle to the floor. He looked to the program for a clue as to what was next. "The Passion of the Lord According to the Gospel of John," it said; "The Congregation shall read the part of the CROWD." Oh, God, he thought, meaning it both reverently and in exasperation, what now?

Again there was, to his growing irritation, no one in the pulpit, only a voice narrating. The CROWD took up its part on cue and, here and there, David read with them, or mouthed the words. The CROWD of which he was a member, acting the parts of temple guards, priests, Pharisees, and citizens, proceeded to arrest Jesus at night, try him before morning, and manipulate the Roman governor, on threat of a riot, into freeing a murderer as a Passover gesture and condemning the man he had just declared innocent.

David's mind, flitting back and forward through the quotations in an effort to find evidence against Jesus, suddenly sought reprieve. He focused on the large empty cross above the altar, and then on the white cloth that covered something on the table in front of the pulpit. Two small towers with conical tops elevated the cloth. An inscription—"This Do in Remembrance of Me"—was carved into a panel of the table. His program referred to "The Lord's Supper." He hadn't counted on that. How did it work? What would he have to do? Or avoid? He could handle it, he told himself; maybe he wouldn't be the only one who chose not to eat. He looked around uneasily, wondering if Ben felt the same. Ben, the Messianic Jew. But Ben stared straight ahead as the CROWD beleaguered the Roman governor Pontius Pilate with "Crucify him! Crucify him!" and another voice with no visible bearer, taking the part of Pilate, asked in astonishment, "Shall I crucify your King?"

The CROWD read dutifully, but without zeal, the words of the chief priests, "We have no king but Caesar." David sensed that the man beside him had, like Ben, stopped reading, and when the man turned to meet his gaze, he saw moisture in his bloodshot eyes.

The narrator concluded with a measured and deliberate sadness:

Then he handed him over to them to be crucified. So they took Jesus, and he went out, bearing his own cross, to the place called the place of a skull, which is called in Hebrew, Golgotha. There they crucified him, and with him two others, one on either side, and Jesus between them. Pilate also wrote a title and put it on the cross; it read, "Jesus of Nazareth, the King of the Jews."

Softly, the congregation sang "Were You There When They Crucified My Lord?" and David could see drawn faces not only to either side of him, but there...and there...and there, throughout the gathering, while he himself felt accused, convicted of the summary execution which this evening recalled. Was he alone? Or were these others, these Christians, experiencing something more than sorrow for a crucified Messiah? This reenactment had made the worshipers capitulate in every way in the condemnation of their Savior. Had that, in fact, been its purpose?

At the side of the sanctuary, a man and a woman stood to sing a song now doleful, now victorious, called "Don't Feel Sorry for My Jesus." Then the elders brought broken *matzoth* on silver-colored platters to the pews, and David prayed it would not be obvious that he was passing along "the bread" untouched, not at all because it was foreign to him—the yeastless cracker was part of his heritage—but because it symbolized acceptance of this Messiah who was, indeed, foreign to him. He implored God not to let him drop the platter as he hurried to pass it on.

The minutes in which all behind him were served ticked on endlessly, and the moment when all ate together brought sweat to David's back and underarms. His relief in the completion of the rite was supplanted immediately by the realization that "the wine" was yet to come. By the time it was in his neighbors' hands, he had so effectively steeled himself that he felt, like the disembodied voices, invisible, a phantom onlooker. When they had drunk the juice together, the parishioners rose to sing "When I Survey the Wondrous Cross." Wondrous, David thought; these people are the personification of confusion. A deluded man dies a humiliating torture-death twenty centuries ago and they commemorate it even now as something from God; they wallow in self-imposed guilt, for which the same event is supposed to be the antidote. Where is the intellect, where?

The song of sorrow and love flowing mingled down in blood was finally "amened." David turned to leave the pew but felt upon his shoulder a hand laid lightly. "LeRoy Willis," the man said, extending his hand, the broad, perfect smile incongruous with the

reddened eyes. David stuttered his own name, and LeRoy continued, his nose inserted into a white handkerchief, "Don't mind me.
Every time I think...if I'd been the only sinner in this world...he'd
have done it for me...." He blinked, shaking his head.

"I-I-I understand," David said, knowing he didn't, and to
LeRoy's expressed hope that they would meet soon again, he said,
"Yes, thank you." There were people going to the front, by invitation of the program, for quiet prayer and meditation. David had
not come to pray and meditate. He had come to request a miracle—
or more exactly, to test the power of the so-called miracle-maker—
and there was not even a pastor in sight to show him how. He
melted into the quiet groups walking toward the door at the back
and headed out. If his challenge to Leah was to work, he knew, he
needed only that one, specific draft—the one which, if he could
swallow it at all, he must drink to the dregs.

Chapter 23

WILOMENA GRANTE TOOK HER MOTHER'S CERAMIC RABBIT from the center of the dining table and wrapped it carefully in the old tissue paper. Lovingly, she positioned it inside the thin cardboard box that was its protection for fifty-one weeks of the year and carried it to the closet in the hall. Its exposure had been short-lived this year. She was surprised at herself for not remembering to take care of this before she left for the evening service. What if they had arrived before she and John had come back? She picked up the scissors. How fortunate that the parsonage, for frugality in the provision of altar flowers, had its own small greenhouse attached. It would take only a few minutes to cut daffodils and arrange them.

"Very much in love," Jon had said on the phone. She had thought, until she met Leah, that she would never welcome that kind of news. Alicia had been a pleasant girl, but not bright enough for Jonathan; Caitlin was strong-minded on the wrong subjects. Rarely, in fact, had Jon lacked the company of girls who lacked. But Leah—Who'd have thought it? A Jewish girl—had won her, point by point: thoughtful, domestic, chatty enough—just enough—intelligent, decent to look at if not exceptionally pretty, and obviously giving of the tender, loving care Jonathan needed. A spiritual girl. Everything Wilomena would specify if she were personally selecting a young woman for her son. Passing through the kitchen, she picked up once more the menus she had handwritten for the weekend. Leah preferred kosher foods. She knew Jesus had come, she'd said, to fulfill every whit of the Law, but the dietary rules still offered health. Pleased with her correctly butchered hens for Sunday, Wilomena put down the scribblings and drew from a low cupboard a cube of florist's clay and a shallow white bowl into which it fit. Taking these with her through the front door, she sang softly to herself, to the night, and perhaps to a neighbor or two: "Blessed assurance, Jesus is mine! Oh, what a foretaste of glory divine! Heir of salvation, purchase of God, born of His Spirit, washed in His blood...."

HAVING OPENED WIDE THE CAR DOOR, Jonathan ushered his love onto the asphalt of the driveway. In the absence of snow, the yard looked even smaller than it had through the winter months. The dwelling was unpretentious, a gingerbread house in springtime. Purple, white, and yellow crocuses defined the flowerbeds along the walk and, blade-like, the leaves of tulips and jonquils thrust through the loam around the maple tree and lamp. The little greenhouse that encased a front window of the house was alive with early hyacinths and greenery not yet peppered with buds. Jonathan reached inside to snap off a spike of lavender clustered bells; this he presented with gallant flourish to Leah as he pulled her toward the stoop.

The inner door to the house was already ajar and the Reverend John Grante was unlatching the storm door and grinning. "Well, if it isn't the little prophetess who quoted Jeremiah 10 against my Christmas tree!" He enclosed Leah in a tight hug and passed her along to Wilomena, reaching next for Jonathan.

"Sorry we missed the service, Dad," Jon offered promptly, the words shaken, along with his shoulders, by the encircling arm. "Leah had a client."

"Come get a cup," the pastor said, hauling him up the doorstep. "Mother's made your lemon pie."

At the table, Wilomena shared her disappointment that Janiene, because her spring break did not coincide with the holiday this year, could not get home from Michigan—disheartening news, she knew, to Leah, since the two of them had so enjoyed each other at Christmastime. John added that Jeremy had accepted an invitation to a friend's for an hour or so after the service, and yes, it was he who had dyed the eggs nested in green cellophane grass around the centerpiece, but by next year, he'd have outgrown that. Leah, coloring a little, said she hoped she hadn't offended the Grantes during her December visit. The pastor laughed as if she had given him a new anecdote for next Sunday and said he couldn't imagine *then* why she had hedged over the answer to a simple question like what kind of tree she liked. But he was glad he had pressed it, or the whole thing about how she celebrated Messiah's birth might never have come up. He said she had given him material for half a dozen sermons on genuine Christianity, faith as opposed to senseless ritual. He and Min, he said, were considering celebrating without the tree next year, pagan as the custom was, might even buy a menorah instead. "Christ among the churches, y' see, including the church of Israel," he enthused. "Have you thought about that? Min, now where's the bunny? Tell Leah."

Wilomena blushed scarlet, finished chewing, and applied the napkin to her mouth, holding it there until she was ready to speak. She said she had put it away, she would have confessed, and he really ought to let them say hello first. He apologized, reaching to touch her, and said he just wanted Leah to know they appreciated what she had shared. After all, he said to Leah, it was they who had become part of the olive tree by grafting, not she, the root. Pulling a notepad from his vest pocket, he said he was anxious to hear how she celebrated the Resurrection. She laughed, glancing at Wilomena, and he added with raised brow that he was serious. Wilomena's forehead knit, and Leah said simply, "He *is* the Passover."

"The Lamb, yes," Grante said, "but I've heard that new Messianic believers are amazed to learn they've been celebrating the Resurrection all along in the *Haggadah*, in the *aphikomen*, and redemption by blood in the third cup of wine."

Leah nodded, coveting—and Wilomena knew it—the picture she had painted of a weekend free of academic and clinical involvement and void of cohesive thought. She promised to send him the *Haggadah* and to talk about it next time.

"Yes, John," Min said gently, "next time." She poured more herb tea into Leah's cup and then into the others, and John turned the conversation, obligingly, he thought, to Min's "lovely new piece of stitchery," a soft blue-on-white greeting, the Hebrew symbol for *Shalom*.

Beneath the tablecloth Jonathan, however unconsciously, traced a message with his thumb on Leah's hand. He had tried to be attentive to the exchange with his father and mother, to which she was more a party than himself, but he looked ardently to the hour when his parents would retire and Leah would turn to him and draw from him his hopes and plans and share with him her hopes and dreams, and sit close to him and talk of little things, and sit very close and not talk at all. These thoughts his thumb continued to write on her hand from time to time until Jeremy returned home and then the Grantes, because the day had drawn much from them, could stay awake no longer.

And as Wilomena climbed the stairs ahead of John, she knew from long experience in the art of watching faces that Jonathan had communicated something to Leah that she had acknowledged in some way, perhaps only in the serenity of her expression, and that Jonathan, somehow, had drawn from that communication a glowing new serenity of his own.

ON EASTER MORNING, David sat on the side of the sanctuary that was not the side where LeRoy Willis sat. He entered late and chose the back row, so as not to complicate things by tangling himself up with anyone. He guessed, as the time for the service drew near, that the atmosphere today would be upbeat again: the choir, in pastels and bright spring colors, was already in the loft; in the pews little girls in long dresses or bouncy ruffles sat with patent-leathered feet thrust out in front of them; and every male, old and young, was suited. The nave was packed. The choir, organ, and brass struck up "Sound the Trumpet," the people followed it with their own full-throated singing of "Christ the Lord is risen toda-ay, A-a-a-a-a-le-e-lu-u-iah," and David checked off another one called right by the Jewish boy. No one was holding back today; the choir beamed; the mourning was for Friday.

He tried to open his mind to what he had to do. If he really believed his Bible foretold the coming of a Messiah, why couldn't he have already come? Maybe—maybe King David's psalm of dying in that gruesome way was a glimpse into the future, to the time when Jesus lived, you know? A prophecy or something. These people were singing at the top of their lungs that "Christ" was alive again. How important was it that he know before he asked a favor? The singing swam around his ears: "All hail the power of Jesus' name, let angels prostrate fall," then "Crown him, crown him, crown him; crown him Lord of all." In the swell of voices he heard joy and praise, but he saw near him, as well, an expressionless face or two just uttering words in tune.

The silver-haired pastor came to deliver the message of the day—for some, of the year. He spoke of "Jesus' obedient sacrifice, God's instrument of grace. Grace, the unmerited mercy of God offered to humankind across the chasm of separation, the chasm dug deep by our inherent sin and our continuing desire to sin; grace for forgiveness, for salvation, for the healing of spiritual wounds and of physical and emotional hurts..." Getting down to cases, David thought. "...for restoration of fellowship not only with God but with others; grace for growth, grace for service." He cited Luke 11:9 and 10, and David listened:

And I say unto you, Ask, and it shall be given you; seek, and ye shall find; knock, and it shall be opened unto you.

For every one that asketh receiveth; and he that seeketh findeth; and to him that knocketh it shall be opened.

It sounded simple; the pastor purported that it *was* simple. He urged his listeners to "take the step of faith, and see that the Lord is good. Believe him, receive him, and know the bounty that is life—abundant and free."

David knew that to do what he must, by sermon's end he would have to strip off his armor and lay it down; he would have to submit to vulnerability for a little while, to give Jesus the "Messiah" a chance to prove himself. He wanted to be fair. He would ask, seek, knock—and let Jesus make his move.

The message ended; from the choir came a quiet song: "Peace, perfect peace, in this old world of sin? The blood of Jesus whispers peace within," and the pastor exhorted worshipers to come forward for "anything at all" that they needed "from the abundance of the grace of God, in the precious name of Jesus." He reiterated the benediction of perfect peace, and David, ruminating on the fact that he felt no peace whatever, let alone a perfect one, waited until the last note of music had sounded and the people had departed to places better suited to the exchange of pleasantries and news. He walked forward slowly, to the altar rail, where there remained a man and a woman kneeling separately. Two elders were speaking to the man on the right end of the altar, and David stood near the center of the rail, a respectful distance from them, trying not to—and at the same time hoping he did—hear their conversation.

"And you believe he can?" one of the men behind the rail asked the one who leaned upon it with folded hands.

"I do. "

"Then he will do it, won't he?"

"Praise God, he will."

The two elders placed their hands on the man's head and one prayed, "Our Father God, we come before your throne believing with all our hearts that, in Jesus' atoning sacrifice, you have already healed Bob's neck, that this pain that he has had for so long will leave him because we are today laying the cause of it at your feet, at the foot of the cross...." The pastor, who had been counseling and praying with the middle-aged woman at the other end of the rail, was now standing and holding both her hands in his. "According to his faith, Father," the elder's prayer continued, "may it be accomplished in him, now in this moment, and maintained through the coming days, in the *name* of Jesus, Amen." The other elder prayed and they both talked a moment more with the man. David saw the pastor look his way and then, bidding the woman goodbye with a blessing, begin to walk toward him. His heart began a thudding in his chest and he forgot what he had planned to say. The two elders now moved toward him as well, and as the group converged, three on the ministers' side of the rail and he alone on the petitioners' side, David felt a wave of panic engulf his innards and overflow into his limbs. He tried desperately to recall his opening line, and when at last he conjured one, no sound would come from his open mouth. He remembered, at seven or eight, watching a black dog hurtling toward him, ears back, hair raised, teeth bared, yapping. He had not been able to move or to scream; not until the animal was tackled and dragged away by its owner— burly, under-shirted, cursing—did utterance return, and David had shaken for long minutes afterward, as much from his impotence to act as from fright over the incident itself. Now, standing in the "sanctuary" of this church, feeling himself as unsafe as ever he had been, he would have sold his inheritance for a stuttered word. The block was a wall, immovable.

He knelt at the rail and the pastor and elders knelt opposite him. "What is it you want Jesus to do for you?" the pastor asked in the low and soothing way that such men can. "The voice? Is it the voice?" David strained to force the words through a throat turned stone and then, reminding himself that he had been trained in the use of better means to overcome this kind of thing, tried to be rational, to bring his skills to bear. The pastor, seeing that his probing only injected the petitioner with increased discomfort, laid a hand on his shoulder, touched a drop of anointing oil to his forehead and began to pray. "Father, in your mercy, in the name of your Son Jesus, restore this voice, we pray; release this young man from his bonds, for our Savior promised that where two or more are gathered in his name, there he is, in their midst, and that if we ask anything in his name—"

"Nnnot the v-voice," David blurted, and then, the more chagrined, in a lower tone, "A-a-a-I st-stutter." He attempted nothing further.

The minister's hand remained on David's shoulder and it tightened as he said, "My boy, I'm sorry, I cannot recall your name, and I would like to know it." An elder leaned to the pastor's ear and supplied the name in full, for which David was at once grateful and anxious. He did not remember ever meeting the man. How well was he known here?

"Do you want to trust Jesus with this, David?" the pastor asked gently. "Is that why you've come forward?" David nodded. "You know him, then, as your Savior?" The implication was ridiculous. How could he know a man who had lived and died 2,000 years ago? Or even one supposedly alive again in heaven? If the question was, did he accept Jesus as the Messiah, well, if he could heal him today as he had the blind man in the story, he, David, would concede that he, Jesus, was, indeed, the Anointed One of God. This was Jesus' chance. He nodded.

The three men laid their hands on David's shoulders and head, and the pastor prayed. "We thank you now, Father, for the work you are going to do in David. We trust you to give to him the ability to communicate clearly and fluently, for Lord, we know that it is neither your design nor your will for your children to be hindered in this way. Rather, it is an indication of the condition of our fallen world. And although you enable us to serve in your strength while we are yet in our weakness, we humbly ask that you bind the powers that constrain this young man, your servant, that in Jesus' love, he may be made whole. By your grace, Father, remove the source of this disability and take away the symptoms, we pray, in the name of our Lord, Jesus Christ, Amen, Amen." By their echoed "Amen, Amen," the elders declared the singular prayer sufficient. Were they aware, David wondered, that they had pressed each "Amen" into his head and body? Was that part of it?

It was over. He arose slowly. They shook his hand by turns, leaving openings for him to speak, eager, David surmised, to see the work of God in him. "Thank you," he said, watching the smiles light all around. "A-a-a-a-I appreciate your t-t-time—very much." The smiles were tempered.

"Ignore the symptoms, now," the pastor said. "Don't let Satan rob you." He touched David's arm and said, "God bless you, Dave." In disfluent phrases, David thanked each man again then turned to walk the aisle between the empty pews. The deal was, he silently reminded Jesus as he walked, that if you would heal me, I'd believe you're who they say you are. Remember? That was the deal. He pushed the door open and headed for the car. Tomorrow, one way or the other, he'd do some straight talking with Leah.

THE CONGREGATION POURED from the doors of both wings of the red brick church in Lewistown. Was everyone talking about it, as Bonnabeth Nilssen claimed, or was it only she who, in making her rounds with such care, had thoroughly spread the word? Hadn't they all known for more than a year now, she had exclaimed to Grace Weber, that Jonathan Grante had backslidden to the point where a body wondered whether he had ever really committed himself to Jesus in the first place? Witness his chosen profession, she had remarked to Barbara Lohring, so avaricious, so tied to earthly gain. And hadn't they heard he had grown up quite the lady's man, down there near the state line, runnin' down to Baltimore with a different girl every weekend, frequenting the discos and who-knew-what-else? Don't you bet those young women would have a story or two to tell! It was all in the open now, seeing as he went forward this morning in such a state.

And little wonder. Wasn't that the finest sermon they had yet heard from the able Pastor Grante, the call to full commitment as heartrending as she, Bonnabeth, could recall in all her days? Had anyone missed the look the good pastor gave his son when he spoke of allowing Jesus, the Bread of Life, to fill us, body and soul, with himself, so that he became fully a part of every cell of us until—Oh, the thought of it—until we walked this earth, truly, in his stead? Had anyone failed to see, she wondered, the look of penitence on the handsome face of Jonathan Paul as he approached the altar even before his father had voiced the call, as if the Holy Spirit himself had drawn him by the hand? Such a peace in his countenance now; can you see it? And do you suppose, she asked Elise Whitney, his change of heart had anything to do with the young woman who came to church with him today? She's Paulette Legaillard's niece, you know—a Jewish girl. Saw her here at Christmastime, sitting next to Jonathan, so there must be something there. Fancy it. A Jewish girl.

Ernst Nilssen descended from the foyer to the graveled parking lot to wait for his wife in the car. He ran a hand over the back of his head where the halo of hair began and settled back behind the wheel. Why people like Elise and Barb put up with Bonnie's suppositions and embellishments he could not fathom. Too well brought up to tell her off, he guessed. Subtle correction had no effect on Bonnie; she didn't hear it. He supposed that at fifty-three, she might just be the woman she would forever be. The only thing he was certain she was right about was the sermon. Beyond the sacrament of communion, he had never understood that passage where Christ had told the crowd of followers that he was the Bread of Life, that if they wanted truly to belong to him, they must eat his flesh and drink his blood. More than once, he had wondered if he, like many of them, would have turned away on hearing those words. What Grante had said this morning made it, for the first time, make sense. To chew on Jesus' teachings and drink of his life every day—regular as breakfast, lunch, and dinner—wouldn't that be the way to become totally Christ-like? And to walk the earth in his stead is what he asked us to do, isn't it? Till he comes back. It was such a revelation to Ernst that he wished now that he had gone forward, too, at the close of the service, to commit himself to the idea. He wondered if he had what it took to follow through without some kind of consecration to it or someone to hold him accountable. But then, Ernst had never been much of an altar kneeler. It was so humbling, so—public.

He looked at his watch: 12:25. Bonnie would not only be the last one out of the church today (nothing new about that), but the next-to-the-last one out, whoever it was, would be detained well into the lunch hour on this one. By Bonnie's book, the pastor's prodigal—whom Ernst had found in the two years he'd known him a likeable sort anyway—had come home.

Chapter 24

IT WAS MONDAY. The Clinic office had closed at five, but Hurland was observing a group session. David and Leah were in the room where they had begun his therapy seven months ago. She leaned forward in a vinyl-covered chair, elbows locked straight, holding onto the edge of the cushion, looking at the floor, and David, pacing, hoped she was not going to play unfairly again: He couldn't cry; neither could she. His frustration wore the mask of sarcasm. "How long does it *take*?" She was silent. "In the story, it was *zap*—the blind man sees." Still no response. "You should've been in Steinberg's office this morning," David stuttered, "when I asked for more time on the talk. Tell *him* I'm healed."

"David," she said, speaking his name pleadingly in its Hebrew form, "don't do this to me."

"Don't do this to you? I'm walking proof you're wrong, and you t-tell me if I have faith, it'll happen. If Yeshua had *power*, it *would* have. Admit it." He walked to her and sat on his heel to look at her; he had never seen her so smitten. Tenderly, he placed a hand on her cheek. "Admit it."

"Some people say that once he showed us who he was, there was no more need for miracles. I don't believe that. You hold the key, David—you."

He saw himself reflected in the delicate irises of her eyes. Was she devastated more by her disappointment or by the evidence that she was wrong? He would not ask. He pulled her gently to her feet and, saying nothing, walked her to her car.

🌺

DAVID OFFERED THE WINDOW SEAT to Evan MacAteer. He would spend most of the flight to California sleeping, or at least secluded behind closed eyes. He had not had time to rest or reason in the last ten days. He fastened his seatbelt. It's the horserace all over again, this thing with Leah, he thought: I've won, but she won't concede. I've won—and I've lost. The hollow feeling in the pit of his stomach was there long before the plane lifted from the ground, and it remained, he was sure, long after everyone else's had normalized. His thoughts went back to Monday. Leah still clung to the myth. "David, don't do this to me," he heard her say. *Dah-veed* she had pronounced it, to remind him of their common bond. Did she know it meant Beloved? How he wished she had meant it that way. He tried to hear the word in her voice: *Beloved, don't....* How long does it *take?* he heard himself chafe. *You hold the key, David—you.*

The only thing to which he held the key was All-American status at the championships. He was the select product of a select team, and he was ripe. He'd show them what the Jewish boy from Penn State could do. He was a shoo-in. That would have to be enough. It was enough.

So why did he feel hollow.

Chapter 25

THE RAPPING WOKE DAVID from a fitful slumber. Asleep, he had been on the still rings; awake, he could not recall what day it was or in what room he lay. Dawn or dusk seeped through the window; the clock said 8:55 with a red P.M. light, but it felt like morning. The knocking came again. He rolled over groaning, "I'm not home," slowly gaining awareness that, if the dorm was home, he was. No one was answering the door. His brain worked soggily: Mac's not here; his last final was today.

"David?" the rapper said.

He meant to answer that it was open, when he realized the voice was female. He pulled his jeans from the floor onto his legs without fastening them and, taking a shirt with him into the bathroom, called toward the door, "In a minute." It was Leah, had to be. He picked up a toothbrush and tube with one hand and a comb with the other and, having unscrewed the lid of the tube, applied the toothpaste to his comb. With a curt comment on his intelligence, he rinsed it away and tried again, this time with success. What had made him so certain on the flight back that he didn't care anymore what anyone thought of him?

He opened the door with feigned surprise as he said her name.

"I haven't seen you for...weeks," she said, "since you left for L. A. Did you get my note?"

"Yeah. Yeah, thanks."

"You'll be going home. I wanted to say goodbye."

He glanced at the room, unaided since the beginning of time. "Uh, shoes. Let me get some...shoes."

The streetlights were lit when they left the dorm. Under the trees that lined the walk, the light was diffused, soft, like the spring air. "Your parents must be very proud," Leah said. He walked, allowing the balm of the May night and her presence to soothe him. He said he had hoped to do better than just the bars. It hadn't come together. That bad break on the horse, and then he couldn't hit his vault. He wasn't psyched. Thought he had it in his pocket, but maybe he wasn't enough of a team man out there. She told him nine-one's and two's at the NCAA's were fine; everyone knew the scoring was tougher. "All-American on the bars and you're not happy?"

"I could've taken the all-around."

"I'm sorry."

"Yeah, well, there's next year." He could not believe he had said that; it wasn't at all what he felt.

She told him that for whatever it was worth, she was sorry to have put him under stress before the championships.

"You didn't push. I pressed the issue. But all I proved is that your Yeshua doesn't work for me. Sometimes I think if he *were* God, it wouldn't matter; there is no help for me. That's just the way it is."

"Rothman," she said, facing him, "you don't do this. You don't quit. And I've got news for you: neither does God." He tried to see her face as they began again to walk. It lifted him to hear her scold. He listened to her build him up then chide him for not re-specting himself, for not finding joy in God's gifts to him, his prom-ises to him, his love for him. And when she was finished, he wanted to close her in his arms and tell her how very much he would miss her till September. She was reminding him to write, telling him that her address would be the same, her work right here in town. And, fearing her next word would be goodbye, he prodded her to tell him about her clinical for the summer and whether she would swim or ride to break up work, anything he could bring to mind. She was, he knew, walking a course back to her car, and when goodbye seemed a step away, he took hold of her arm and turned her.

"I can't leave w-without saying this. I'm in love with you, Leah. I don't care who else is. I don't care what he thinks or believes. I'm...drawn to you all day, every day. And I'm tired of being noble. How do I reach you? How do I make my feelings matter to you? They're there, they're real, they're deep—so deep." He would not kiss her when he knew she did not want him to, but there was no way she could make him stop loving her. He had said it; she had only listened. There was nothing to do but go home. His throat suddenly swollen and hot, he stepped back and began to turn away.

"David." He waited, breathing stopped. She walked slowly to him, and the lamplight shone on wetness in her eyes. She reached for his shoulders and placed a soft kiss on his cheek; her voice was a whisper. "Goodbye, David."

Chapter 26

THE HOME OF NATHAN ABRAMOWICZ was in no way more sumptuous than the sprawling thirteen-room country residence of D. Jacob Rothman outside Lansdale, Pennsylvania. To each of its three visitors, the appeal of the edifice was entirely, although for different reasons, in the place where it stood: overlooking the Mediterranean from a broad private beach site in Herzliya, Eretz Israel.

The Americans had spent less than a day in Tel Aviv. For the following five weeks the drive wheel in the planning and implementation of Rothman's proposed ten-story emporium had been powered from the conference library in Abramowicz's villa. Meals fit for honored guests, served with fine wine at the planning table, and the breeze from the Sea through the open balcony doors were the fuelers' sole relief through sequent days of concentration.

But Samuel Feingold was not in Israel to labor. The intensity of the conference room, the studying and shuffling of the drawings, the stewing, the phone calls were his concern only insomuch as he loved Jacob Rothman and his son as deeply as could any godly teacher his proteges. While the pleasures of the house and grounds were his, it pained him to see them so consumed by the project that the wonder of the Beloved Land was no part of their thinking. He looked forward to the release of young Dov—David—to accompany him on a sweeping tour that would, midway, ascend to its zenith in the Old City. The thought of his return to the site caused gooseflesh even now, in his seventy-fourth year.

Dinner with Nathan's wife and teenage daughter had been exquisite, as usual. He closed the conversation by saying so and excused himself. Reclaiming his walking stick from the place where he had leaned it and utilizing it as the extension of himself that in the last three years it had become, he moved his considerable frame outside, over the flagstones, and through the arbor toward the water.

So sad about Dov. The boy had had his lumps. If he had not been so strong of spirit and so bravely dogged in pursuing his career plans, this stuttering thing, his nemesis for all the years Samuel had known him, would have already reduced him to tasks degrading to a Rothman—doing the books or, at best, paperwork orders—and it still might. Worse than psoriasis, this disfluency; no end to its plague. And now, the young woman, the rejection. Maybe the trip abroad right now was good; David would have little time to brood. So far, there had not been a daytime hour left to him here to give full sway to depression. How much of the boy's mind, Samuel wondered, was on business while he worked with Jacob and Nathan? Ah, probably as much as was on the Summer Games as he sat with eyes unfocused, late at night, before the television screen. The rabbi knew people. David had the look of a young man haunted; the girl was still on his heart, and what was on Dov's heart was on Samuel's. There was a permanent place inside him for the boy who, years ago and to this day, devoured the Scriptures in silence.

It was kind of Jacob to ask him, Sam, to come along. Not only would he absorb all he could of the air and sun, the expanse of sky over the ancient Land, but he would be sure that David felt safe in undressing his hurt before the rabbi who could, perhaps, bathe the wound in love.

He reached the overlook puffing, let himself down onto the wrought iron bench, wishing it wood, and surveyed the sight. The seascape was more beautiful each time he came here. Today it was marred only by an elongated speck moving, although hardly, south along the horizon. An outbound freighter, he guessed, and so close to the shore that it was surely from no farther north than Haifa.

Three more days, Jacob had said, three more sunsets, and Dov would be free. Then, following the Sabbath, the two of them, Dov and Sam, would go.

"GOOD NEWS, JACOB, THAT YOU CAN COME WITH US," Samuel said. There would still be, he told himself, time with young David in Jerusalem. "I wish it weren't a business trip for you."

"Just the few days in Jerusalem, one or two in Tel Aviv," the elder Rothman answered, his clipped sentences making Sam's, by comparison, a drawl. He was a wisp in the shadow of the rabbi. "The rest is a lark, and well earned, eh, D. J.?" He took Samuel's luggage from David and set it on the driveway. The smile animated his thin moustache and displayed even, angular teeth. "Sam, you wouldn't believe the input this boy has had," he said with a nod toward David. "I am impressed; so is Nathan." He fit the last suitcase into the trunk of Abramowicz's Volvo and, closing the lid with a "chuk," walked around to slide behind the wheel. Samuel, at David's insistence and with his help, eased himself onto the other front seat.

They drove south to Tel Aviv, stopping there the better part of two days and then continuing southeast through Lydda and Latrun toward the City. To David's expressed pleasure in at last heading down to Jerusalem, Samuel replied happily that one always went *up* to Jerusalem.

But for the rabbi's comments as they drove, the two D. J. Rothmans would not have known that they were passing through the ancient tribal land of Dan—homeland of Samson and site of his burial, somewhere between Kibbutz Zorah and Eshtaol—or that they were now entering Benjamin's territory, with Judah to the south. Benjamin—beloved little brother of Joseph—from whose seed arose Israel's first human king ("for isn't the only true king God himself?" Sam added), and Judah, the root of her greatest warrior-king ("for whom you, of course, David, are named," he said). Sam jabbered on about Saul's and David's birthplaces and how the prophet Samuel had anointed each to be king—first Saul, the self-willed, and then David, the "man after God's own heart."

The Valley of Ayalon, through which they were now driving, Samuel told them, had been the scene, later, of many battles between the Greeks and the Maccabees—in fact, the scene of much bloodshed over the centuries, including the recent War of Liberation. Clear passage through this valley had always been, and probably always would be, he said, critical to the safety of Jerusalem.

As they approached Abu Ghosh, Samuel explained that it was to this town, to ancient Kirjath-jearim, that the men of Beth-shemesh brought the Ark of the Covenant when it was returned by the Philistines, who had realized to their horror that it was not a good luck charm. There it remained, Samuel told them, until twenty years later when David, dancing before it, brought it with joy into Jerusalem.

As they approached the route south into the heart of the City, Samuel reached to touch Jacob's arm and beg his indulgence to take them "just a few miles to the north" before they went on to the hotel. He wanted to show them the route of the Fathers, only as far as Tel el-Ful and el-Jib. "You'll remember that ancient Gibeah was Saul's hometown and later the site of his palace...."

"And before that, the s-source of the trouble b-b-between the Benjamites and the rest of Israel," David murmured, taking in the stone mansions through his window.

"Yes," Samuel said, intrigued that the boy recalled it, "the rape unto death of the Levite's concubine by the Benjamites of Gibeah." He turned to glance at David. "An interesting war. Now, there, see it on the rise? Tel el-Ful—Gibeah."

The old man's vignettes continued as they drove past the minaret of Nebi Samuel toward el-Jib. He began them with the excitement of a schoolboy and then developed them a stroke at a time into articulate paintings, finished at the edge with the fine brush of awe. His passion for the Land was communicable, and David could not help but begin to give himself over to its contagion.

On the drive back toward the City, they passed for the second time a Bedouin caravan also heading south, and David, seeing the herd of camels about which the weathered nomads traveled, commented that if their bartering went well, he guessed a few locals who were walking today would be riding tomorrow.

"Not necessarily," the rabbi corrected. "The ship of the desert is as often sold for its hide or milk, even for meat these days. I wonder why these people are in this place at all, let alone traveling toward the City from the north—they're from Gaza." David chuckled and asked how he knew. "The woman's coins," he said. "The strands fall from her headband in an inverted V-shape over her face; she could only be from Gaza. Hmm...maybe trading camels for finer wares to take to Beersheva for the Thursday morning market."

"They don't look friendly," David said.

"Ah, but they are," Samuel said with a chortle. "If you were their worst *enemy*, they would entertain you with their best fare, up to three days."

"Then?" Jacob asked.

Samuel's face crinkled. "No holds barred."

David laughed, and Samuel sensed that he had won the boy's respect anew for the scope and depth of information he had laid before him in a single hour. He must be more careful, he reminded himself, to encourage him in his observations, to build the boy's self-esteem.

"Camel meat," David stuttered. "Not for Israelis, I hope." He added pensively that the economic climate must be hard for American immigrants to bear; he had read that increasing numbers were heading back home, unable to cope with fiscal uncertainties, not to mention terrorism.

"The meat," Sam assured him, "is for export to developing nations—and you're right, too, about the economy."

Jacob lit. He said his sources told him that controls, as much as they seemed the answer now, could not be kept. When they came off, inflation would soar again. He turned to David, smiling. "You know what that'll do for profits."

Right, David thought, if people keep buying; never had he heard the principle stated with such anticipation. He was surprised at how crass it made his father sound.

"Intriguing," Jacob was saying, "to invest now, take the losses, watch consumers discover they can't do better than at Rothman's." He beamed over his shoulder at David. "We'll pump those first profits back in till the ink turns black, D. J., you see? That's good management." David stuttered that he knew how glad Israel was to have American investments; he had heard radio spots in Philly selling Israeli banking. Jacob was speaking while David's last words were still in his mouth. "Israel needs us," he said, "no question— but the interesting thing is, the States need Israel more. This skinny shalk of wheat in the middle of the brew," Jacob said, looking about him, glowing, "is America's best oasis of stability in this part of the world. We must support our friends here."

"We have," David responded.

"Ah, but have we?" Samuel chirped. "An excellent question, my boy...."

POLICIES OF AMERICAN PRESIDENTS regarding Israel since statehood in '48 ignited a runaway debate as they climbed the holy hill, and although David was assimilating much, he was also feeling more and more the little boy in the back seat of his father's car, the pupil in the rabbi's classroom. He was tired of the stuttering—it would not obey him while he was with them. Why could he reveal to Leah in fluent words the most intimate emotion of his heart, while with these men... They loved him. *They loved* him.

He missed her. There was hardly a thought he did not relate, somehow, to her. Leah. Even here in the wasteland heat, her name was a sweet-scented breeze through a willow. Strange. To say it—*Leah*—brought him peace. Don't think goodbye, he told himself. She didn't mean that. Oh, God, she didn't mean that, did she?

He felt small, disabled, weary. Relating to two people with whom he could not communicate as a man drained him. In any other circumstances, the ascent to the City might have taken his breath away. Now, he was relieved to have it ended. Tomorrow, at least, he would have only one companion—as it happened, the one with whom he needed most to talk. As much as he loved his dad, two on one was one too many.

Chapter 27

WITH JACOB DELIVERED TO JERUSALEM and all of their reservations secured, Sam and David, having agreed to keep the Old City for the final coup, left early the following day to drive northeast to Jericho, where, following a light breakfast, they toured. In 110-degree heat and nearly unbearable humidity, David—concerned for the rabbi, who was overdressed and sweating profusely—abbreviated the visit and called a retreat to the car for the trip south through Ein Feshcha to Ein Gedi, which Samuel had assured him would be better. Today, behind the wheel, David was quiet. With no task before him, he found Leah Rachelle Beaumont the guest of his mind through every impression. She had gone with him through the amazing marketplaces of Jericho. She was with him now in the midst of the farms and orchards. Yet how could he speak of her here? What would Samuel think, while they were surrounded by so much else that the rabbi wanted to talk about? He chose to mention the unbelievable bounty of Israel, and as he expected, it set Samuel off again.

"The Land will bear in this way only for God's people," he said lustily. "Ezekiel foretold it, and the marvel of it is all the greater in view of the relentless creeping of deserts into arable tracts everywhere else in the world. Since the Chosen have returned, even the Negev blooms. Everywhere, flowers, everywhere, dates...mangoes, papayas...look, bananas," Samuel exclaimed with open hands, "a garden. Here, even the cows give more milk."

They were headed toward the Dead Sea, but Samuel's zest was undying. It was not for David to create conversation when Samuel was harvesting produce, unearthing the Scrolls, explaining the symbolism of the seas. "Ah, but this lake is like a woman aborting her child," he said with wide eyes. "Pure and beautiful as she appears, she has destroyed all life within herself in solution saline. No fish, no algae live; a bird, according to the Bedouins, could not even fly across the Dead Sea without dying. Next week," Sam promised, "we'll go north along the Jordan to Lake Kinneret. It sparkles with life," he said, himself asparkle, "receiving it, nurturing it, bearing it."

From Qumran they drove to Ein Feshcha, ancient home of the Essenes, and Ein Gedi, the oasis of David as he fled from a jealous Saul—the most beautiful oasis on Earth, Sam proclaimed as he gazed at the falls and felt its cooling mist on his face. At Masada, they took the cableway up to the fortress, and by the time they descended David knew the mind of an eighteen-year-old primed for service. How could an Israeli perform less than heroically with this kind of history seared into his heart? Believing he could face any obstacle of mind, spirit, or body, David suggested they get on with the trip west, but Samuel insisted otherwise, saying "Beersheva keeps." They drove south toward the plant stacks of modern S'dom, the rabbi chatting about ancient Sodom and Gomorrah and David listening. Beneath the thick silt at the lower end of the brine, Samuel said, lay the two cities so utterly destroyed by God for their sin that not a single artifact had ever been found. Nests of lewdness and sodomy among the male and female populations alike, he said, taking in the desolate beach, to the extent that God could not find even ten for whom to spare Lot's city. A line came to David's mind—from Jeremiah, he thought—but he did not utter it: *This city hath been to me as a provocation of mine anger and of my fury from the day that they built it even unto this day; that I should remove it from before my face.* Appropriate, but not said, he knew, of Sodom or Gomorrah; God had pronounced it upon Jerusalem just prior to the Babylonian captivity. Disobedience. He heard Leah speak of it softly, hesitantly at first. Was it, to her, a topic painfully discussed with someone else in the past? Or just too personal a subject for comfort? Of what disobedience was she insinuating he was guilty?

Now, Sodom's, that was sin, and he'd certainly never do anything like that. What, then? To reject her Yeshua? How serious could that be? Why had she, over this, put their friendship on the line?

When he realized he had not heard Sam's voice for several minutes, he glanced at him. He was watching David, his mouth lined with concern. Here was a desert highway, privacy, and the rabbi's full attention. They both knew the subject. "A-About Leah, Rabbi. We had so little t-t-time to ourselves on the plane, you and I."

Samuel sat forward. "*Sam*," he corrected. "We are friends, Dov."

David nodded almost imperceptibly. "She's a beautiful girl, a wonderful girl. I wish you could meet her."

Samuel looked at him, surprised. "She's broken your heart."

"I'm not giving up," David stuttered.

"I want to understand," Sam said gently, "but 'wonderful' is not a person who turns her back on someone because he stutters."

"No, no. Leah's not like that." David recalled the faces of two who had been. "It's not the stutter, S-Sam," he said, fighting disfluency and familiarity at once. "I'm not sure, but I think it's ideological." The word came out in pieces.

"What, exactly?"

"It's that...she...b-believes...in Jesus." A wave of embarrassment swept David's face. He had not realized it would sound so rude. Glad for the "necessity" of keeping his eyes on the road, he absorbed Samuel's stare.

"*Dawid*," the ancient name was pronounced with compassion, "you don't want to get involved....You told me she was Jewish."

Suddenly, words were less important to David than need. "Help me, Sam."

The luster fled from Samuel's eyes, and he looked back to the road. He said he had seen it before. These people rarely changed their minds. Mesmerized—by what, he did not know. A cultist thing; a religion of guilt and blood. His voice carried no balm; maybe, David thought, because there was none for it. The doctrine of Jesus, Sam was saying, was hopeless: *Be perfect, even as your heavenly*

Father is perfect. "How can a person aspire to be as God is?" he said. "It was the downfall of Lucifer."

"Leah claims her Messiah made a gift to us of his perfect life, through his death. All we have to do is turn around and accept it. The Psalms, Sam, you know them well?"

"Of course, many by heart.... Mm." He looked at David.

"Twenty-two. *They pierced my hands and my feet.*"

Erroneous, Sam said; the Hebrew read *like a lion*—a favored phrase of King David, who had faced more than one as a youth in the hills of Judah. *Like a lion at my hands and my feet*, referring to his enemies. He pulled a booklet of travelers' checks from his vest and wrote on the flap the symbol for *kaaru*, they have pierced. Pierced, ending with the letter *vav*, he said. But the symbol in the text, he reminded David, did not have this line descending that far, and so, what was the last letter?

"*Yod*," David said, dividing his attention between the writing and the road.

"And so it reads *kaari*, 'like a lion,' does it not? Get out of her Bible."

"It was mine."

"Go back to the Hebrew," Sam said without missing a beat, "the earliest you can find. And Dov, study *carefully*, as if it were life and death."

The Dead Seascape shrank as they headed across the Negev, analyzing the assertions to which David had been exposed in the two months before school's end. They talked on the road, over lunch in Dimona, at Abraham's Well, and at Tel Sheva, again on the road, and over dinner in *Bayt Lahm*—Bethlehem—of Torah, Talmud, Mishnah, of Christianity, and "the girl." They returned late to the hotel, and David, although bodily tired, was encouraged in spirit by Samuel's patient rendering of rabbinical thought. Lost and burning in the desert, he had come upon a lake—a reservoir so clear, so cool, so protected that he could walk into it and drink of it and swim in it. Already refreshed inwardly, he splashed away the grit of the day in the shower and fell into bed in his private room. He had only a few more questions, and perhaps by day's end tomorrow, his stuttering would cease altogether in the company of his mentor and cherished friend.

Chapter 28

NOT UNTIL THEIR THIRD DAY IN JERUSALEM were David and Samuel ready to embrace the Old City; there was much to see in the new as well, and a study to be made, for David's benefit, of the Holyland Hotel's exquisite diorama. These things done, they set out early on Thursday morning.

Samuel lifted his old frame up the high steps of the bus and, having given David the window, collapsed cheerfully on the aisle. As the vehicle moved away from the curb, he spoke close to David's ear of the day when the West Bank would truly be Israel's—for didn't God promise the restoration of Ephraim in due time?—and of how things might have run a different course historically had Britain wholly honored the Balfour Declaration and not sent Lawrence "of Arabia" to nationalize the Arabs—for was that not the beginning of their heightened agitation against the Jews? How long would it be until Hagar's offspring understood that they would *never* possess the Land and that their determination to rid the Middle East of Israel would only bring their own ruin? That was the prophecy of Joshua, was it not? And furthermore, God promised Isaiah, didn't he, that he would extend Israel's borders; and to Micah he said that she, Israel, would judge her enemies.

Samuel's commentary on the prophets was interrupted only by his commentary on the passing scenes, and in his low, confiding voice, David read that he was pleased to have a listener as willing to ruminate upon his gleanings as he was to share them. How few were the times, David mused, that people had argued the Bible's prophecies against the Quran's interpretations of the same without starting another little war. He was glad for the noises of the bus that confined the rabbi's morning lesson.

When they were again on foot, Samuel was slowed considerably by his uncooperative leg and a shortness of breath, but here there was no need for hurry; hurry was, in fact, seldom thought about in these narrow streets, lined even now in the off season with tourists and tradespeople. The two made their way steadily toward the mount of the vanished temple, allowing stops for Samuel to regain his breath and too soon to expend it in conveying to David all that he was able of the sights about him.

They reached the remnant of the Western Wall, and the rabbi went immediately to prayer. David first occupied himself in observing the supplicants. How many, like Sam and he, were visitors? And with all the old and new immigrants, who could tell who was Israeli? He watched a man, probably in his late thirties, strap the thongs of the phylactery about his arm—carefully, so as to form the letters of the Almighty Name—and then begin to pray. Clothing, European; features, Semitic. Tourist, citizen? How could one know? Now, there was a *sabra*: a uniformed Israeli soldier, probably not yet David's age, leaning with both hands on the wall and staring open-eyed at the ground. *Sabra*, David thought, yet his profile was Martin's, in his younger years. Beside the soldier, a black man, North African by dress, was folding a snip of paper to near nothingness. He inserted it as deeply as it would go into a crevice in the wall, and David invented in his mind the man's family, somewhere in the heat and famine of Ethiopia, praying the same prayer. Maybe soon, as Sam had said, this pulling them on board quietly, a few at a time, would end and the gates could be opened to great numbers from that strangling land. He watched a man near Sam pull his white-and-blue shawl over his head, invoking divine protection. In a moment he was gone, and another took his place. Prayer shawls the same, faces all different, David thought; was there a place on earth where God had not scattered at least a few of his people? And these, or their forebears, had returned. Maybe this was what Isaiah meant when he said the Lord would gather up the children of Israel one by one and bring them back to worship on the holy mount. One at a time these had found their way here. Not to the Pyranees or the coastlands of Greece or to any other seductress, but to Israel, to the Land of Him Who Struggles with God.

Not to Italy, Spain—Greece? he remembered asking Leah. *Israel*, he heard her dream—only Israel.

He pushed his *yarmulke* forward a little and watched a Hasidic Jew near the wall; his head and torso were a metronome, nearly tapping it. And then his gaze returned to Samuel, who was standing open-eyed before the wall, before the Lord, and he knew at least a portion of his prayer. David lifted his hands toward God and, making the words his own, whispered his adoration and prayed: *Gather our dispersions from among the nations, assemble our outcasts from the ends of the earth, conduct us unto Zion, thy city, with joyful song, and unto Jerusalem, the residence of thy holy temple, with everlasting joy.* His thoughts flew back to Leah, and he wanted to pray for her. Would it help to write it down and leave it here? He moved nearer the wall and, with closed eyes, stood thinking. Then he tilted back his head, touched the wall as he would dare to touch the footstool of God, and pled in a whisper, "*Adonai*, help Leah. Bring her to me to talk. Thank you for Rabbi Feingold's wisdom; guide me as I share it...."

AS THEY MOVED THROUGH THE GATE and up the ramp, the devastation of the temple engulfed David. This was Mount Moriah, the place most holy in all the world. Here Abraham, taking God at his word, bound Isaac for sacrifice and was granted, for his faith, the covenant. Here King David had made his altar, and King Solomon had built God's temple of cedar and gold. Here had stood Herod's magnificent reconstruction of white marble, seventy-six years in the building. And here, upon the meager remnant of the splendor of Israel, the very House of God, gleamed Islam's Dome of the Rock. Built upon the rubble first of wood and then of finer things, the Mosque of Omar with its shining golden dome now housed the rock where, according to Islamic belief, Mohammed departed on his night journey into heaven. At first David thought it curious that in this of all places, the rabbi did not so much as look up; he plodded toward the subterranean stairway alongside el-Aqsa Mosque. It was as they descended that it came to David that they would not have climbed the temple mount at all had it not been important to Samuel that his young friend Dov see Solomon's stables beneath the ground. Solomon, son of the warrior-king, wisest and wealthiest man ever to live, Sam puffed with an eye full of meaning, until, to please his Gentile wives, he built other altars, and the kingdom was never the same. It was Samuel's way of telling David, in the strongest terms possible, to let Leah go.

Having ascended again into the sunshine, the rabbi and his charge wove through the Arabs and tourists and donkeys that tramped the holy ground; they worked their way back down to the street, and David noted that the old man's gait was more wearied than it had been all day. He again reversed authority and declared the tour ended, and Samuel did not object. The two climbed onto the bus, and there, their party became three.

Moishe Simon was a lifelong friend of Samuel, if one considered grade school in Brooklyn their cradle. How wonderful it was to see Samuel, he said, after all these years and all these miles. Yes, he would join Sam for dinner at the hotel, and indeed, he was happy to meet David.

From his seat across the aisle, David learned that Moishe, when he retired eight years ago, had succumbed to the wish of his grandson, who had no other family, to emigrate. Always a skilled jeweler, Moishe had had no problem finding reserves of ambition and capital to begin again the old trade in Jerusalem, for he had never wished to give it up at all, but had so much needed a change when his "dear wife—May she rest in peace—died in 1974." Here, he was free of the overmanagement of the younger partners to which he had, with later regret, acquiesced in New York; here he had his own shop. "Young people," he declared, with an apology to David, "sometimes they 'know' too much."

Grandson Daniel, Moishe told them with scarcely buffered pride, was hard at work in a *kibbutz* twenty minutes away, a good boy, soon to be eighteen. Brought up right, before his parents' tragic accident. Not like a lot of the young people you see these days—yes, even here in Jerusalem—casual attitudes, into drugs. Of course, here too, and yes, they knew where the stuff was coming over the border; no, they had not been able to stem the tide. An insidious weapon, drugs, he said, against Israel's youth, and against the army's strength.

They crossed over into the New City, and as David listened, he watched through the window the passing of the sixteenth flatbed carrier he had seen since Tuesday morning, when he had started to count. Odd tanks on them, not Israeli. Probably confiscated in Lebanon a year or more ago, now to be modified or, having been modified, to be stored, because, obviously, the drivers were in no hurry; the region was beginning to look like Moscow on May Day.

War. The Accords had declared it over, yet it hung low over the Land like a dark cloud, curling, churning. How long could tiny Israel pour all of herself into defense? Where would it end? When?

He leaned back into his seat and wondered what he would do to amuse himself while two old friends resurrected Isaac and Ishmael. He needed to work harder at keeping in shape—but not tonight. Tonight he needed some fun. He had almost forgotten what it meant. Did anybody here remember? Where was the *fun* in Jerusalem?

Chapter 29

David had had better conversations with his father. The opportunity to have dinner, just the two of them, was rare. He, the younger D. J., feeling the freedom of unplanned hours for the first time in months, was open and talkative, ready for wherever their exchange might lead, hopeful, in fact, that his father might eventually discern his need to discuss a deep concern or two. As they ate, he shared several thought-provoking reflections on what he had seen and heard in the last few days while touring with Samuel, but these missed the mark. D. Jacob Rothman's preoccupation was impermeable, yet by the tone of his occasional responses, one would have thought he believed the exchange coherent. He was not the father who had treated David to a tag-along trip from time to time in years past; neither was he the man who had so lavishly praised his son's suggestions a week ago. If his mind was still on business, even that was not evident, because when David switched to the planned innovations in design and decor for the store, these also fell on ears out of tune with the subject.

They parted ways without dessert or a second cup of coffee. David found himself on the street, irritated, wondering what could be so engrossing that the man would need to stay in Jerusalem while he and Sam took their journey up the Jordan. What could merit changing their itinerary, to come back south for him in six days? Now they would not see Haifa at all. He headed down the sidewalk telling himself the night lay wherever his feet would take him. His thoughts turned inward, to the days at Nathan's. He was sure the two elder planners were sincere in their appreciation of his ideas, a couple of which came right out of his marketing books but many of which were the product of his own reasoning. They had utilized nearly all of them, with or without refinement. Why, then, did he feel so out of his element? Why was there no joy in it? He saw Sam's confiding eyes as they had sat on the bus and walked the streets together. *There* was a man who had enjoyed his work, his interests. In these past few days, he had taught David so much, pouring drink for him, as it were, from his own love of the Scriptures, the Promises, the Land. Forget the pall of war; it was good to be on holy ground. If only Leah were here, she could taste the sweetness of the wine and savor its bouquet. He hadn't written her, not even a card from Tel Aviv. How could he start? *Dear Leah, about the way we said goodbye...* Uh-uh, try again.

He had walked for nearly half an hour when he heard it. An incredible sound, perhaps more so because there had been no time for music in all these days. Not just clarinet, trombone, piano, trumpet, sax—but fantastic clarinet, great trombone, a wonderful, light hand on piano, an unmistakable jazz sound, and now over it, eight, maybe ten voices, good ones, singing what seemed a—what?—a spirited folk song, a *horah*? He had never heard anything like it.

He could see the group as he came to the corner of a wide, shop-lined street called Ben Yehuda and peered down its length; a crowd had already gathered. He quickened his pace, smiling at the popcorn vendor who stood looking down the street, an instrument, David thought, much like a dulcimer out of the Appalachians hanging limply from his hand. As he drew close to the music, there welled in him an urge to clap to the beat; it was one to which somebody, everybody, ought to dance.

Five of the singers were, he guessed, in their early to mid-twenties, three were close to thirty, one side or the other. Four male and four female, they were dressed in bright blue, brown, and white Israeli folk costumes, alike only in triad of color. Their faces glowed; their hands and feet moved in a way neither amateur nor professional, but somewhere between. David moved along the side of the gathering toward the front, trying to catch the words.

They were singing a song of praise to God, now in Hebrew, now in English. The music flowed into an improvisation on the clarinet, one of such virtuosity that it did not matter to David that the band played through a soundboard; he fed on the rhythm, consuming next the sax solo and then the piano. The singers were also enjoying the music, and when they vocalized again, they improvised as well, or seemed to. They sang that Israel's enemies would all be turned away, and the crowd was clapping, having a good time. The song ended and there was applause with genial shouts, then a new number began. It was in Hebrew—*Ivrit*—and David caught phrases here and there. Again, he could not believe what he was hearing. He looked around him at faces, all attentive except for two people here, and one there, who walked on. Two men in Hasidic dress appeared near David and stood listening. The song was lively. When it was over, the bearded baritone greeted the audience and explained, mostly in English, that *HaMashiach* had indeed come to Israel and that he hoped that each man, woman, and child in the gathering had taken note of the testimony given in the song as to how he had been identified by Moses and the prophets as the Anointed One. He said that all the singers on the platform believed what they sang and had experienced the power of *Yeshua HaMashiach* in their lives. The men near David said something to each other, short, low phrases in Hebrew. It was when the tenor had stepped forward to tell, in English, of his "coming to know Yeshua, Jesus, God's Anointed, whom Moses called a prophet like unto himself" that one of the men in black *kapote* and *streimel* interrupted in a resounding voice. "Blasphemy! There ought to be a name for you."

The young singer lost his grip on the microphone but retained its wire in the other hand. "There is," he said, his voice breaking; he was grabbing at the mike that had escaped. "There is, sir," he said into the recaptured mike. "I am a Messianic Jew, a believer in the New Covenant promised in Jeremiah 31. Do you believe the Bible?"

"I believe you are a heretic," came the even reply. "You come from the States? Go home."

The crowd began to buzz. A man near the center told the two interrupters to move on if they didn't want to listen. Someone else shouted at them, "Let them say what they came to say," and one of the men in black, deciding against further confrontation for the time being, cast a look at the performers and, with his companion, turned away. The baritone stepped toward the younger singer and placed a hand on his shoulder. He spoke into the microphone the words of the prophet Jeremiah, to which his young friend had alluded, a promise by God that his people would, under a new covenant, know him, and that he would forgive and "remember no more" the sin of the houses of Israel and Judah, who had broken the old covenant. "Will you believe your Maimonides, gentlemen," the baritone said to the departing two, "or will you believe God, whom I have just quoted? To Zechariah, God said,

> I will bring forth my servant the Sprout of David...and I will remove the iniquity of that land in one day. In that day shall ye call every man his neighbour....

"In Yeshua the promise is fulfilled," the singer declared. "God asks only that you believe."

The air was still. A man near the front of the crowd moved forward, spat toward the platform, and followed the two *Hasidim*. His spittle hit the instep of the bearded singer and ran under the leather strap of his shoe. The singer kept his eyes on the man. "I stand in Yeshua's sandals," he said. "I offer you life." The three continued on their way and the younger singer, nodding to his associate, resumed, in better voice, the story of his "meeting Yeshua, Jesus."

When a new song began, David took up his observation of faces, this time, the performers by turn. There must be some fear behind the fronts, he thought; there has to be, to sing these songs in this place. At the far side of the singers, the arc of people began, and he saw a young man and woman, both in Army garb, standing with arms folded. David studied the man. Certainly over twenty, perhaps soon to be discharged, he was square of jaw with a bearing that radiated battle savvy: comfortable in Army shorts and tee shirt, he wore an Uzi on his back as if it had always been there. In his mind's eye, David imagined him instantly one with his weapon. It was at that moment that he heard him exude a singular phrase: "*Hallelu Yah.*" The young woman wore an olive Army blouse and skirt and carried a shoulder bag. In the tranquility of her face, she reminded David of Leah, yet she scanned the crowd slowly as if observing quietly, carefully all that was happening here. The show continued for three-quarters of an hour more, people coming and going on the periphery while the core of listeners remained. David kept the two soldiers in sight, and when they began to leave before the program had ended, he moved as swiftly as he could around the back of the crowd. He caught up with them at the popcorn vendor's and passed fully around to confront them face to face. He introduced himself, not caring that his name was stuttered, and asked whether they spoke English and then whether they would sit down with him at the cafe across the street. He wanted to know what they thought of the concert, if they didn't mind.

It was 11:15 when David emerged from the little restaurant, his brow furrowed. He walked briskly toward his hotel, looking as he went for *sherut* or cab and hoping for the latter because it would take him express.

Chapter 30

FIVE DAYS FROM THE SUNDAY on which David and Samuel left for Galilee, they returned to find at the hotel desk an envelope bearing the *mishtorah* seal; it was marked Urgent. David had not yet torn it open when a man sprinted from a lobby seat to within six feet of him and flashed a photo. Another closed in, notebook in hand, asking, "David, why was your father here in Jerusalem?" David squinted as eight others surrounded him and Sam, some flashing circles into their eyes, some thrusting portable mikes at them and demanding:

"Is it true the Tel Aviv store is a front?"

"How long has your father known Ben Sheva?"

"Where've you been, D. J.?"

"Rabbi, you were seen with Moishe Simon Thursday. What'd he tell you?"

No one waited for a finished question, much less response. David and Samuel answered nothing, but sought refuge in David's room. Locked inside, David opened the message in his hand. It instructed him to contact police headquarters for "information on the condition of Jacob Rothman." He handed the note to Sam and reached for the phone. Ten minutes later, Police Inspector Baruch Metz and two uniformed officers led David and Samuel through the hail of questions and flashes to a waiting car and thence to the hospital. They stayed the night at Jacob's bedside.

IT WAS LUNCHTIME SATURDAY. Suzanne tossed a handful of mail onto the kitchen table, sat down across from her roommate, and said she had blown the whole morning at the library reliving last night. "How did he hear what I never said? Leah?"

She handed Suzanne the morning paper folded back. Sue glanced at her and thought she saw redness in Leah's eyes. She looked at the photo and caption, twice.

"David?"

Leah nodded.

"That's not like him. What'd the guy *say?*"

"The names of the dead and injured in that explosion in Jerusalem have been released," Leah said, starting from the beginning.

Sue unfolded the paper. "Oh, Leah." She pulled her chair close and, her hand on Leah's arm, read quickly to herself:

JERUSALEM, July 27. American department store entrepreneur D. Jacob Rothman of Philadelphia died today at 4:41 a.m. (9:41 p.m. July 26, EDST) of injuries sustained in the Thursday morning bombing of the residence of Ari ben Sheva south of Jerusalem, bringing the death toll to nine.

Following the alleged attack on ten American, European and Israeli businessmen gathered at Ben Sheva's home, authorities had placed police guards in and outside the hospital rooms of the two survivors. Ben Sheva remains on the critical list under police protection.

No group has claimed responsibility for the bombing. Speculation in the city that the ten had met as core members of Ma Machir Zion, an underground activist organization, has not been substantiated.

"Increased activity on the part of several terrorist groups based in and outside of Israel has not escaped our attention," Police Chief Baruch Metz said. "Any one of them might have interpreted this meeting, if they knew of it, as a threat—or as an opportunity."

Reporters requesting information from 21-year-old David Rothman as he left the hospital room following his father's death elicited a violent reaction (photo left) from the co-heir to Rothman's multi-million-dollar estate.

Efforts by hospital administrators to curtail press activity on the Sabbath had met with varying degrees of cooperation: While some of the press confined themselves to the hospital lobby, a contingent of American reporters waited for the younger Rothman and family friend Rabbi Samuel Feingold at the nurses' station on the medical-surgical floor. Questioned about his father's last words to him, Rothman lifted reporter Alan Henning bodily by his shirtfront and shoved him across the hallway. Henning, claiming he sustained bruises of the head, would not comment on whether he would request that charges be filed by his agency....

Suzanne handed the paper back to Leah, called the question insensitive, and asked what they should do. She wasn't sure, Leah said, staring across the table. Burial was to be in Israel. The family would, most likely, fly over today, and that would complicate things. She picked up a windowed envelope and tapped it on the little heap of mail.

"And here I was jabbering on about nothing," Sue said sheepishly.

"You didn't know," Leah said, fingering a letter trimmed in blue. She pulled it out: addressed to her, postmarked Jerusalem. "David," she said. She inserted a knife blade into the corner to slice the seal, ran it deftly around three sides, held the tissue-thin paper a moment, then unfolded it slowly. There was something in the way she did it that made Suzanne stand up and say she would try the news channel, and Leah was left with her letter.

Friday, July 19

Dear Leah,
        You've got to experience this Land—I can't send even a part. Maybe when I see you, I'll be able to share what it's done to me.

Funny. Two days ago, even yesterday, I harbored the hope that when I got back, I could draw you to where G-d could reach you. I'm beginning to think now that you're where you belong.

I met two sabras last night. They were on their way to a friend's, but they gave it up for me. For all they told me in the more than two hours we talked, I could have been sitting in that little cafe with you. It's too much: The songs at the street concert where I met them were a refrain to what you've said. Even Mac came at me on the plane back from L.A. in April, and I'm left wondering whether it might be G-d himself who is hounding me from so many directions.

As we talked, Jesse and Tova began to see that I could handle Scriptural Hebrew, so they showed me some fascinating things— several places in the Tenach where the Messiah is referred to as separate from G-d and yet deity, and others where G-d refers to himself as if he and the Messiah are one. Tova pointed out that G-d-given prophecy is by definition correct and that if the Messiah hadn't been born in Bethlehem of the tribe of Judah and had his life "cut off" before the second Temple was destroyed, then Micah's and Daniel's prophecies would be incorrect. I don't have space for all they showed me, but this one came off the page—12th chapter Zechariah, verse 10, G-d speaking: "...when they look on him whom they have pierced, they shall mourn for him, as one mourns for an only child, and weep bitterly over him, as one weeps over a first-born." No way can "pierced" be read here "like a lion," as someone I know would have me believe.

The point is—Haven't we always been honest with each other?—I wanted to practice on these two Israelis the arguments I had planned for you. But, ready as I thought I was, they had out-studied me. They were always a step ahead—and patient. Leah, I could feel their love.

Jesse grew up in Sde Boker, Tova in Jaffa. They said they wished I could have been at a meeting in Yafo (Jaffa) following the

Passover, in which they and about 200 other people, mostly sabras around their age, celebrated "knowing" Yeshua. To hear them talk, it was an Event, capital E. Jesse said it would be ludicrous to call them non-Jews for their faith, since they were all Israeli, most of them Army, and he laughed. Tova asked whether I knew there was an international convention in my own state, at Messiah College— her uncle came back calling it "electric."

I haven't completely figured out these two. They light up talking about Arab Christians. And they told me the first person to trust when the tide turns is a "true Christian" no matter where he or she is from. Jess said the acid test of a Gentile believer is love for the Jew.

So much thinking to do. Tova gave me her New Testament, claimed she needed a fresh one. I felt almost driven to get back to my room and try to read it myself. Like Jess's Tenach, it's in Hebrew. You never told me it was written by Jews in the first place! I read Matthew (Levi) last night and brought it with me into the Old City today so I could look at some of Paul's— Shaul's—letters. Haven't had much sleep and my eyes have about had it, but sitting here on the Mount of Olives, I'm seeing the scene in front of me in a new light. I don't know what I believe. The trip up the Jordan to Galilee (with Rabbi F.) will no doubt pull me both ways. I want, more than I've ever wanted anything, to be right in the choice I have to make. I can't believe in Yeshua because you want me to, or because it might bring us closer. It's got to be right. And if he is real, I want to know why he let me down.

Miss you, Y'didah,
David

Leah read the letter a second time, then put it down. He had refused to compromise his beliefs to gain her love, but neither would he shut the door on hers until he was sure. She closed her eyes and tried to remember the English word for *Y'didah*. She could not, but something inside her told her she knew. It meant Beloved.

Chapter 31

HE SHOULD HAVE BEEN TIRED. The week had been arduous even without the night drive to New York for Friday's briefing on his new responsibilities. Having opted to overnight in Manhattan after the meeting, Jonathan slept in till nine or so Saturday morning, showered, had his eggs and coffee, took his time at the jewelry store, and left from there to see Leah. On the road now, he felt fresh, virile, in command of his life. Truly, since Easter, he had been a new man and the recipient of more blessings than he had ever asked. The promotion and pay raise aside, his gift for handling clients and investments had blossomed as never before. The *old* salary had already provided a substantial nest egg and a cash flow that had enabled him to send Janiene some help each month and to contribute a little toward Jeremy's braces. It had bought the new carpeting for his parents' dining room. And it had afforded him and Leah some wonderful evenings together. Talk about blessings—she was the ultimate, an angel in silk *or* denim. She had challenged him to be the best he could be, simply by believing that he was well on his way; she could light his day with a single word, a touch, yet she asked nothing, disdaining all but the smallest gifts. As soon as he got to town, he would reserve their favorite table by the side window at *Le Renard* and then stop at the florist's. From beneath the armrest he took a tape filled with love songs and, yielding to a wide, grateful smile, pushed the cartridge into place.

FROM THE FIRST DAY JONATHAN HAD KNOWN HER, there had been a depth to Leah that he could not fathom: reflection ever moving, appearing, eluding. It was so tonight. She stood in her doorway dressed in ivory, restrained. He pulled the single rose from behind his back, saw the moistness in her eyes, and smiled. He kissed her, led her to the car, and headed for *Le Renard Argent*. Unable to wait longer, he told her the news as they drove. When they were seated at their window, he ordered for them both: fresh cut fruit, roast duckling, wild rice, champagne. The promotion, he reasoned, should be accented over the transfer, since the greater distance that would lie between them, it seemed, had clouded her spirits. It was when he was describing the soaring eagle he would hang above his desk that he remembered she had flown a day ago herself, to a new clinical assignment at the rehab hospital outside town. She answered it was going well...fine. And yet the cloud remained. He tried blowing it away with a promise to get down to see her almost as often. Just as often, he amended, knowing the pledge would wear him down in weeks. The pianist, through no device of Jonathan's, began to play the song that Leah loved and Jon, permitting circumstance to align his sights, felt the precision of the moment. He took her hand and, lifting a bubbling stemmed glass, said confidingly, "A toast." He knew he would remember always her face by candlelight this night. "To the lifelong alliance of the Beaumonts and the Grantes—to Leah Rachelle Beaumont-Grante." He pressed her fingers to his lips and saw her own mouth open like a fragile flower. Her gaze fell to his tie, his vest button, he was not sure.

"I'm asking you to marry me, Sweetheart. Name the date. We'll get you certified in New York, apply to the best clinics in the city. The bank's finding us an apartment, and with your knack for... Are you all right?" A spasm moved her hand; she said she couldn't think about it now, she couldn't answer.

Can't answer? he thought. "Can't *think* about it?" he repeated.

She leaned back and drew her hand from his. "It's been a hard day," she said, tears welling in her eyes, "so hard."

Work, she had said, was fine. His stomach felt heavy. She told him Jacob Rothman had died from wounds after what appeared to be a focused terrorist attack on a meeting in Jerusalem; it had been on her mind all day. She was sorry, she said, reaching to touch him; such a special night he had planned. Half relieved, he said it was too bad about Rothman; he hadn't heard. The coming Monday took form in his mind: he would start—and probably finish—the week behind a stack of Rothman's accounts. He patted her hand and kept it. "You knew him?"

"What'll it do to...?"

"His chain of stores? The family reputation?" She shook her head to both. "D. J.?" he offered. Had she forgotten his name? To her silence, he answered that he imagined it would be a pretty tough blow and it might set him back for a while—as a speech pathologist, she'd know better than he about that—but they could only send condolences and pray for peace for the whole family. He looked for signs that he had been of help. Instead a tear slipped down one cheek, its path catching the flicker of the candle, and she said they would have no peace.

"Leah..."

"He didn't believe."

"D. J.?"

"Mr. Rothman."

"Mr. Rothman didn't believe." He felt a stare from the next table. "That's why you're upset?"

She smudged the tear with her fingers and said that was part of it. He told her the family would survive; people didn't miss what they had never appropriated in the first place. "Do you think losing his father might make D. J. worse?"

She shook her head and another tear brimmed. She couldn't say, she told him, but she was afraid it might set him back in more ways than one. Jon tried to remember her talking to him before about D. J. and could not. All he knew of him had come from watching his performance against UCLA and listening to Rick.

The woman and then the man at the neighboring table cast a

look at Jon that implied he was the cause of his companion's state. Covering his annoyance, he suggested he and Leah talk elsewhere and, leaving the duckling *à l'orange*, rose to pull back her chair. They drove without exchange to a spot above Pine Grove that over-looked the valley. He turned off the motor and pushed deliberately on the brake. She offered no word, so he began. "D. J. was close to his father?"

"Very."

"He has an empire to co-manage now." She nodded. "And you're worried because Mr. Rothman died without Christ. That's the last thing on D.J.'s mind." Leah clutched a tissue and bit her lip. "You said Mr. Rothman's death was *part* of what's bothering you," Jon ventured, the leadenness back.

Her eyes closed. "Jonathan...I love you." Until now, it had been a light expression: *Love you, Jon; see you next week.* He waited, knowing there was more. She swallowed and, hugging her arms, looked into the valley. Jonathan sat with his own thoughts: the bracelet refused; the weekend she had been "too tired" to have him come up; Rick's words while the women were in the kitchen that night after the gym meet. As a friend, he had said, he'd spent several hours a week in therapy sessions with D. J., but if he ever overcame the stutter, it wouldn't be anything he, Rick, had done; it would be Leah.

He felt himself sinking. "You're in love with him."

She turned to face him, her eyes flooded. She told him she had been at war with herself for five months. Today a letter had come...."Jonathan, I love you too...but it's not...the same."

As before? Or as with D. J.? He told her she was letting herself get all mixed up. "You're confusing p—compassion—with love."

She looked toward the lights of town and said David had frustrated her, irritated her, challenged her to the core. He had also taught her that circumstance can kneel on people's throats and on their lives. "But he's never done anything—or *been* any-thing—that made me pity him...never."

It burned the more for her softspokenness. He traced the crease of his pants with the ignition key for three, four inches, to his knee and back. "You said you had forgiven me for Easter."

"That has noth—"

"I've been straight as an arrow since, *un gentilhomme du premier ordre*. Haven't I?"

She told him he was killing a moth with a hammer; he had simply lost his head a little and then been so angry with himself that it was enough for them both. "What we're talking about here," she said, "is whether our love is the kind a person marries for...or not."

"And whether it's mutual...or not."

In her hand lay the tissue, squashed and stained with makeup. Her color drawn, salt tracks drying on her cheeks, she sat small and voiceless, sculpted in moonglow, and he remembered the sun on her hair the day they had met. Slowly he placed a hand behind her neck and pulled her to him, held her for a time, then kissed her forehead tenderly and let her go. He did not speak as he drove her home; he could not have if he had tried.

Chapter 32

SAMUEL LAID AN ARM ACROSS DAVID'S SHOULDERS. "Come with me, son. We'll walk." Leaving Enid Rothman in the care of her older son, Martin, and the ministering rabbi, they made their way among the above-ground tombs to the graded path and, one shoe of the four scuffing its own arrhythmic rhythm, climbed the Mount of Olives. Imperative, Sam told himself, this interlude with Dov. Unlike his mother and brother, the boy had not expressed his feelings on Jacob's passing; they still lay deep inside. Grateful for David's measured pace, Samuel spoke when he could, of the service in which he, himself, had taken part, of Enid's need for David's support and closeness now.

When they reached a height from which they could look down on both the cemetery and the Old City, they sat on the hard ground until the old man's wheeze had fully come and gone and he was able to say that it had always been his desire to die in this place. It had entered his mind weeks ago that perhaps from this trip, perhaps from the next, he would not return. He—not Jacob, his friend, and not Moishe. He shook his head. "Such plans he had, Moishe...such energy still to give...and Jacob..." He felt the rush of emotion and fought it—this was not helping Dov; he must choose better words.

David sat with his mouth against folded arms that bridged his upraised knees; his eyes were on the dome. He tilted his head to give the old man a wan smile. "You'll see *me* into the ground, Sam," he said, then returned to his thoughts.

"Incredibly good of Ya'akov to offer his plot," Sam said with a note of wonder. "Two weeks ago you met?"

"Jesse? If you knew him, you'd understand. Samuel, when my

father was going on like that about the temple, why did he apologize to you?"

It had not escaped Samuel's notice that on the trip north and even under the stress in which they had been submerged on their return, David had become increasingly fluent—not with everyone, certainly not with Enid or Martin, but with him. They had become so close in these weeks; whatever barrier of formality had existed was now fallen. Sam was gratified. He mused on David's question and said he didn't know; many times they had discussed the rebuilding of the temple, talked of the prophecies. Jacob was fascinated by them. "He questioned me one evening at my home about the temple envisioned by Ezekiel, asked me—it must have been several weeks later—whether, on further thought, I still took the passage literally. If what we've pieced together is true—that he was involved in a plan for the rebuilding—I guess he felt he'd failed me in some way. I had no idea...."

David nodded pensively.

"Your father was a good man, Dov. He tried to rush God, that's all. The same honest mistake our father Abraham made, and look what it brought *him*: Ishmael." He chuckled, but the smile faded quickly. "I should've shared that with Jacob. Why must we rush God? Jacob of old and Rebekah, King Saul. We're the same." They sat quietly, scanning the City bathed in sunlight. *"A father to the fatherless...is God in his holy habitation.* Remember that, Dov. How beautiful for Jacob and Moishe, to rest on holy ground until the coming of the Prince." They sat in silence once again, until David spoke.

"I wanted to talk to him." His gaze was far away. "He couldn't hear me."

Tough little Dov, Samuel thought, let it out. He rested a hand on David's arm. "He knew you loved him."

David tipped back his head and shut his eyes; he drew a long breath, in, and out. "I've heard you talk of a woman named Deborah," he said. Samuel looked on his profile; he had not been aware that he had done so in the presence of the boy. "She loved you."

"She...*said* she loved me," Sam replied hesitantly. "She was...very young."

David looked at him. "You didn't believe her."

"I... How could she have loved me? I was forty-three. Already portly; hair thinning. My responsibilities were my life. What could I have offered?"

"Trust," David said softly, as if he himself examined the word. "Where is she, Sam?"

"I...don't know. What..."

"I love Leah. God brought me to Israel to show me she'd told me the truth. I wanted Dad to know, but I was too late. You've known it all along." David rocked back and forth and then was on his feet. Sam felt himself, if only in the uncertain little movement of his head, draw back. "No way, Sam, no way could you have missed it. In the pages every day—you know the Prince has come. And you...never told...my dad."

Samuel looked at him, stricken. They had both been bludgeoned by the events of the last few days. He had lost two dear friends; David had lost his father, and perhaps, because of the violence, more. The boy's stress, he allowed, might be the greater, and this crush on the girl, a vent. He'd take the sting.

David paced, his eyes fired with tears. "Do you know what God call-calls you? The dried-up root of Ephraim that will *never* bear fruit but only 'bring forth his children to the murderer.' My father died without Yeshua." A sound escaped his throat, and suddenly he knelt before Samuel saying, "I'm sorry. I'm sorry, Sam. You've been my friend so long." His fingers squeezed Sam's arms and he asked, his face contorted, "Why couldn't you say it to him, to me? Why...when you knew?" Samuel stared at him. He felt the fingers slide down, catching sleeve. "You *don't* believe it," David said, incredulous. "If you doubt Sacred Scripture, Sam, what *can* you believe?"

"You talk of truth," Samuel said, his own eyes blurred. "Why would you convince me?"

"The covenant's cut in the blood of *God*," David pleaded, the sleeves still in his fists. "Deny it...and you deny him."

Sam heard love in the words, and fear. He looked long at David and then at the ground and said Jacob had, once, said a curious thing. "It had occurred to him that if a man could forgive his captors for nailing him bodily to a tree and could say so in the midst of his agony, his mother and his friends in mortal trauma, watching...he had to be more than a man."

"He said that to you?"

Samuel did not raise his head.

"And what did you say?" David asked.

"Nothing."

"*Nothing?*"

"Curiosity. A hole in the dike." He felt David's eyes upon him and looked up. He had explained this in Beersheva: Pinning a withered leaf to a tree did not make it green, much less God. "Even to *handle* the so-called New Testament brings grief. I listen to you, and I hear Jacob. Just remember his dying words. Remember your father's words."

He struggled to rise, saying the dampness was getting to his bones, and David, standing, hoisted him. "Samuel," he said, his dark eyes softer, "you've tried to help. And you have." He walked close beside the rabbi so that his arm or shoulder could be leaned on, and Samuel, leaning from time to time as they descended the stone-paved path, said, only in his mind, *Dear Dov, my son, I didn't realize you loved her that much.*

"CABLE FOR YOU, MR. ROTHMAN," the desk clerk said. David noted the source and tucked the message, unopened, into his pocket until Sam, Enid, and Martin had returned to their rooms and he was alone in his. Aware of his fatigue, he stretched out on the bed and pulled the cable from his breast pocket and from its envelope. He read:

MY GRIEF ON HEARING OF THE DEATH OF YOUR FATHER IS INEXPRESSIBLE. PLEASE UNDERSTAND HOW VERY MUCH I LOVE YOU. LEAH

His heart beat faster, and he sat up to read it again, and then a third time. The more he read, the less it said. She was well schooled in the amenities. She might have sent those words, he thought, the first month they had worked together.

Surely it was their divergent thinking that had blocked the release of the kind of love he wanted. Even supposing that she had received his letter, which she probably had not, there was no way she could know that he had stopped struggling with Yeshua, that the conviction that had so appalled him in her, he had now espoused on the basis of overwhelming evidence he had accumulated on his own. If she had known, maybe the cable would have been more than a polite condolence; maybe it would have meant a turning on her part. And maybe not. Witness the rejected Benjamite, unaccepted on the romantic plane even after his conversion.

He closed his eyes and lay back on the pillow. How would it be, the day that he would tell her? The image of his father's eyes, imploring, filled his mind. Then Jacob's hand was raised to clutch his forearm weakly, and he felt again the residue of strength seep from the man, this one who had fathered him, who had, above all others, loved him. And he remembered the words. In one breath, Samuel had comforted him as much as it was possible to do, and in the next, he had laid on him a burden too heavy for any man.

Chapter 33

ON WEDNESDAY NIGHT AND THURSDAY MORNING, a cool rain swept down from Canada and washed away the swelter of July. The next day Leah, forsaking the Beaumonts' better-equipped car, drove the turnpike in her own red Mazda, east toward the City of Brotherly Love. The name of the suburb and number of the rural route were all she had. She reached Lansdale soon after lunch and pulled into a gas station to inquire of the attendant whether he knew of the Rothman place. He leaned on her door and told her everybody did. "There's this lake Rothman built," he told her with a smirk. Leah did not smile. "Ah, but you can't see it from the road," he said, standing upright. "Go down here a mile..." He did not tell her that the house was a singular mansion dolloped along with many trees and an expansive garden on a gentle rise. But once she had found the country lane and driven half a mile, what he had said was right—she could not have missed it.

Yet seventy yards from the house, she pulled to the side of the driveway, thinking herself perhaps less welcome than the owners of the three cars nearer the veranda. That the widow had been home only two days gave rise to sudden doubt; she considered another day's wait, an overnight in town, then put it away. It was as incumbent upon her as upon any friend, she told herself, to come quickly. She put the keys into her bag and walked toward the door.

A voice came from the house, a man's, and not in mourning: "You don't *know*?" A voice responded, but it was neither raised nor as close, and she could not hear what it said. The first exploded, with a curse, "You were *with* him." The speaker ranted, moving toward the window and away. Leah, walking in front of the house, placed the tete-a-tete in a room on the second floor. Her view, had she cared for one, was blocked by the portico. She heard the second voice again, nearer, low, firm, "Marty, there are people d-d-downst—" The window closed on his words. Again she doubted her timing and, having climbed the crescent of steps to the porch, was contemplating retreat when the door opened and a striking woman, holding, as if in parting, the hand of a stout old man, said, "Nor did he with..." She realized Leah's presence and gazed at her.

"Oh, uh, excuse me. Mrs. Rothman?" Leah said, offering both hands. "I'm Leah Beaumont...David's friend?" Leah's brows knit and she continued. "Please accept my sympathy. I was so sorry to hear of your loss. Mr. Rothman was well-loved and appreciated by so many people."

Enid Rothman, slightly taller and more mature of build than Leah, looked at her with unmoving eyes. The few graying strands in her hair served only to highlight the black, to enhance her bearing. "Thank you, Miss Beaumont. Get some rest, Samuel. I won't call."

"Call," the old man said. He surveyed Leah head to toe once and then departed, a formally attired servant assisting him down the steps.

Granting Leah the fingers of her right hand, Enid addressed the servant as Thomas and told him that when he had seen the rabbi into Allen's care, he should tell David that Miss Beaumont was waiting. "Come in." Closing the door behind them, she thanked Leah for coming, but her tone neither conveyed gratitude nor confided sorrow, and Leah hoped that Thomas would be quick about his work. They entered a sitting room off the foyer, and Enid excused herself. Leah looked up. High ceiling, conditioned air, yet she felt stifled. The portraits on the walls, the sculpted alabaster urns in their timelessness bore no life. She thought the place too heavily draped and, seeking openness, walked to the panel of light that marked a paned door leading to the porch. Blinking away its brightness she looked through it, past the balustrade toward the lawn. It was a radiant day. She placed a hand on the slender handle of the door and, discovering it unlocked, opened it. The air was all the more balmy and fragrant for her having been denied it. She breathed of it deeply, let it fill her.

"Leah."

She turned from the sunlight to the figure in the doorway. "David?" He met her at mid-room, embraced her, and thanked her for being there. Surprise and affection were in his voice, yet there was about him a constraint that unnerved her—something more than the deportment of mourning. The stigma of murder, she thought. Perhaps chagrin over Martin's raking, fear that she had heard it. Or was it possible...could his feelings have changed? "Did you get my cable?" she asked, searching his eyes.

"Yes, thank you. Come outside." She felt her heart slow. He escorted her through a long hall, a summer room, and a glassed doorway, and she walked beside him down a garden path, replying nothing to nothing. They entered a hedged area where hung a white wooden swing. She felt his hand on the small of her back, turning her toward him. "It's good to see you," he said in the voice she remembered. "It's been a long summer."

"My first news of you was the photo in the Times. The press makes everything harder." She wanted to hold him, to kiss away the hurt, to give him rest.

"They weren't all like Henning," he said, smiling a little. "A mosquito. Thinks he's intimate: 'Come on, Rothman, I'm All-American too. What'd the old man say?'" He led Leah by the hand to the swing, saying it wasn't over yet; the press was there when the family came home Wednesday, but so far, they hadn't unraveled what it was all about. He rested his hand, holding hers, on his knee and looked over the garden toward the lake. His brother, he said, was ticked at him for not knowing what his dad was into, not talking him out of it, not protecting the image of the store. He had no idea how much his father had funneled to Ben Sheva before the attack, and no one could get near the man to find out; he had tried. He took both her hands. "Do you know what my dad asked me to do? Leah, with his dying breath he commissioned me— begged me—to see that the work was finished. 'Talk to Ari,' he kept saying, 'talk to Ben Sheva.'"

"Work?"

"The rebuilding," he said quietly, as if, despite their isolation, someone might overhear. "Think of it. Could they have meant to level the mosque?"

The out of doors was suddenly oppressive, like the parlor. It would mean instant *jihad*, David was telling her. Jess had said there had been attempts; but since the Kaufman dig, a lot of people believed the Holy of Holies wasn't even on that site, but next to it, where the Dome of the Tablets and the Spirits now stood. If that was true, David said, the third temple could be built on the proper site without disturbing the Dome of the Rock or any part of the Mosque of Omar—providing, of course, that the temple courtyard remained in Gentile hands. Leah's palms began to sweat. *No, God, please*, she prayed; *you wouldn't teach me to love him and then do this to me.* "The vision of Ezekiel," David was saying. "The enormity of it staggers me. If God detests even a hewn altar, why does he want such a thing?" The swing moved ever so little; Leah sat transfixed. David was watching a sparrow in low flight, talking to himself as much as to her. "What did God say to King David when the idea first came up? He sort of chuckled, didn't he? He said something like, 'You want to build a house for the Creator of the Universe? Let me build *you* a house.'" He turned to Leah, his face began to light, and the words came, pouring: "When God said David's son could build the temple, he wasn't talking about Solomon." Leah laid her free hand alongside his head, listening, hardly breathing. "Sure, he accepted—even honored—what Solomon did," David said, "but God was building the house of David's greater son. Yeshua. Yeshua called his body the temple, the house of the Holy Spirit, and until he comes back, you and I are his body. *We...*" He began to laugh as he pulled her hand up to kiss her palm. "*We* are the temple!" Gone were Leah's fears, gone the uncertainties. Her fingers in the shining black of his hair, his arms around her, his mouth on hers, she gave herself to his kiss. Standing, laughing, he swung her in a great circle, and with her arms around his neck, she laughed and said she loved him, so much. He held her and kissed her eyes, her face, her mouth and, finally allowing her feet to touch the ground, he looked at her in wonder. "*You* are my miracle."

"You are mine."

"Imperfect as I am. But now I know that God doesn't heal everyone; it'd make selfishness a basis for belief."

"Maybe. But I'd put it more like this: I'd say, the brightest hope is not for the one who grasps, but for the one who is proven true." He looked into her eyes then drew her close, and she felt the strength of his arms.

"Stay *with* me. Y'didah, stay with me."

Chapter 34

THE OTHERS HAD GONE. To Leah's plan to return home the same day, David had said he would have nothing less than the weekend. Now at the dining table, with more space between them than her arm and his could close, she worked at looking comfortable. Once, it had appeared that Martin, sitting opposite her, would, from beneath his thin moustache, make utterance, but he had thought better of it. Enid Rothman, seated at the end of the table, her elder son and daughter-in-law to her right, seemed not to mind that dinner had been eaten in near silence. Only Sheila and Leah had attempted conversation, and it being left in both cases to founder, neither of them had tried again.

Leah liked Martin's wife, if only for the similarity of their circumstances at this moment. Outwardly, they were not in many ways alike. Sheila's "simple" daytime dress Leah compared in cost to that of a good portion of her own summer wardrobe. The blonde hair, professionally done to look windblown, was also chemically treated to look blonde; the makeup, although flawless, was ample, as was the jewelry.

The muscles in Martin's jaw were working, and it occurred to Leah that they appeared better exercised than the remainder of him, which fell not a little short of David's stature and development. The flesh of his neck aquiver, Martin suddenly directed a remark to David, and it was with the same tenor of brotherly concern that had come to Leah's ears at midday. "Beginning today," he said, simmering beneath a polished lid, "you have got to be more careful. You carry a name." David looked at him unblinkingly without response; he resumed chewing the bite of chicken Mornay in his mouth while his eyes remained on Martin. "Have you seen tonight's paper?" Martin pursued. "The cartoonists have got hold of you: 'As one All-American to another...'"

"It did not disparage David," Enid Rothman interjected, knowing full well that the cartoon depicting their confrontation targeted not Alan Henning's behavior, but David Rothman's.

"He's got to think ahead," Martin spurted.

"There is no point in placing blame," Enid said with deliberate calm. "The store will not suffer for your brother's right to privacy, nor for your father's ideals. Consumers," she said, nodding a go-ahead to the servant who had appeared beside the lowboy, "are not ignorant of philosophical concerns."

"She's right," Sheila said to Martin. "Your father will be remembered for the things he did for all kinds of hurting people, not just his own."

"Perhaps neither of you has noticed," Martin said through clenched teeth. "I am not talking about my father's discretion or lack of it; I am addressing David's need to move through the events of his life as a Rothman. Just as I've had to. I *am* the *store.*"

No one replied. Indeed, Leah thought, Martin was the store; he thought of little else. Sheila at length ventured that it was true: Martin was not himself when he was out of touch with Chicago. She spoke the last to David and added that they had booked the early flight back. David stuttered that he and Leah would drive them to the airport; it would give them more time....

"Unnecessary," Martin chimed. "Allen or Thomas can take us. We'll not be needing dessert," he told his mother. "There's still packing to be done, if you'll excuse us." He rose.

"I'll be right along, Darling," Sheila said, taking a cup of coffee from the hesitating servant who had already poured it. She smiled sweetly and, when Martin had left, accepted a small slice of Danish cake as it was served. She told them he hadn't pulled himself together. They understood, didn't they? Enid remarked that he had always been high-strung; the world was on his shoulders now, and he did not know how long he could carry it alone. Martin never was one, she said, to take responsibility lightly. They finished dinner without further conversation, and Sheila excused herself, telling Leah she hoped they would get to know each other better, next time. Enid left to make certain the help would be free by eight, and David took his time turning to assess the effect of dinner, specifically Martin's diatribe, on Leah. She said she remembered best—and so would the public—a photo on the sports page not very long ago: he was airborne over the high bar in L. A., a "No hands, Ma" kind of flip, and the crowd, the paper said, went wild. She walked to him, watching him smile.

"I didn't take the event."

"You landed on your feet."

He stood to reward her with a kiss. "It's called a *Thomas*, just like the man who let me know that you were here." He guided her again through the summer room, saying if she planned to hang around adoring him, they would need to spend a lot of time in very close communication—on the matter of jargon, of course.

Chapter 35

IT WAS THAT NIGHT THAT HE FIRST CALLED HER RACHEL. He had sat with her on the swing and talked of Jesse Ya'akov, of Sam's spiritual blindness and how sad it made him, and of the day his father died—the same day that he forgave Ben Epstein. Looking everywhere for comfort in his grief that day, he said, and not knowing yet that his dad had recognized Yeshua as the Messiah, he had tried, as a new believer, to pray the Lord's prayer. When he came to the part where he asked God to forgive him as he forgave others, he was startled to realize that he was talking about his father's murderers. To forgive them would be the hardest thing he had ever tried to do. Or so he thought until he considered the people who, whether they knew it or not, had formed his own existence into something less than living—a netherlife, where expectations, high or low, like so many caroms, careening, left their nicks and scars on his soul. He could say it was no one's fault, but something inside had kept score; the hate was there. He felt it and began to perceive what he was, and why Yeshua died. Brokenly, penitently, he lifted his brother off the hook, and, one by one, the others. "Then," he said, moving the swing a little forward, a little back, "there was Ben."

"Ben?"

"Because you dated him for several months, I thought I had to forgive Ben for taking what was mine. When I got turned around that day, I somehow knew he never had. ...I love you, Rachel." The name had less to do with her ownership of it than with the unshakable love, respect, and appreciation for her that he implied.

I love you, Rachel. Leah, adrift in his kiss, forced herself back to Andy's apartment. Andy had reentered the room saying no one had bought the baby overalls; they must all be thinking she would be some kind of "priss."

"Rachel Marie," Leah said, smiling at the bundled bit of life in her arms. "A name like that could fool some people." The baby thrust strong little feet, however uselessly, against the blanket wrap. Between her pink fists lay a bald head with a tiny square face, its nose having no elevation to speak of, its eyes squinting. "Ten out of ten for looks," Leah said, remembering the others.

"Gaining on it," Andy lobbed. With the two Rachels content in the rocker, she eased herself into an overstuffed chair. "Cat did okay—sent a size two football shirt, my old field hockey number on it, addressed 'Rae.'" Leah laughed, but Andy's smile went vacant. "Who'd have thought, a year ago, I'd be in Pittsburgh playing house?"

The game had changed; Leah took the ball low and inside. She slipped a finger under four of the baby's and thumbed the miniature nails. "How's Rick?"

"Fine, fine. If you're asking whether I'm happy, I am. ...Lee, if you want the truth, he comes home beat—won't go anywhere, won't look for friends. I can't even talk to him about his work. QBA. Do I look like I know something about quantitative business analysis? I can hardly pronounce it."

Forever at bat. "You've got *one* friend," Leah said. "Fifteen weeks, two grade schools. How much of me do you want?"

Andy mellowed, smiled. "What's this about D. J.? I thought your man had to *believe*." Her hands fanned a rainbow.

Leah laid the baby, face up, on her knees. "He does," she said, "and he's been to the River." How he evaded the press, she thought, only Jesse knew.

Andy's jaw dropped. "Baptized in the holy drink?"

"Water's water; you die to sin and self."

Andy blurted God's name, apologized for it, and mumbled she could never remember. "How did you choose?"

"What?"

"D. J. over Jon."

Both faces came to Leah, and when she focused on Jon's, it hurt. That's what life is, she thought: choices. Andy would not comprehend what she had been through the day David's letter arrived and for two endless days afterward, the fending off of her own will to know the mind of God, the wait for his Holy Spirit to steer her safely through the reefs of her very human reasoning: she needed not just faith that God would complete what he had started, but also knowledge that, as strong and undeniable as the urge inside her was to say yes to David, she could not until he said yes, with all his heart, to Yeshua. Andy would not see why she had to wait for one man to see the light when another perfectly fine catch already did. The factor she might understand best was the obvious one: the bond that David shared with her in the culture and the blood of their people, and in God's promise that their race would not perish before the Messiah came in triumph. Powerful truth, yet perhaps too simplistic even for Andy. Maybe, Leah thought, it was better left undissected. Too many times she had tried with Andy, only to be misunderstood.

"Did you talk to God?" Andy nudged.

"You've got it," Leah replied. "And now, I have peace about it."

Andy rose and took the baby, saying it was time to feed her; Rick liked peace at dinner. Leah said she needed to get back, but Andy held her gently in her chair. "Stay, Lee, please. Please."

While Andy changed the baby and heated a bottle of sugar water, Leah leaned back in the rocker. Why wasn't Andy creative with Rick? With life? Leah tried to imagine doubting her own happiness with David's baby at her breast; not knowing what to do when he came home tired or discouraged; herself and David living without friends. File not found. Yeshua had taught them how to love—and in their believing friends, his blood flowed thicker than anything. Didn't it?

Chapter 36

THE DAYS DAWNED AND SET in orderly if not dynamic progression. Leah enjoyed her work; she lived for David's calls. Tonight the phone had rung at six-thirty as it did every Thursday—and every Sunday and Tuesday—and she nestled in a cushioned chair, the receiver to her ear.

"So he says, 'You think you know it all,'" David's voice beamed. "'Where are you and I in the Book?'"

"I said, 'Mac, we were there when Adam bit the apple, and we were there when Yeshua paid the price.'

"'Good, but not good enough,' he says and he shows me Deuteronomy. 'God says he'll move the Jews "to jealousy with those which are not a people,"' he tells me, and he says, 'That's us Gentile Christians from all over the world. Now isn't that what happened with you?'

"I hated to burst his bubble, but it took more than Evan MacAteer and envy to raise my shades. Try two armed soldiers, the original text, an appointment with the Holy Spirit in the Land of the Patriarchs—not to mention a stubborn little *tulah* named, of all things, Beaumont."

Leah laughed. "I yield to the Man Upstairs."

"Rachel-My-Love," he said in a W. C. Fields, "that's what I like about God: We can't do without 'im, and he won't do without us."

"You've had a good week."

Wrong, he said; he'd had a great week. He'd found a third *yehudit* at Fellowship last night, and one more thing: When he was in the Philly office over the weekend to help unwind the Jerusalem mess, the consultants Martin requested showed up—a Mr. Bratton and a Mr. Pettindill, the secretary said. "When she let them in, the first guy held out his hand and said, 'D.J.—Jonathan Grante. Remember me? My associate, Mark Pfettingill.'" David laughed. "You tell me: do we need help from rung one up? Bratton and Pettindill."

Leah hung on to the phone. He had never even asked what had become of Jonathan Grante. Perhaps he had assumed, and rightly so, that she had tied up all the ends. Now here was Jon still fingering Rothman affairs, sidling into David's life and therefore again into hers. She had hurt him, and she had no accurate measure of his feelings.

"You there?"

"Yes. I'm here," she said distractedly.

They had gone over the books, David told her. Jon was thorough, but they needed more; on the twenty-sixth they would go to Israel. Martin had chosen the team—Case, Irvin, and Grante; David had asked to go. "...Leah?"

"To Israel? You and Jon?"

"David and Jonathan. Can't beat that."

"How long?"

"Six days. If the store still floats, we'll work the rest of the year through Nathan."

"*Yadid*, you do carry a name. Talking to Ben Sheva could make somebody edgy."

"Give me this one. I have to."

"I know. But—"

"Don't go soft on me, *Chabibee*. I can't hold you from here."

"It's more than a bunch of terrorist thugs I'm worried about—as if that weren't *enough*. This arrangement is...strange."

"You mean Jon? What can he tell me?"

She heard the smile. "I'm just not sure he'll have...your best interests in mind."

"Why, Leah," he said affectedly, "Think on that." He said he had an exam in ten minutes, gave her the three little words in Hebrew, and was gone. She replaced the receiver and noticed that something had siphoned her energy. How far could Jonathan be trusted? How bitter might his feelings be? Odd that he, too, had alluded to the biblical characters when they parted at her door that night—he had said nothing else; he had said nothing since: "It's one thing to hand a man your kingdom; it's another to give him your queen."

Chapter 37

LEAH LET HERSELF INTO THE APARTMENT, slid her bag and coat off as one, and sat at the desk. David's call the preceding night had been on her mind all day as she worked; she could not let it go. Now, all at once, there was a nearer, more present danger.

Almost three weeks had passed since her first evening with Andy, Rick, and the baby, when she had stayed to help eat the very food she had brought. Contrary to Leah's expectations, Rick had been like a little kid that night. He had surprised Andy with good news at dinner, and she had received it as giddily as he. As of October fifteenth, Cat would be employed by the same foods distributor for which Rick worked. Leah had been glad for them, too. Until today. She laid her head down on crossed arms on the desk and stared at the brown blotter.

Cat—Jerry—was a quiet man; he ran deep. When he had something to say, he spoke, and when he did not, he was not uneasy in reticence. To some, Leah thought, he must seem backward, even slow, but she knew now that it was only that he lived inside himself; the hours she had spent with him traveling to and from Rick and Andy's wedding had proven him, to her, intelligent enough, and caring. His grief over the circumstances of the marriage had been readable to Leah in his mood in the car, that intensity. Now she wondered how much more there might have been to it. Weren't there, now that she thought about it, traces of something gnawing at him even that first night she had spent time with him, after the gym meet with the Russians? Tonight the four of them had been together again for the evening, their first regathering since the wedding, and to Leah, the electricity between Andy and Cat had been as clear as the light in the room.

She felt herself sinking into despair. She was tired playing counselor, tired of being restraint's only advocate. The canons had always been clear to her: You decide whether you love a man before you marry him, and you marry him before you conceive his child. A mistake in either or both of these is not made better by another error; it is remedied by an act of the will, to love. People forgot. As if freedom from constraints were to be equated with bliss, as if love were some sort of billiards game, where everyone ricocheted off one another until each rolled to rest wherever energy died. She saw Andy veering away from Rick; and there were Jerry's feelings, circling the table slowly, like the hustler measuring angles, calculating.

She determined to be silent. Andy knew her thoughts if she wanted to consider them, if she wanted to consider anything. There was left to Leah, then, only one course, the best she knew. She stretched her arms out straight on the desk and, face down, spoke from her soul. "O God of Abraham, Redeemer, Lord, please, protect my friends...."

LEAH HAD QUESTIONED THE EFFICACY of an assignment in Pittsburgh at the time when her feelings for David, and his for her, had just begun to bloom. Now she perceived a touch of Providence in her exposure to the impulses of Andy's life: her commitment to David was deepening. It was hard to let him go the day he flew out of Pittsburgh for New York, to depart from there for Tel Aviv. She awoke each morning he was gone to switch on the TV news and breakfast in front of it before leaving for work. When she returned, she checked the news to be sure there *was* none. The days came and went. On Tuesday morning, the phone called her from her bed and David told her they had finished their investigation; there was cause to believe the project in Tel Aviv would still fly. She felt release; he was as good as home. A day at Nathan's, David said, then he and Jon would meet Irvin and Case to catch the early flight out of Ben Gurion.

When she got home Wednesday, Leah flipped on the TV and sat down with her dinner plate and cup. The election, Ethiopia, Lebanon, Nicaragua were the news of the hour. She finished eating and thought a pear would taste good with her tea. It came as she stood, like the specter of the seventh wave, out of nowhere, moving over her, monstrous, inescapable, engulfing her like driftwood in its airless tumult: a second bombing incident in Israel, a home in Herzliya, near Tel Aviv. Two Americans were reported to be guests at the house. Police reported one dead, two injured at the scene; details as they break.

"O God, no..." was all the prayer that would come.

When no augmented report was released in the next twenty minutes, Leah placed a call to the Abramowicz home. Unable to get through, she requested it be transferred to police headquarters, only to be told that names had not yet been released. The line to David's home in Lansdale signaled constantly busy. She returned to the television news network and, on her knees, remained there through the long evening, asking God over and over to forgive her for being so selfish as to pray that it wasn't David who had died, and abhorring the thought that by begging for David's life, she was condemning someone else to be the one. She forced herself to pray for Jonathan too, and the agony of her prayers increased as the sound bite was repeated again and again with scant new information and no names. Shortly after 11:00 o'clock, the network announced that a press conference would be broadcast via satellite at 11:30, with an American named Shelby Case representing the D. Jacob Rothman family, on the bombing of the Nathan Abramowicz home north of Tel Aviv.

Chapter 38

CHISELED FEATURES, GRAY SEERSUCKER BUSINESS SUIT, club tie, presence: Case stood behind the podium. That his hair was full and silver, like her father's, passed through Leah's head, but the thought went untraced. There was rustling and the hum of voices, and she wished them stopped. She watched Case look at the throng of reporters and cameras and place his horn rims on the second try. He began a statement, reading: "On behalf of the Rothman family..." The rustling hushed. "...I dare say, on behalf of all peace-loving people in America, in Israel, and around the world, I extend to the Abramowicz family our deepest regret and our heartfelt sympathy upon the death of their daughter, Ruth. It is our hope and prayer that this senseless destruction of life, which degrades civilized society, will see its end in a new climate of tolerance and understanding. Meanwhile, the management of Rothman Department Stores, International, and the family of the late D. Jacob Rothman will do everything within their power to comfort the Abramowicz family in the loss of this, their only child. I realize that you have questions concerning the bombing," Case said, addressing the press, attempting command. Hands went up all over the room. "I'll do my best to answer them," Case continued, eyeing the hands without acknowledging any. The reporters' patience with his hesitancy gave way to consideration that perhaps he did not intend to nod to individuals; they began to call out:

"Was David Rothman here to meet with Ari ben Sheva?"

"Have the terrorists been apprehended?"

"Would you care to tell us why the girl was in Mr. Rothman's room, sir?"

"Why were the names of the dead and injured withheld until 8:30 this morning?"

"Does David Rothman sense his responsibility in this incident?"

Case's eyes darted about the room. If some of what he heard had been anticipated, some apparently had not. He finally pointed to a woman in the second row and order came. "To answer your question: The perpetrators have not yet been identified; two groups have claimed responsibility, but the investigators have asked us not to discuss that disclosure further. As for the withholding of the victims' names," he said, nodding toward a man farther back, "Mrs. Abramowicz was visiting relatives at the time of the incident. Mr. Abramowicz wished, if possible, to inform her in person, and he was able to do that." He pointed elsewhere.

"Does David Rothman feel that his being in the Abramowicz home unduly endangered that family and that community?"

"Mr. Rothman feels," Case began carefully, "that an unfortunate misunderstanding may have promulgated this kind of response to his presence in Israel. He has not come here in any interest other than that of expanding the chain of Rothman stores."

"You're saying he has no Zionist inclinations?"

"Mr. Rothman is not a political activist."

A reporter near the front stood. "Do you deny, sir, that he is here to pursue the matter of the temple?"

There was a pause. Case's face twitched; he looked toward the door to his right, then back at the room full of faces. "The Rothmans wish to assure the public that they have no interest... Mr. Rothman would like it to be known..." The gathering buzzed, a low sound over which further comment, should it come, could be heard. Leah's throat was nearly closed by the lump in it; now her heart began to pound. Case had moved aside. David took his place behind the mikes and the room fell silent. *He looks all right*, Leah thought, and elation surged through her. *He's there, standing up, no wounds apparent, THANK*

GOD, *and he's going to say something to a roomful of reporters—to millions of viewers. Oh, Lord, help!* Tension stole her breath.

David began slowly: "For those of you who don't know me, my name is David Rothman. My associates and I are here this week to review the status of my father's financial affairs and to implement progress on the new Rothman store in Tel Aviv. We are not here to contribute to any effort—by anyone—to build any other structure. It is with deep sorrow that I acknowledge that someone's thoughts to the contrary might have led to the death of Ruth Abramowicz." He stopped to assure composure, and someone fired a question.

"Have you anything but your word, sir, to convince the terrorists of that?"

"It is not the wish of my family to pursue this particular interest on the part of my late father. I, personally, do not believe that the true temple of God, restored, is material; it is spiritual."

Quickly, the reporter near the front stood again. "Would you explain that, Mr. Rothman? A spiritual temple?"

"Yes. A body of believers in the Messiah."

"Is it correct," the same man pressed, "that the girl was sixteen, sir?"

"Yes, I believe that's right."

"Could you explain to us, Mr. Rothman, why she was with you in your room?"

The answer was quick, calm, firm: "We were not in my room, Mr. Henning. We were on the veranda common to all the rooms on the first floor."

"But outside your bedroom, sir, at approximately 1:20 A.M.?"

"Ms. Abramowicz came to me with a personal problem. She had been unable to sleep because of it."

"Would you expand on that, sir?"

"In deference to her, Mr. Henning, I will not. Suffice it to say she had observed that I had overcome a comparable problem since my last visit and she wanted my counsel."

"How is it that she was fatally wounded, while you received only minor injuries?"

"My financial advisor, Mr. Grante, who was asleep in the next room, was awakened by our conversation. Ruth had just said goodnight and was walking back to her room when he reached his veranda door; he saw beyond me two men moving near a stand of trees on the property. One threw something. Jon instinctively knew what it was; he shouted and flung himself at me. As we impacted the balustrade, it splintered and we fell to the ground. Ruth ran toward us just as the...bomb..." The camera zoomed in on David's face, the glistening in his eyes. "When I saw what'd happened, I lunged toward the trees, but Jon—in spite of the pain of his broken collar bone—hauled me down. The terrorists escaped. There was no saving Ruth."

"Was she the victim of a bomb meant for you?"

"That supposition is under investigation. It is possible, yes."

"Will you be detained?"

"No, sir, I will not."

Shelby Case stepped back to the podium and leaned into the mikes. "Thank you, all." David walked with Case to a small group of men standing near the door at the front. Leah saw Jonathan, wearing a sling on his left arm, place the other hand on David's shoulder and David reciprocate, a moment later, with a hand on Jon's back. They were leaving the room as the studio cut to the New York newscaster, a summary remark, and a promo for the late show. Leah, from her place on the floor, pressed a palm against the off button. Pebbles seemed to move beneath receding waves and she knew she knelt again on sandless shore. Utterly spent, she turned her face and sweat-damp hands upward and wept.

Chapter 39

THE APARTMENT WAS A CAGE. Leah paced, stopping time and again at the front window to scan the city of Pittsburgh twinkling in the new November evening. Like a dowager bejeweled, the Monongahela wore the lights of her bridges. Beyond her, over the distant hills, Leah saw the blinking white, green, and red of a moving plane and imagined David, a speck in the sky, inside. But it was too soon.

She had phoned the airline before school in the morning and been told that the flight had departed on time. Her distraction throughout the day had turned to pure tension after school, but blessedly, not for long. At 3:30 P.M. she received his call from New York; he was through customs, taking the 5:45 out of JFK, arriving, 6:59. Nevertheless, thoughts of work had been futile. She tried to rest, knowing he was safely inside the country, but it was a fitful, sleepless rest and, shortly, she gave it up. She showered, put on beige slacks and pullover with a sienna sweater, light jewelry, and his favorite fragrance. She made herself a sandwich for dinner but could not eat. There seemed nothing to do in the remaining time but keep company with the window, and so she paced, and the clock ticked apathetically: more than an hour until he landed, another hour and a half to claim his luggage and get a limo into and across town.

She would have met his flight at Greater Pittsburgh at night; she had driven before through the city after dark. But he had asked her to wait, had nearly insisted. She picked up a magazine and, sitting down, leafed through it, not seeing anything. Thoughts of David and Jonathan and Ruth walked constantly across her mind. She was relieved that the men were safe, and thankful to God for it. But why did someone have to die? She had never met Ruth, had never even known she existed. If she had prayed for her, would God have spared her, too? Not even a sparrow falls but he knows of it, she thought. So God was there when it happened, but murder is never his idea. Was it the fallen state of man that brought tragedy in such random ways? Yeshua intimated it was. Still, she mourned for Ruth and, remembering the grief in David's eyes when he spoke of her even to total strangers, she allowed herself to feel fully the pain of Ruth's loss. She had no prior emotional ties to the Abramowiczes, but she grieved with and for them all. She began to pray for Nathan and his wife, entered into a long and searching talk with God about Ruth, and afterward, prayed for David's safe return, and Jonathan's. She praised him for his kindness.

Leah was still in prayer when, at 8:15, the phone jangled once and she fumbled getting the receiver to her ear. "How are you doing?" Suzanne asked.

"All right," she hedged.

Sue said she had only a short time to talk, so she needed to get to the point. "The day after you and Jon stopped seeing each other, he called to apologize to me...."

"To you?"

"On his way down to the street that night, he bumped into me on the stairs, and I don't mean politely. The next day he called, and I saw no reason to mention it to you. He only did what he should have. But about ten days ago he called again, just to talk."

"I'm glad."

"Lee, he's flying here, to University Park. It's a hard thing he and David have been through."

Leah's throat squeezed a sound for *yes*.

"He knows I'm free. If he wants me to be more than a friend..."

"I have no claim on Jonathan. I owe him."

"It's tacky."

"It's not tacky. How long from New York?"

"There's no commuter from JFK. An hour from Pittsburgh."

She laughed. "I've wasted precious time agonizing."

"Well said."

"I love you, Leah. Thanks."

NOW THERE WERE THOUGHTS to occupy her mind, thoughts of Jonathan and Suzanne meeting tonight in a way not too unlike her own meeting with David would be; thoughts of David's sparing her an awkward situation, with Jon and himself disembarking together; thoughts of victories each man had experienced—Jonathan, clearly, over past hurts and jealousies, not to mention the fearful circumstance he had faced in Herzliya; and David, evidently, in conquest over his disfluency, that rude and relentless enervator, the giant that had taunted him so long. Both he and Jon had faced the odds in Jerusalem; both had suffered trauma in the bombing at Nathan's and in the death of Ruth Abramowicz. They would seek comfort now in waiting arms.

Her gratitude to Jon could not go unexpressed; yet David knew she would want to choose the moment, and this was not it. Eventually, she would write or talk to Jon; it would be hard to find the words.

Her thoughts were still cascading over one another when a rapping sounded on the door. She hurried to twist the knob, to remove the barrier, to throw her arms around David, hold and kiss him, draw him into her safety, her home, away from the land of danger. He shut the door slowly behind him and held her. His left cheekbone was discolored and his hair had been brushed loosely over a higher wound, a jagged cut, stitched closed; there had to be other bruises. She communicated in kiss and tender caress her gratefulness for his return, for his very being, wishing to give to him of her comfort and strength. What she received from him took her off balance: More than she had ever sensed it before, there was an aura of peace about him. Yes, he had need of her warmth and love; she felt him draw them from her. Yet it was she who was the recipient of comfort and strength; it wrapped about her like a mantle. He led her to the couch and gently pulled her down beside him to sit enfolded in his arms, her head on his shoulder. He did not speak; it seemed he did not want to, until at last she, wishing the closeness and safety they felt would last forever, turned to him. "Don't you ever leave me again," she said half in jest, half in dire seriousness.

He smiled. "I have to see Martin Sunday," he said, raising one eyebrow and trying not to wince.

"Can't you call?" she asked, surprised and disappointed. She kissed his temple just below the cut.

"Uh-uh. Face to face."

She sat up. "Let Case."

"Sweet Rachel. Among other things, Nathan should have a much higher percentage of the Tel Aviv store. He's manager now, and he's earned it."

"And it's up to you to nail that down? What are chances?"

"I'll approach it gently, maybe start higher, maybe lower than the figure I have in mind."

"You want to *negotiate*? With *Martin*? You're that sure you...?"

His smile was relaxed. "I'm anything but sure of Martin's capacity to be reasonable on this; I just want to get him thinking about it. But yes, I *am* sure of my fluency, been gaining on it for weeks. With the team and at Nathan's, I was fine. When Ruth came to me that night, we talked for a couple of hours about how I'd been able pretty much to wrestle it down."

"How did you? What did you tell her?"

He studied her with a patient smile; of course, she would want to know. "I told her how long I had tried to conquer it myself and how I never could until I met Yeshua. He held out to me what I needed—his forgiveness, his lordship over my life—and I took him at his word. He accepted my trust—he accepted me. I told Ruth all I knew about who he was and how he'd been framed by jealous, fearful Jewish leaders and a fickle mob who expected a different kind of Messiah. I explained how he died willingly, for her sin and mine, exactly as God planned it, and how there's nothing I believe more strongly than that he's alive in heaven and in every follower. Ruth said it was more than she could comprehend all at once, but she had 'a funny feeling that it all made sense,' and she'd 'give it some thought.'" He rubbed Leah's fingers with his thumb. "Three times in my life I've been too late. I was too late to save Ruth's life *or* her soul. When she died, I knew God was talking to me. I told him I would do what he expected whether or not I felt ready. Now."

Leah's grieving and prayer had helped her through her own struggles with Ruth's death. Now David needed comfort in his. "God knew Ruth's heart," she said, "and that's enough. You've got to believe it is." She touched the bruised cheekbone with feather-light fingertips. "Your talk with her planted the seed of Life, and that's all she needed. She's with him, Love, I know she is." David listened intently, then kissed her fingers. "As for your fluency," she said, "you're right to credit him—your press conference was nothing short of miraculous. What could have taxed you more?"

"Try calling my mother," he said, his mouth droll. "She was as hot over my causing another incident as Martin was about the first one, and livid over the temple thing being exposed. But I handled it with her—no stutter, none."

Leah went straight to the concern of a therapist—maintenance. He gave her a little smile that made her, again, forget feeling motherly. "Miracles don't need maintenance," he said, "but if it will make you happy, three years of coursework should provide opportunity enough." She questioned him with a look. He took hold of her, and his eyes were serious. "I'll need training." She waited, held by something compelling in him, the something new. "People have to meet him," he said. "They don't know the proof is in their hands."

Him. Comprehension came with a sensation high in her stomach. Hadn't he said something about doing what God expected? And she really hadn't heard him until now.

"Peace will only come when Yeshua brings it," he was saying, "and he won't do that until his people recognize him. They'll come to him by the thousands, Leah—the Word says they will—if someone will tell them, show them, who he *is*."

"David," she said and kissed him, "nothing could make me happier."

"Do you see now why it has to be face to face with Martin?"

She nodded soberly. "How will he take it?"

He let go to rest his head on the back of the couch and close his eyes. "Like I said, I'll try for a higher share for Nathan first."

"He'll cut you off? Can he?" she asked softly, so as not to "waken" him.

He told her, eyes closed, that when he was ten years old, his dad began to play a little game with him—a share of stock for every year of his life, given annually to him on his birthday. He now owned, in addition to those 186 shares, a few bought with dividends and interest. His laugh was wry. "I'm not yet *into* the company. To be a partner, I'd surely be expected to be personally involved. And as far as Martin's concerned, I went off the deep end in the Jordan."

"Your mother's defended you."

"Not on that."

Leah, sliding one arm over his chest and one behind him, touched her head to his chin. "*I'm* proud of you."

He cradled her, drew a great breath, and let it out. "You'd be the wife of a preacher of the gospel?"

She turned herself to him; he was awake, all right. If this was his proposal, she would not treat it lightly. "I'd be honored," she said, deeply solemn. Seeing no smile, she closed her eyes and waited for the sealing kiss.

"And live with me in a *kibbutz*?" Her eyes opened, widened, and she pushed against the cushion. His smile was brief. "God's called me, Leah. No thunderclap, no vision. No Aaron. Speech, for his purpose."

She sat silent a moment. "To give him your life...is wonderful." It just didn't *sound* wonderful anymore. Preach to Israelis? In *kibbutzim*? "Living on what? Never mind, I know—a *kibbutz* is a co-op."

"Exactly. One *kibbutz*, then another—management, labor." He sat up searching her eyes. "A minimum of two years in each to establish a bond, plant a synagogue, teach people to share what they *know*."

Leah was quiet.

"The bones and flesh of Israel are standing," he said. "God's breathing on them even now. Y'didah, are you *willing*?" Her eyes on his, she shook her head no, no, no. She was not ready for this. This was not what God wanted her to do. This was not what he had called her to be. She ran nervous fingers, once, through her hair, but those deep brown eyes would not let go. "Tell them, Rachel...the way you told me."

The duties of a Messianic rabbi's wife in the States—the speaking, teaching, sharing—were not unpalatable. But in Israel... Her world—neat, familiar, predictable, comfortable—began to whirl into misshapen images: work, heat, sand, and stubble; rejection and loneliness because of their beliefs, danger because of David's family name, and near pennilessness in a situation where a bottle of pop a week was pure luxury. And, because there was something indomitable about David now, something she knew would not give up, their sojourn would not be short. She could not conceal her fears. He held her, but they did not go away. "If I said I wouldn't go..." she said haltingly into his ear.

"Look at me. I've put my hand to the plow."

"You'd go without me? ...You would. You would go."

He held her close to himself, and she felt the beating of his heart.

"I need time," she whispered. "David, I love you. Give me time."

Chapter 40

Never had they had so little to say. She lay in his arms until after one, when he moved her gently away saying he would see her in the morning.

"Don't go."

"What happened to 'appearances'?"

She hesitated. She had told him her feelings on that matter, but some of her neighbors would think it stranger to see him leave anyway, and tonight..."You need to be with me—here." Her invitation was to the couch only, and she knew he would not violate it; if he had been a man of honor before his consecration, he was that and more now. This night, in point of fact, nurtured no form of union. Her thoughts were in tumult, and his eyes told her that regarding her decision, he was sure of nothing, not even tomorrow.

"In the morning, Leah. Nine," he said, and kissed her with exquisite gentleness on the mouth.

She lay in bed remembering his kiss, reliving it a dozen times. It was clearer to her now why he had not wanted her meeting Jonathan at the airport. It was not just to protect her from an ungainly social situation; it was to protect them both on the night he intended to ask her to marry him. Why throw into the mix an old flame who had become a hero and had done it by saving her current interest's life! Oh, they had gotten through that one just fine. But she had sabotaged the occasion much more thoroughly all by herself.

She tried now, lying there, to see blossoms in the desert, trees laden with fruit, a shimmering lake. But contorted mouths and shaking fists appeared instead; explosions and fire, merciless pursuit, and yes, beheadings and blood—for she knew the warnings of Yeshua for the end days, and if Israel was, as David said, on the brink of discovering its Messiah, that would indeed herald the time of culmination: "You will be handed over to be persecuted and put to death," Yeshua had told his followers and those who came after, "and you will be hated by all nations because of me." It had happened, exactly as he said, after he ascended. It would happen, more so, at the end, as the finger of God touched the finger of Judah...of Reuben, Gad, and Asher...of Naphtali, Manasseh, Simeon, Levi, Issachar, Zebulun, Joseph...and Benjamin. She had been reading in the Revelation to John all week, and now her questions became urgent. Why was Dan not named at the end? she thought. Would the Danites be "a serpent by the way, an adder in the path," as Israel said? And if the half-tribe of Manasseh was there, why not that of his brother, Ephraim? "This one is the firstborn," Joseph had said to his father, speaking of Manasseh; "put your right hand on him." Israel refused; Manasseh would be great, he said, but Ephraim, greater. Even God called him his firstborn. Yet his name was not sealed in the end, except in his father, Joseph. Who would be enemy and who friend, Leah wondered, and how would she know the difference? Questions without answers; fear with no relief. She lay on one side and then the other, turned her head into the pillow, and tried to pray; and when sleep came, it was because her mind was too exhausted to examine one more thought. She wandered in and out of slumber until dawn and then, remembering the night, worse than a bad dream because it was real, she pushed herself to shower, dress, and lay the makings of breakfast on the counter.

The rap on the door came at 8:30 and she, supposing David, too, had had a sleepless night, greeted him as warmly as she could. Heaviness clouded the Sabbath hours, even as they walked the wooded roads of South Park. October was past, the colors fading, falling. Infrequently they spoke, and when they did, it was with strained little laughs or superficial exchanges, void of intimacy.

She drove him to the airport after dinner. The sun had vanished behind the hills when he boarded the plane, and having watched his flight into the bleakness of the sky, she walked the windy lot to find her car. She drove the route back toward the tunnel, crossed the river, and continued along 22. Signs appeared that warned of the parting of Route 30 from the highway. She held her course, not knowing they were murmuring to her need. It was not until she had passed the turnoff to her apartment that she understood where she was going. She would stay on the northern route, better anyway. In an hour she could talk to someone not tangled up in David, in religion, or emotion. She would see Uncle Paddy—tonight.

Claire answered the door. Surprised, she invited Leah in out of the night air and went to the cupboard for a second cup and saucer. "How nice you could come," she said, not very well veiling her bewilderment. "Is...everything okay?"

Leah laid her jacket on a chair and held her hands over the kettle heating on the stove. "Fine. I love my work. How've you been?" She glanced into the living room at Paddy's chair while she acknowledged Claire's reply with "Good, good. Is Uncle Paddy at the barn?"

"At the lodge for rabbit," Claire said, "he and the boys and Peter. I thought you might have come to see your brother. Did you know your father brought him down yesterday?"

"No, I... No," Leah said, trying to recoup. She asked when they would be back, and Claire said tomorrow about midday; they couldn't hunt on Sunday, of course, but they would take their time improvising a big breakfast and admiring the kill. "Paddy never comes home empty handed," Claire said as she set the saucer and cup on the table.

Leah tried to smile. An evening with Claire. The kettle whistled, and she took it to the cups. Claire had sat down and was saying,

"It's been months since I've seen you, honey." Leah caught the glance at her waistline and the easing of the lines in Claire's face as she took a chair opposite her. "How is your friend, what's his name...with the speech, uh, problem?" Claire asked.

"Fine, considering," Leah said, wondering if she looked as offended as she felt. Claire was blank. "David Rothman," Leah supplied, thinking surely her aunt had listened to or read the news.

"Ohhh...the same David Rothman... Oh, you're not still seeing him, I hope."

"Why?"

"*Why?* Let him set foot in Israel again, you'll see why. Tell me he went to watch them lay brick for a store. What's he take us for? He's in with that Ben-what's-his-name. Hand me those, would you?"

Leah moved the pack. She found herself smiling in near disbelief at what she was hearing. "Forgive my wild extrapolation, but could it be you don't like David very much?"

Claire lit a cigarette and exhaled away from her. "A hothead. Ask that reporter. And giving the girl advice?" She gave Leah a "come-now" look. "*Are* you still seeing him?" Leah put down her cup and looked at her. "Oh, honey, don't be taken by a face or go soft over his problem; you can do better. There're plenty of fish, and your ocean's wide." She drew again on the cigarette and said Israel had launched reprisals against the PLO for that bombing. Leah had heard it in the car. She took two sips from her tea, rose slowly, carried her cup to the sink, dumped the ample remnant, and told Claire she'd certainly cleared her mind on the subject of David Rothman. The corners of Claire's eyes crinkled; the smile bloomed, and she said she had a surprise. Paddy had bought her *some* anniversary gift in May; she'd been afraid to ask what it cost. "Run upstairs for your jodhpurs while I finish. No, just grab your boots. You won't believe this."

Chapter 41

At the upper barn, Claire led Leah between the long rows of stalls that housed the Saddlebreds. They passed an empty stall near the end of the corridor and, seeing no more heads jutting over the half-doors, Leah thought perhaps Claire's surprise, whether horseflesh or tack, had been taken from its place by one of the boys. It was then that she heard the deep nicker and saw, with its gray patrician muzzle jutting over the next to the last door, the most beautiful equine head she had ever seen: white, dished, with large, dark, low-set eyes and flaring nostrils, velvety to her reverent touch. His delicate ears pitched forward, and a well-combed white mane flowed over his full, arching neck. Arabian. The animal nuzzled her hand and, finding nothing, tried Claire's.

"Well?" Claire said, grinning at Leah as she flat-handed him a piece of carrot and opened the door. "I've scheduled nine parades. Good for the farm, don't you think?"

"He's so...regal," Leah said, running a hand over his flank. His skin was dark under the white coat, his conformation flawless from poll to croup to slender legs.

Claire slipped a halter over the head and snapped a longe line to it. She looped the 25-foot fabric line several times over her palm and, with the Arab behind her, chatted to Leah the length of the corridor: "Close to green when I got him. Wait'll you see. Jack won't even canter in here; this baby's a ballerina." They walked to the entrance end of the barn, where there were no stalls but a modest open space. Bales of straw lined the walls on three sides of a well-trodden rectangular track. Claire took a longeing whip from its hook and moved to the center of the ring. When she had let the horse out nearly the length of the line and commanded him to walk, she laid it at her feet. He walked until she said "trot," and when he had earned her praise for his discipline, she called for the canter. Leah stood entranced by the beauty of it—easy, spirited, the long, full tail its proud banner. She had to sketch him, she told Claire, tomorrow, while she waited for Paddy—and Peter, who she hoped would stay out of her hair long enough for her to get some advice. What was it Claire was calling the horse?

"Arabah, like the valley he came from," Claire said, bringing him to a stand. She bridled him and gave Leah a leg up. The stallion pranced. Leah put him into his fast walk and, when she sensed rapport, signaled collection with her legs and little fingers. It was as if she had only *thought* "canter" and begun to shift weight when he gave her the gentle, rolling gait. Effortlessly he moved around the ring, a Pegasus, a spirit of white fire at one with her whim; he made of her a princess ascending to a celestial palace. She willed him across the ring and signaled a change in the pattern of his moving feet. She had it.

"He'll change on the fly," Claire called, beaming.

Leah took the figure eight, signaled change of lead for the cross point, and got it precisely there. Claire called out his show skills by name, and Leah tested each. The minutes ticked away and when she had taken her fill of elation, Leah cooled him down and rode to Claire. "Fantastic. Does he jump?"

"The breed isn't built for the hunt, of course," Claire said, "but when his legs mature, I might try a little easy cross country."

Leah swung to the ground. "He's magnificent."

"My dream come true," Claire said, leading him into the corridor. "Come talk—or are you tired?" Leah's room was always ready—never dust-free, but all hers—unless Peter had moved in. She said it was late; she'd turn in if Claire didn't mind. She walked to the house, got rid of her boots, and climbed the stairs. Washed, she headed down the hall. Some of Peter's things were in a heap on the floor of Danny's room, so she continued down the hall to the room that had been hers every summer for almost as long as she could remember. She'd been tired after the drive; now she was wide awake. She sat on the bed, and David flew into her mind for the five-hundredth time since he had left. She saw him say again, his grip strong on her arms, "Peace will only come when Yeshua brings it. And he won't do that until his people recognize him. Y'didah, are you *willing?*" Absently, she reached for the Book of answers, of help and comfort. Her hand fell on the nightstand where it should have been. Neither was it on the desk. She lay back across the bed and tried to remember something, anything that would ease her mind. All she could think of were end-times passages where Yeshua warned of wars, revolutions, earthquakes, famines, and pestilences. In Israel believers, until he came back for them, would be jailed and many martyred. She strained to remember more. It came in snatches and gave no comfort; if anything, it made humankind's terror tactics sound like child's play: signs in the sun, moon, and stars, the roaring of the sea, the heavenly bodies shaken.

"Oh, Lord, you've said in your Word I can't cling to my family," she whispered. "I belong to you. Show me safety." She looked again for the Bible, any Bible. There was none. She walked into the hallway and down two doors to Danny's room, flicked on the light, and saw the Book on the table next to the sleigh bed. She scooped it up, flipped its pages to a gospel. Luke. Where—where? Twenty-one. She sat on the bed and read the words of Yeshua:

Heaven and earth will pass away, but my words will never pass away. Be careful, or your hearts will be weighed down with...the anxieties of life, and that day will close on you unexpectedly like a trap. For it will come upon all those who live on the face of the whole earth.

All those who live, she thought. Everyone left at the end. She lay the Book in her lap. Suddenly a verse she had learned as a child came to her, and this, too, was Yeshua speaking:

Fear not, little flock; for it is your Father's good pleasure to give you the kingdom.

Another came to mind:

For whosoever will save his life shall lose it: and whosoever will lose his life for my sake shall find it.

And another:

These things I have spoken unto you, that in me ye might have peace. In the world ye shall have tribulation: but be of good cheer; I have overcome the world.

Overcome. Overcome, overcome. So many times he had used the word in his revelation to John. She turned to it, to her own underlinings:

To him who overcomes, I will give the right to eat from the tree of life, which is in the paradise of God.

Do not be afraid of what you are about to suffer....

To him who overcomes, I will give some of the hidden manna....

To him who overcomes and does my will to the end, I will give authority over the nations.

Leah moved page to page, gleaning:

I am coming soon. Hold on to what you have, so that no one will take your crown. Him who overcomes I will make a pillar in the temple of my God. ...I will write on him the name of my God and the name of the city of my God, the New Jerusalem....

She flipped pages to where the angel spoke of the city—*the bride, the wife of the Lamb*—and read what John wrote:

> *I did not see a temple in the city, because the Lord God Almighty and the Lamb are its temple. The city does not need the sun or the moon to shine on it, for the glory of God gives it light, and the Lamb is its lamp. The nations will walk by its light, and the kings of the earth will bring their splendor into it. ...Nothing impure will ever enter it...but only those whose names are written in the Lamb's book of life. ...and they will reign for ever and ever.*

To sit at his feet, Leah thought, *would be more than I deserve.* A tingling sensation rippled through her. There was no escape from danger, terror, or death, except in Yeshua—no constant friends but those who were his, no sanctuary but in his sealing and his promise to return. If she must die before he came, could she give her life for any purpose better than to share that knowledge with her people? If she were brave in the time given her, how many lives could she help turn to him? Thousands, David thought.

Dear, beloved David. He had decided. Even his love for her could not change his course. She had seen the look in his eyes when he left the apartment Friday night, as if, over this, he might have lost her. And at dusk tonight, when he boarded the plane, he must have carried a weight in his chest. How could she have allowed him to think she would let him go alone? "Stupid, Leah, stupid," she said aloud. She wanted desperately to talk to him. She looked at her watch. He was somewhere in Chicago, making his way to Martin's. She replaced the Book slowly and turned to run a hand over the bed where he had lain. How would she sleep, wanting so much to talk with him? She knew better than to interrupt his conference with Martin. Nor could she call at some awful hour later in the night when everyone there was asleep. It would have to wait till he was back at his apartment tomorrow night. She sat distraught on the edge of the too-soft bed, looking up at the portrait of her great grandfathers, meeting them eye to eye. All at once she stood and made her way back to her room. Blue would do nicely. Fidelity. She found a pen and, sitting at the desk, pulled the paper from the box and wrote.

> *My Beloved David,*
>
> *That you would do what you've been called to do, no matter what the cost, makes me love you all the more.*
>
> *Yes, I will leave my family, my country, anything that would separate me from you. I'll go anywhere you are, cope with anything I must to be with you, to be a wife worthy of your love. I want to be a part of everything you do, to make wherever we are a home for us. I want to bear your children and help you with your work. We will be his witnesses "in Jerusalem, and in all Judea and Samaria"—and the circle will be closed.*
>
> *I love you for being patient with me, Yadid. I'll have talked to you by the time you get this, but I was going out of my mind, unable to reach you tonight. I can't wait to see you.*
>
> > *Forever,*
> >
> > *Leah*

She sealed the blue envelope, addressed it, touched it to her lips. Blue was the color tonight. She drew from the dresser drawer a soft nightgown the hue of a summer sky and laid aside her clothes to slide it over her head. The chill of the room was in the gown and in the sheets and coverlet as well. Warmth came slowly to her bed, but it was total warmth, of body, soul, and spirit. She surrendered to the night with a smile on her lips and David in her dreams.

Chapter 42

NO ONE WAS IN THE KITCHEN WHEN LEAH CAME DOWN. She laid the sketchpad and pencils on the table and poured some juice. A scrawled note under the salt shaker read:

Arabah—north pasture. Chores are done—shopping now. Do one for me.

Leah took the last half of her English muffin with her. She would stay long enough to see Paddy, Peter, Danny, and Mike, then head for Pittsburgh and mail the letter on the way. She walked the dirt road to the barns and beyond. The temperature already neared fifty. This was a day made for keeping; there was joy in the air, in the earth, in the trees—in the muffin—there was joy.

It was barely 9:30 when she reached the gully that the creek cut through the north acreage. The Arab was grazing near a big old oak in the upper pasture; he started when he saw her, frisked in a circle, and came back to the tree. She walked the bridge of stone and boards and continued along the fence to the second gate. A newly oiled halter and a much-handled lead rope were hung over the latch post. She let herself in and settled against the fence where the sun had dried the grass.

He was beautiful from any angle; she sketched him from three sides while the young tiger cat that had bounded behind her from the barn rubbed its coat against her jeans, its tail an arrow aimed at clouds. Once the feline, playing games, came under moving hooves and scampered for protection up the oak. Leah finished the sketch of Arabah in a gambol over the pasture and turned her attention to the cat that peered down wide-eyed from the lowest branch. In carbon strokes she captured fur and bark. Finished, she laid down her materials and took in the brilliance of the day and the stallion standing, an ethereal vision, a hundred feet away. Gratefulness welled in her toward God for his leading through her valley. She wondered whether Claire—or, for that matter, Peter— would allow her to talk with Paddy long enough just to share with him her love, her deepening love for the man who had come here with her last spring. Her watch said 11:45; time had fled. She stood, and the tiger meowed from his suspended prison. Silly cat. They wouldn't see him at the barn till he was hungry enough to be brave. She pulled a chunk of carrot from her pocket, slung the halter and rope over her forearm, and moved toward Arabah, talking. He walked to meet her and allowed her to halter him and snap the lead to the ring. He munched the carrot and rubbed his nose against her sleeve. She led him to the tree, dropped the lead, and scuttled onto his back. He moved two steps or three, and Leah wished he had been trained to ground tie, like Dinah. She had to circle him with weight, leg, and hand to get him back to where the coward crouched. Arabah stood, head up, ears pricked. She reached the cat and lifted him, a long, dead weight, from the branch. From out of a far field, there came a sound like a shot. The horse moved sideways nickering, and the cat squirmed free of Leah's hand. Needlelike, its claws fixed in the horse's neck. Arabah sounded his pain, reared crookedly, and bolted forward as the cat slid down his shoulder, leaving thin, bloodless tracks. Leah leaned to catch the flailing lead rope, calling, "Whoa," her forward weight impelling her mount all the faster toward the fence. She stopped groping; he was bound for it, his stride precisely right if he could take the height. She held tightly to the mane, squeezed with her heels, and leaned aside of the lifting neck. Up and over, a not-so-bad landing, and Leah thought half whimsically as she regained her seat, *Who said he wouldn't make the hunt?* She tried again to snatch the rope, to make him circle and stop before it tangled in his feet. She saw no gully, just the lead that whipped beside the shoulder now raked with red. She caught it fast, eased back and to the right. He would not turn. His muzzle nearly to her shin, Arabah pounded forward until the ground vanished from beneath his feet and he plunged and slid toward the creek, his head tucked so that he could not see or judge or balance. She felt herself lift from his back, bounce off his croup and, apart from him, fall toward the rocks along the stream. Time for just one thought: *Oh, God, why not on grass....*

ALWAYS, MARTIN HELD THE CHIPS. Not till morning, he had told David; he was tired. He had gone to bed, and David, after having talked with Sheila, had done the same. Lying awake on the king-size bed, he watched the stars through the penthouse window. What had happened to the boyhood bond? Had it been imagined all these years?

At breakfast, Sheila told David his brother was already at work in his office/den and wished not be disturbed. David smiled into his coffee. She apologized, as annoyed and embarrassed by her own lack of resourcefulness as she was by Martin's tactic. Yet it was not the first time she had witnessed his hardheadedness. "You're not peddling vinyl handbags," she said to David, stirring the brew she had already stirred. David finished, thanked Sheila, and walked to Martin's door. He opened it with "Good morning!" and seated himself before the desk, spreading papers where they both could see. He confirmed Case's telephoned report—no transfer of funds to the temple project had yet taken place when they talked with Ben Sheva; and as Martin had requested, Case and he had, from Nathan's, on Wednesday, given the construction people the go-ahead on the new Rothman's. Second thoughts, David said, presenting it as a question.

"I don't indulge," Martin answered, and David felt heat; he said that brought them, then, to his proposal. Nathan was not just a family friend; he'd been indispensable to the project from its outset. His counsel was expert, reliable and, as always, free. And now, as per his and Martin's prior discussion, David had broached the subject with Nathan of his managing the branch. "Till now, he's been in for twelve-and-a-half per cent of the new store."

"So?"

"Offer him fifteen."

First came color, then eruption. "You call that business? You learn that in the Cow Pasture? Toss stock when your conscience cuts?"

"You know as well as I do that we've been the beneficiaries of Nathan's generosity ever since Ruth and I got our families together at the speech clinic in New York. Marty, that was nine years ago. Isn't it about time we did the right thing? Isn't it time we did something *good* for Nathan?"

Martin walked the length of the room, holding the back of his neck, and turned with clamped jaw. "I used to think...all we needed on the Coast was a Rothman. But after that televised *fiasco*, after all you've done for the store, you need time...on the ground." He worked to calm himself. "What's happened to you?"

David's mouth rested on a tent of fingers. He stood and walked to the window. Hands in his pockets, he watched the traffic below. Everyone was going somewhere, or thought he was. "I'm finished bowing down to baubles. That's what I came to tell you."

Martin's teeth parted behind closed lips. "What?"

"Chip off the old man, I guess; I'm picking up his dream."

"You can't mean...the temple. Your new *religion*..."

"...is an offer you can't match."

Martin stood measuring. He nodded. "Jumping ship. Some first mate."

Cabin boy, David thought. "It'd take me a week to give you Dad's view of the temple, and mine, Martin. Let me just say, you're right about one thing: I carry a name."

"*You* don't care about Dad," Martin said, his voice gravel.

This was clearly not the day, David thought, when Martin would see Yeshua's name as anything but a stone to be sunk in mud, or David's call to minister in Israel as anything but insanity. He had offered no condolence for David's trauma or the death of his friend Ruth. He had made no mention of David's being the only one Ben Sheva, in the end, agreed to see, and proffered no thanks for his risking all to do it. And there had been no "Say, you sound good." David extended his hand. "I'll miss you, Marty. Take care." He thought he saw wetness in Martin's eyes, but there was no move toward him. Maybe he was mistaken.

DAVID CLOSED THE OFFICE DOOR BEHIND HIM and, with a hug, said goodbye to Sheila. He took his bag to the elevator, and through her window Sheila saw him head for the curb. She walked to Martin's door and opened it. Silhouetted by the light from his window, he stood looking at the street, arms folded, his teeth on the tip of one thumb; his shoulder moved. She retreated, but he looked up, startled, then walked quickly to the case and pulled down a book. She offered coffee, but he motioned her away, and when she stayed, he put it to her clearly: he would be left alone. Quietly she closed the door. David was getting into a cab when she returned to the window. She waved, saw him do the same, and as he pulled away she felt a knot inside. Hadn't she sensed the crossroads? They had chosen separate ways. Which was Jacob, which Esau? Which had his father's blessing? And would they ever seek to mend the slash?

Chapter 43

THE WALLS WERE CLEAN, AND BEIGE. The bed was hard, and beige. The spread was thin, and soft...and beige. Leah lay on her back, finally alone, and the scene began to play itself again: the slam on her breech, her head against her knee and, as she watched the stallion struggle in vain to get himself out of the shallow stream, a sensation, warm and tingling, creeping down her legs. She lay back on the dirt because she had no choice. She worried that Arabah would drown in six inches of water and that no one would find the two of them for days. But in minutes, she heard running footsteps and Peter's face was suddenly above her, flushed and streaming tears. He kept saying it was all his fault; Uncle Paddy'd said if Danny went home without a kill, Aunt Claire'd have Dinah for dinner. "I went for rabbit," he told Leah, crying hard, his hands on her face, on her shoulders. "It went off." She pulled him down to her and stroked his hair. She said she forgave him, hush now, and was Arabah still holding his head out of the water? "He's okay," he said, the words catching. He tugged her hand. "We'll pull him up."

"Peter, listen. I can't move my legs. Get Aunt Claire." He choked back a sob and ran. Leah heard the sound again, farther away, and then the minutes dragged. She watched Arabah work relentlessly to stand, and when he succeeded, she saw he was muddied from shoulder to barrel and hobbling toward her on three legs. He stood over her, a wounded sentry, nickering comfort.

It was not long after Claire and Peter reached them that the helicopter landed on the bank. Claire steadied Arabah while the rescue team placed Leah on the backboard. By then the pain had begun, sharp pain in her back, all over, and still she could not move her legs. She had said it before, and Claire had told her it was all right, but Leah longed for something more in her tone, her eyes, and so she said it again as they lifted her, level, up the embankment: "I'm sorry, Aunt Claire. Forgive me," and she felt sick to her stomach as she caught a glimpse of Arabah, his left foreleg twisted strangely above the fetlock, the hoof held so it barely touched the ground.

"You're not gonna cry now, are you?" one of the rescuers said, flashing her a smile as they slid her into place. She shook her head and bit her lip and fought the sob that convulsed her chest without permission. When the young man returned to Claire, the older one touched her arm. "You cry, Sweetheart; it helps the pain. That's why God made tears."

ANTOINE BEAUMONT, SMALL-BONED AS HE WAS, hastened to keep up with his wife as she made her way toward 309. He caught her elbow. "Miriam, wait." She stopped. He took a breath, then nodded and proceeded to the room; he entered beside her, smiling. "Now what've you gone and done, Tom?" he teased. "Tried to jump a canyon on a cow pony?" He reached for Leah's foot; there was no life. The smile wavered; he had hoped to find them altogether wrong.

"Papa, I have hands," she teased back. She pulled him close and tapped the cheek her mother had not kissed. "Even me up." Miriam told her they had talked to the doctor; the prognosis was good. She ran a hand up and down Leah's arm. "She told me," Leah said. "Four, maybe five days."

"Then for just a while, a little leg brace," Antoine said as cheerfully as one could talk about a leg brace.

"How's Arabah?" Leah asked softly.

Antoine kept the smile, but the crank on the tray table required his attention. He moved it back and forth and started to say something, but nothing came of it.

"Papa?"

"Tell her," Miriam said gently. Antoine glared at his wife. "Before someone else does," she whispered.

He let go of the crank and sat on the hard, flat bed, taking Leah's hands. "A splintered cannon, damage to the shoulder. Frank offered to do it...but Paddy did it himself." Her anguish found voice, and he felt the stab of grief. Forbidden to lift or hold his daughter, he could only squeeze her hands, detest the burning in his eyes, hot pools that overflowed and trickled down his face and off his chin. And, remembering that singular word of uncertainty Leah's doctor had used when she spoke to them of possibilities and alternatives—*chance*—he stopped fighting it and let the sob come too.

TUESDAY. NO WORD FROM DAVID, in spite of her family's efforts to locate him. Leah lay listlessly on the pillow, holding the phone receiver in place and telling Suzanne she should've let the Arab have his head; he'd have stopped short of the ditch. So meaningless. She had just given God her life; why this now? Suzanne said she must be onto something important, or the enemy wouldn't have bothered with her. "Just remember God doesn't waste anything." Glad she had called, Leah asked how she knew what had happened. She'd been trying, she said, to call—two days—and, thinking it a little strange Leah was never at her apartment, had dialed her parents' home. They had been unable to contact David about the accident, so she had offered to do it.

"And did you?"

"Today."

"He hasn't called."

"He's on his way."

She wanted to hug her. "You, friend, were born in Zion. How's Jon?"

"Incredible. Twenty-two years it took, but I have met a gentleman. Rest, Lee. I'm praying."

IT WAS AFTER TEN when she felt his kiss on her mouth. She opened her eyes to a huge bouquet of mums and, beside it, David's smile—only for lack of the uplifted arm, the same as followed triumph on the gym floor. "How did you get in here?" she beamed, touching suede to be sure he was real.

"On the road since 6:30 to see my fiancée. How could they say no?"

The mums were citron sunshine, vibrant, pungent. He had remembered. She saw him again across a table, the first time she had blushed to see his love. "I needed these." He kissed her, pulled a chair close, and asked how she was feeling. She said her legs were still zero; the doctors wanted to use something called Harrington rods on the damaged vertebra, a fusion process using bone from her hip. They were glib enough, but she wasn't sure what to do, or why this was happening to her.

"To us."

"If they're wrong, I don't want you feeling...bound...."

"I'll *carry* you."

She looked at him. He meant it. She smiled a little and took his hand. "To Petach Tikva and Negba?"

He pulled the blue envelope from his pocket. "To Petach Tikva and Negba."

She laughed. Claire must've mailed it Sunday morning, thinking it said goodbye. Suddenly it wasn't funny. "I don't want to be your cross," she whispered.

His fingers brushed her hair back into place above her ear. "You'll walk. You'll ride. ...Believe."

Chapter 44

On Wednesday, Andy barreled into Leah's room lugging an eight-by-twelve-by-six-inch box. "All right, what are they doing for you here?"

Leah laughed. "So far, steroids. They're talking surgery, but David—"

"He's right. Try these." She put the box on the bed and lifted the lid. Rows of plump, yellow fruit circled a chopped-short shock of leaves. Leah looked at her.

"Papaya," Andy said, biting a yellow sphere. "Takes the swelling right down. You know, between the discs." She pulled up the green blades. "Pineapple," she said with her mouth full. "Finish the job."

Leah turned a papaya in her hand and took a bite. She munched down to the little black seeds while Andy confided that she had targeted her frustration over Rick the way Leah had shown her to do. Encouraged, Leah listened to her describe her commitment of the situation to God and the settled feeling that had come with her decision to give Cat a chance to be to her what Rick had failed to be. The papaya fell from Leah's hand to the sheet. "I have peace about it, so I know it's right," Andy said, and Leah recognized the words as, many times, her own.

"You're not playing by the rules."

Andy didn't hear. She wanted to kick herself, she said, for not giving Cat more of an opening when they were in school. "Who'd have guessed behind that hard face there was this sweet, sensitive guy? ...You need something? A nurse?"

"I'm fine; tired."

Andy left soon afterward, buoyant as she'd come, and Leah wondered whether God had heard her prayer to protect her friends.

He had protected David and Jon. Was he listening on this one? Did *they*—Andy, Rick, and Cat—have to be believers for her prayer to be answered? Or was he answering "no" to some of her prayers?

THURSDAY WAS THE FIFTH DAY following the accident, and Leah tried to banter through her phone conversation with David in spite of the unchanged paralysis. The doctor who had read the x-rays had told her, after all, that it might take a little longer. But Leah had heard no assurance in his tone. David, on the phone, made her talk about wedding dresses and honeymoon plans and instructed her to read Psalm 46 before she turned off the light. It helped. The reading sent her spirit soaring, out of the sterile room, away from the city of three rivers, to the faithful God of her fathers, to the Land of Jacob, to her dreams of selfless giving and fierce, courageous love. She hovered there almost an hour, until the lights were dimmed, and she fought to keep the vision in the night. But the last thought that crept across her mind, awake, was of her lifeless legs and numerals on the clock beside her bed: 11:54, 55, 56.... And so the fifth day ended.

IT WAS NOT EASY FOR DAVID TO TRAVEL in the opposite direction now, but he had not seen his mother since Yom Kippur. There were things he had to tell her in person—his intention to marry, his plans for the future. Leah understood. And so on Friday afternoon, he drove to Philly.

Friday evening he took Enid to temple, and they talked with Samuel. Something was missing now between him and Sam. David tried all the harder to greet his old friend with warmth, and Sam tried, too, but they both knew that behind it they were, each to the other, alien. Enid was much aware of it, of course, and David was sure it grieved her.

Back at the house in the large front room, she stood at the mantel as if to communicate to him that there was a matter to discuss before they could sit down together here. David, standing also and remembering the days when to share with her his pain brought motherly response, told her first of Leah's accident. When she had expressed a passing kind of sympathy, he dropped a word on his encouragement to Leah concerning wedding plans. It seemed a natural way to ease into the subject.

But not to Enid. "*Wedding?*"

Ignoring the odds, he offered, smiling, "Under the canopy, *Ema*—the Jewish way." The line had worked in *Fiddler*.

Torment, disbelief, and fury strained Enid's voice. "You'd turn your back on everything you are?"

"What am I, Mama?"

"The girl has sold her heritage."

"The *girl* is the most Jewish person I know."

Her hand moved swiftly, striking his cheek. He turned back to her slowly. She sat down, stunned. "I'm sorry. ...I'm sorry." Never before had she struck him on the face. Yet he did not sense the act wholly rescinded; she had recognized only its lack of gentility and, therefore, its inappropriateness. She groaned his name repeatedly. "Haven't we taught you, loved you...given?"

"*Ema*. I would die for her."

"You would die for her. Would you die for me?"

He felt his eyes widen. "Yes, I would."

"Would you give her up for me?"

He sat down facing her and moved his head twice back and forth. Silence hung heavy between them, then a smile came to Enid, wan, melancholy. "You're all I have, David. Wait."

"I won't change."

"You don't *know* she'll walk."

"That's not like you, Mother."

"What is God telling you through this?"

Another first: Enid interpolating God. "You think he's telling me I've made a mistake? Punishing me? Punishing Leah?"

"Correcting you...perhaps. Think about it." She kissed him on the forehead and left him with his thoughts.

EARLY SATURDAY, HE STOOD AT MORNING PRAYER, holding Leah's letter God-ward in one of his upraised hands. He knew he had not misunderstood the call; he knew he was not wrong in loving Leah; he prayed God would continue to assure him her healing was sealed. If any being stood in their way, it could not be God. Simply he prayed, like a little boy carrying too heavy a bag, thanking Dad for hurrying while he edged toward him bearing the load. The door behind him stood ajar; it opened more as Enid rapped. He turned and knew she had been watching. "I was thanking *Adonai* for healing Leah," he said.

"You've talked to her?"

He shook his head. "He will."

She sat down on his bed and said she was worried about him. He was missing classes. Off to Tel Aviv, Chicago, Pittsburgh, and now here, with her. When did he study? He said he was not behind, she shouldn't worry. She told him that to take on all Martin had in mind, he had to study carefully, not just hold his own; his father would have wanted excellence. It was clear she had not talked with Martin. He sat on the bed beside her and told her that he would, indeed, invest himself in Father's business, totally, untiringly. In the time he had, he did his best to make his meaning clear.

She lashed with all her strength. "There is as much chance that *you* are the Messiah as that Yeshua is." She spit the name and called it lunacy, to go where, even now, he might be killed. "To spend your days in labor and sweat, to tell people who do not want to hear it that some long-dead, self-proclaimed prophet is about to reappear and save Israel—from herself?"

The words did not sting; they made him sad for his mother. He smiled and said he couldn't have put it better. "I'm not asking permission, but your blessing would mean so much. Could you believe in Father, if not me?" She watched him form his unmarred words and take her hand. *"Bevakasha, Ema*—please—let me go."

ON SUNDAY AFTERNOON, PADDY CAME through Leah's doorway, hat in hand. He tried to say something cunning on his way across the room, but it was the eighth day, and he knew it. While he had sought courage to face her, her time had ebbed away. Claire, he told her, had had to stay and tend the horses. But he and Leah both knew that even Danny was old enough. He stood against the heater wringing his tweed cap, and when he had apologized to her for his untimely teasing of the boys and she to him for her dubious horsemanship, he continued kneading the cap until the last rampart of his self-possession crumbled and he stood weeping, looking anywhere but at her. Leah held out her arms. He leaned a moment into them—awkwardly, too heavily—and told her he'd give anything to undo what he had done. She placed a soft kiss on the callous of his hand and said she wanted him to know: God would give her back her legs—it was no longer her concern. "Tell Aunt Claire I understand; I've found it so hard to forgive myself. Tell her I love her." The words came with tears, and neither of them was able to say more.

He had been gone only ten minutes when Antoine and Miriam appeared. Antoine took Leah's foot as if it were a throttle, then caught himself and let it go to take her hand instead and kiss her cheek. Her face was damp and pink, like Paddy's when they'd seen him in the hall, and the corners of her mouth turned down. Antoine, thinking to cheer her, told her David had come by Friday to ask permission to marry his daughter; he liked that. Now Miriam was filling up too. He lectured them on trusting, if it took ten times the wait, and he pulled Leah's hand from the sheet she clutched to rub it with resolve. And then he knew. She was laughing—the way she did sometimes when Matt said something funny and it hit her right, as it had, Matt had told them, the other day, when he was here. He looked at her, confused.

"Papa, hold my foot," she said between the sounds. He did, and momentarily he felt a moving toe. "It's happening," she cried.

Three people laughing, crying, and exclaiming all at once became ten people laughing, crying, and exclaiming all at once. Nurses, aides, and one congenial patient on his way to find the lounge beheld the sign, and it meant much more to Leah than the wisest of them guessed.

THE PHONES RANG IN THE ROTHMAN HOME soon after David left. Thomas came to Enid in her sitting room to inform her that Ms. Beaumont was calling, and as she exchanged banalities with Leah, she forced a friendly voice, saying she was sorry, he was on his way back to school. "How are you feeling? ...What's 'just what you wanted to tell him'?" She sat on the Chippendale, where no one ever sat. "Well, I'm so happy for you. ...Surely."

She replaced the receiver and sat thinking, then picked it up and dialed Herb Caplan to ask a few questions. No, he told her, he wouldn't say it was terribly unusual. Most often a flicker of movement would occur within four or five days, but sometimes a little later. Eight days would put understandable strain on the mind of a healthy young woman. He'd have been nervous himself in her place, would have opted for the surgery. But now that they knew some function had been preserved, the prognosis was good for complete recovery, especially in view of her age and strength. Of course, there were cases that turned out quite differently, but if Enid was looking to call it a miracle, she'd do better to consider the way David's friend had landed on the surface she hit. "That young woman will surely look at wheelchair cases from now on and think, 'There but for the grace of God...'"

"...go I, " Enid said with him. "Yes."

"Amazing, our resilience and capacity to mend," the doctor said, "and faith plays no small part. But more amazing, I think, is the patient who'll never in this life be whole, and yet will trust. To me, *that* is a miracle."

Enid thanked him for his help, told him to give her love to Marjorie, and hung up. Sometimes a miracle, like beauty, she thought, is in the eye of the beholder. How should she behold this circumstance? How should she behold Leah? And what about her strange new son whose tongue was now as fluent as her own, who peppered his speech with *Ivrit*, and who would be seeing to his *father's business*—whatever in the world he meant by that—all over Israel?

Chapter 45

THE WINTER WAS PAST; the rains were over and gone. Flowers appeared on the earth, and the season of singing had come. It was May, and the media, having watched David through Keystone, Maccabean, and national competition for four years, wanted to know: Now that he had taken the NCAA all-around and been tapped for the Olympics trials, what was his first thought? Still in his sweats, David smiled but did not answer. "The Rabbi here," Mac proffered with a hand on David's shoulder, "will take a bit of a break to get married, but take my word, it won't cramp his style—quite the opposite." The reporters chuckled, teased, and congratulated David, and when the story hit the papers, the nickname stuck.

Leah had returned to take a job within thirty miles of University Park while she completed her thesis. The work's conclusions, based on quantities of case studies, demonstrated no strong correlation between, on one hand, the patient's ability to identify root causes of disfluency and cleanse away related anger, bitterness, and guilt, and on the other, his or her success in transferring and maintaining fluency; but David's case was not an isolated one. Leah would receive her master's degree on the same weekend that David received his bachelor's.

The wedding was planned for the third Sunday of June, little more than a month away. On the day that David took his last exam, he and Leah drove with his belongings to his home in Lansdale. They laughed and sang loud and silly songs that both remembered; they reveled in the glorious, sunny day, and in their freedom. Soon enough they would face the mission at hand: to be reconciled with Enid Rothman, who, feeling that her presence in a receiving line on June 17th would clearly imply approval, had said that she would not take part.

The betrothed spent Wednesday evening and Thursday morning in purely being themselves with Enid in the hope that she would realize their love for her, their love for each other, their love for the God of Abraham, Isaac—and Jacob. She gave them no measure of their progress. Thursday afternoon, David and Leah took time off together on the shore of the lake on the property's south side lowland. Beautiful, set among the trees, it was quiet, so peaceful. They settled on a wide, soft blanket in the sun and baked contentedly, exchanging only sleepy-sounding words.

A quarter-hour passed and Leah, never one to bask for long, sat up to take in all that was around her—forest, water, the air of spring. She picked up a plastic bottle, opened it, and smoothed lotion everywhere she wanted to brown, then turned to David, dozing on his back. She warmed the lotion in her hand and applied some to his nose, cheeks, and chin, already brown from daily runs outside.

"Mmmmm," he murmured drowsily.

She kissed her finger and touched it to his lips. "'My lover is radiant and ruddy,'" she said, smiling down, "'outstanding among ten thousand.'" He opened his eyes. "'His hair is wavy and black as a raven,'" she continued, smoothing lotion gently over his neck and onto his shoulders. "'His arms are rods of gold, set with chrysolite. ...His legs are pillars of marble....'"

"Leah," he said, raising his head, one eye closed. "Lover?"

"Song of Songs," she said, grinning. "The bride to the bridegroom."

He snatched her wrist and pulled her to him. "You, woman, are looking for trouble."

"'This is my lover, this is my friend, O daughters of Jerusalem.'" She was in search of a kiss, and he helped her find one. She said she was so into their life together, she didn't think of them as separate, even now. "Do you?"

"Get me thinking any more 'together,' I'll plead involuntary rape."

"Five weeks. I'm counting minutes."

He kissed her, quoting Solomon. "'Do not awaken love before it so desires.'"

"*Now* you tell me," she said, her mouth on his. He finished the kiss—well. Then, holding her head in his hands, he smiled a little smile that melted her, that made her not so sure where this was going. He picked her up and carried her to the water, walked in up to his waist, and let her down. She squealed and splashed until she found her footing. The water was too cold, but he disappeared beneath it and surfaced swimming toward the other shore. She stumbled back to the blanket laughing, dried her hair, and watched him pull himself the width of the lake, then turn and start back, shoulders glistening bronze in the water—right, left, right, left. When he stood and made his way to her, five weeks were a year. Breathing hard and dripping, he flopped on the blanket, and she handed him a towel. "I'm sorry," she said, laughing at them both behind contrition.

He shot her a look of reproach, then lay back and began to laugh, himself. "It didn't work." He roared in mock attack, lowering her too carefully to the blanket for a man out of control. He kissed her madly, and for good measure, not so madly, and then, for very good measure, quite seriously. She felt his cool, wet legs and body warm slowly, tantalizingly on her own, and the hardness of them sent a tremor through her. He kissed her neck, her chin, her mouth, as her fingers traced the clay of his shoulder and wove through the wet curl on the nape of his neck. A ray of sunlight gleamed golden on her ring—a floweret of small stones, curved to meet its twin not yet placed on her hand—and euphoria enfolded her. *I belong to my lover, and his desire is for me,* she thought. Song of beautiful Songs, parable of Messiah and his bride searching for and finding each other, reflection of the spirit in complete and perfect love.

The sun glinted off the ring. Complete—incomplete. Perfect—imperfect. The Leah who waited for the twin band called to the Leah who longed to give her love: Stop him. ...Stop him. Say his *name*. Suddenly, with a self-reprimanding gasp, he lay face up beside her, his hands beside his head declaring innocence. "I have to take you back."

She sat up sluggishly, rested her elbows on her knees, her head between her hands, and nodded dismally. "I know. To the lake."

He gave her that same smile, for Leah only, then slowly rose and pulled her to her feet. Taking the blanket for a cloak, he drew her inside. "Tomorrow, New York—a boat ride, whatever." He held her close as they walked up the long grade to the house. "Suzanne's at Jon's. What d'you say?"

Chapter 46

THE DAY WITH JON AND SUZANNE was of multiple value. Enid's parting words that morning had been that she would "never, till *HaMashiach* comes," see David through seminary, which to her meant never at all. Insolvency, David said, was breathing down his neck—to which Jonathan replied that no one could touch the trust fund.

"What...trust fund?"

"Yours," Jon said, confused, "the day you graduate. Your dad—"

"Will it see me through the year-and-a-half I can't cover on my own?" David asked urgently.

Jon chuckled and gave him a quick computation: "With tuition, say, at twelve-thou a year, plus housing and food, let's see— roughly...seven times."

David thrust a fist through the air and hooted, "Thank you, *Father!*" He kissed Leah soundly and asked if she'd meant what she said in the car. Smiling, she told him that she did, and he picked up the phone to change honeymoon plans. "He's still taking me places," David murmured as he dialed, "still making me feel like Number One. Thank you, God, thank you, thank you. ...Hello? I'd like to book two flights...."

Leah looked at Jonathan. His eyes were tender as she met them. She remembered calling Suzanne from her hospital bed to thank her and Jon for the flowers. Sue had said, "He loves you, too, just like a sister," and she had laughed and repeated, "Praise God, just like a sister."

Leah squeezed Sue's arm on her way to him. Taking David's hand in one of her own and Jon's in the other, she kissed him on the cheek and whispered, "Thank you, Jon—again."

❦

THE DRESS LEAH WORE ON THEIR DAY was imported by her father from Tiberias. It was styled and embroidered in the fashion of Israeli wedding dresses, white on white. Leah was too busy to nurture feelings of nervousness as the hour approached and so, in fact, had none. Suzanne, aglow in azure and in her imaginings of a wedding where all things were done perfectly, practiced the unveiling, trying not to alter Leah's hair. Suzanne's knight would be her partner today, a foretaste, both down the aisle and up it. In the abstaining Martin's place, Jonathan would be David's best man—a title Leah deemed no less than fitting.

The ring that would, within the hour, belong to David was in the way, tucked as it was into Suzanne's palm as she worked. She handed it to Andy. Leah glanced at her and was struck by how different Andy looked today, in her face, in the very way she carried herself. She knew the why; the degree was what surprised her. Because of height considerations, Matt would escort Andy, but in attitude of mind, her walk now excluded all but Rick. Cat, in the end, had refused to compromise Rick's friendship and had taken a job on the coast, in Oakland. But that was not the whole of it. In the weeks following Leah's accident and, in particular, those following her stay in Lansdale, Leah and Andy—a more humble and compassionate Leah and an Andy ready at last to listen—for the first time since they had known each other, talked. Today Andy understood Love; today she was living Love and, through it, living Life.

Suzanne took away the veil, and Dessa, Matt's diamond sparkling on her hand, refurbished Leah's hair, touching up the loosened wisps to remind them of their place. The bedroom door burst open and Paulette's seventeen-year-old Nicole, in blue, flew in. "Grandpa's outside," she said to Leah, breathless. "He wants to see you." Roseanne, blue-gowned as well and calmer, followed, saying there was time.

When Leah was ready, they admitted Pierre Beaumont. He saw her and, rapt, declared her radiant beyond an old man's words to tell; how he wished *Grand-maman* Josephine were here. He sat beside her, leaning close and speaking quiet French. There was, he said, a place about which he must tell her before she went away, a place where, he knew now, her destiny had long ago been sealed. As she might be aware, he said, in the time of his father, Jean Baptiste Beaumont, there had been much anti-Semitism in France, which caused some to recall with uneasiness the vicious purging of the Huguenots a few generations prior. So when Israel Katzar, Jean Baptiste's friend, left the French cavalry in 1883, the new civilian took his wife and young family to Palestine, to a place near Joppa where Baron Rothschild had only the year before helped establish a new settlement—Rishon le Zion. While he was living there, Israel befriended a young Russian Jew named Eliezer ben Yehuda, one of sixteen students who had survived a migration of 300 from Kharkov to found their own settlements. They had no money, no tools, only their own zeal to redeem the Land. These things Israel and Eliezer had in common, and they formed an iron bond. In Eliezer's house as the Ben Yehuda children grew, Israel heard a sound not heard in the Land in 2,000 years—the language of the Scriptures *spoken*. Even the little ones prattled in Hebrew, and soon Israel began to study it too.

Then came the months, Grandpa Pierre continued, when Palestine's orthodox establishment, believing the language of the Scriptures did not belong in the street, gave Eliezer no peace. They slandered him, accused him of heresy and treason, and finally, persuaded the Turks to arrest him. While Eliezer was imprisoned, Israel, in spite of his efforts to help, saw the family of his friend persecuted, deprived, indeed, starved. The children who survived clung to the Scriptures day by day—they *would* learn and use the language, they would. In those days of diligence and prayer, they learned something more than the tongue of the patriarchs: they saw that the messianic prophecies had been fulfilled with precision, in Yeshua of Nazareth. It was the oldest who came to Israel's village to tell him, and two months of study later, Israel saw that it was true.

"He wrote my father once," Pierre went on, "of the day fore-seen by Moses, Isaiah, and David when their people's blindness would be healed. He wrote that one night, in a half-dream of some kind, he saw Yeshua standing there on Zion with the thousands—and he knew he must convince his family of the truth. But Israel's wife refused to listen. She feared imprisonment and found no joy in their life in Rishon le Zion. When their youngest child was only two, Israel was indeed arrested. In prison, he took a fever and died, and his wife returned to Paris with the children. She lived to see all of them wed."

"The youngest child—my Grandma Josephine," Leah said in French, and Grandpa nodded.

"While she lived in our home as the widow Hausmann and, later, as my wife, I shared with her her father's discovery and his dream—and my Josephine believed. Can it be mere coincidence that you now return to the Land to open your people's eyes?"

"Pray for us," Leah said, taking his age-specked hands in hers. "We'll need all the courage of the Huguenots...and it will take time."

"Time is a form of grace," he said gently, "and grace must end. As it is closing for the Gentile, so it will, even for the Jew. May Israel see, through you, his vision come of age."

Chapter 47

MATT BEAUMONT STOOD BESIDE his mother's flower garden. His cousin Nicole and her classmate Brian were in song. The chairs were filled with friends from church, friends from campus, Beaumonts, and friends of Beaumonts. During the photographing of the groom and groomsmen, his brother Bernie had told Matt to worry later, and now he had the time. "Call me from Lydda," he had told David. Too fresh was the ordeal of his classmate, whose kidnapping, along with his bride's, had made front pages around the world—proof that honeymooners, much less Jews, were not exempt from terrorist madness.

"Israel is a *nation* of hostages," Bernie had whispered to counter Matt's argument and defend David's plans, "until they're told the ransom's paid." He was speaking in spiritual terms, which Matt understood quite well. He wasn't asking them not to go, but he wanted to worry, and worry he would.

"You call, you hear?" he repeated to David without disturbing his grin, and the photographer's shutter whirred.

Now it was nearly zero hour. Paddy Farrell stood in the trellised gateway, surveying. Matt waited to offer Claire his arm. Sheila Rothman sat alone in the second row on the groom's side. Enid, her mother-in-law, was nowhere to be seen. So David's kin have set him adrift, Matt thought. That's all Uncle Paddy needs: if Claire won't rise to the occasion, he'll lift her out of her little shoes. He watched Paddy lean down to Claire's ear. She stepped back looking, it seemed, for a place to think. Seeing Miriam standing on the porch with Antoine, she smiled in her direction, then took Matt's arm and hugged Peter as he gave her the order of service. "Groom's side, next to Sheila," she told Matt clearly.

Moments later, the procession began: Dessa and Evan, Nicole and Rick, Andy and Matt, Suzanne and Jon. Miriam and Antoine themselves were aglow as they, in the Jewish manner, escorted Leah toward David. With the party gathered, the young minister spoke. "This," he said, "is a day of beginnings. And so it was for the Lord Jesus on the day he attended a marriage festival and there began his ministry of power." Today, he told them, they were all gathered to witness the vows of David and Leah as they celebrated the world's earliest rite—instituted by God their creator and performed the first time by him. Thus it would become David and Leah, the minister said, to realize the sacred bonds by which they would be united and to take heed to their solemn vows. He told them they would find great joy in their marriage to the degree that they would be self-sacrificing, one to the other. Then he yielded his place to Rabbi Joseph Eppelman of Beth Yeshua, Miami, who charged the bride and groom to love and bond with each other as the Messiah loves and bonds with believers. "And now, who gives Leah Rachelle Beaumont to be married to David Jordan Rothman?" Antoine and Miriam replied, kissed their daughter, and gave her hand to David.

"Before the Omniscient God and in the presence of these witnesses," Uncle Joseph said, his deep voice resounding off the white front of Leah's home, "wilt thou, David Jordan Rothman, take Leah Rachelle Beaumont, here present, to be thy wedded wife? Wilt thou love and comfort her, honor and keep her, and in joy and sorrow, preserve with her this bond, holy and unbroken, until the coming of Yeshua, or God by death shall separate you?"

"I will," David said, and Leah saw the vowing in his eyes.

The same was asked of Leah and she squeezed the promise hard into his hand. "I will." David lifted the veil, and Suzanne laid it back—perfectly, Matt thought—behind Leah's shoulders.

"Your personal vows," said Rabbi Eppleman.

"My beautiful Leah," David said, still holding her with his eyes, "before God and these witnesses I pledge to you that I will marry once. You are my beloved; to you I give, without condition and for all time, my steadfast love. You have led me to see the Glory of Israel, the Light of the World, and according to his teaching, I will cherish and protect you as long as God gives me breath. I pray he will grant us, together, a long and fulfilling life. Yet, please, my Rachel, know...that by your assent to spend your life with me— *whatever* God's plan for us—you have made me supremely, and forever, happy." He kissed her hand and said softly, "I love you."

"David, man after God's own heart," Leah said, holding his hands fast, "because you love the Lord above all else, above all other persons, names, and purposes, I love you with all of my being. I know that it is through your love for him that you are able to love me more deeply than I deserve or comprehend. I promise you, Beloved, that I will always be at your side to uphold you with encouragement and prayer. It is with joy that I submit to your leading. God has taught me, himself and through you, that I must never quench the Holy Spirit in your life or in mine—that he will guide. Wither thou goest, therefore, I will go; wither thou lodgest, I will lodge. Together, in the power of our God, we will see the eyes of our people opened...to Yeshua HaMashiach." She touched his face. "May our hearts be young and at his call, until his kingdom comes."

The young minister stood gazing. He swallowed, stepped forward as Rabbi Eppleman relinquished his place, and asked David what token he gave in acknowledgement of these vows. Jonathan handed the ring to David, the symbolism of which act was not lost on certain members of the party. Matt tried to imagine Jon's thoughts. He guessed that Leah, standing where she alone could see his face, might know them. As she offered her hand to David, Matt noticed that she moved almost imperceptibly to her right. He saw her smile and knew that Jon could now see her lady in waiting; he watched Sue blush, but Leah watched the band of flowerets that David placed.

"Leah, do you, in evidence of your love and sincerity, accept this ring?" the pastor asked.

She cupped a hand to David's. "I do."

"This ring is a perfect circle of precious metal," the pastor said. "The circle is a symbol of completeness and an emblem of eternity. The precious metal is that which has been tested and proven true. It is a fitting emblem of your love for each other and your everlasting bond with the Lord." David and Leah exchanged a glance that Matt could not decipher; there was something in what the man said that had surprised them and made them smile. "In the test of time," he concluded, "like gold in the fire, may your love and faith prove true and endure until death do you part." He asked Leah for a token to acknowledge her vows.

In quiet desperation, Suzanne turned to Andy and whispered, "Do you have it?" Andy placed the ring carefully in Suzanne's hand. There were smiles all around, and Matt thought, *The classic goof. We all survived, and suddenly I'm more relaxed than I've felt in weeks.* Leah slid the ring onto David's finger, and the pastor asked for his acceptance, then placed his own hands over theirs. They knelt as he prayed, received the bread and wine, and heard his blessing, his pronouncement that they were, in the pure and holy bonds of wedlock, man and wife—and those whom God had joined together, all present heard the pastor warn with considerable spark in his eye, let no one put asunder. David needed no reminder to kiss his bride.

It was, however, Bernie's prerogative when they had left the canopy to point out to him and Leah its posts of cedar and cypress, representing, in Israeli fashion, their uniting in marriage. The cedar was from the juniper David's father had planted for him in Lansdale, Bernie told them, but he and Roseanne had brought the cypress from Florida at Mrs. Rothman's request. He had told her he'd take care of it, including the purchase price, since Leah had no tree. But she could not, she had said, give her new daughter a gift that hadn't cost her anything.

Chapter 48

ALL DAY THE MEDITERRANEAN BREEZE had moved the warm air of Bat Yam, refreshing the bathers and others come to rest and recreate. While the sun was still a half-globe on the horizon, its fire reaching wide to hold the day, lights of white and maize and blue began to mark the restaurants below. With a lingering last embrace, the twilight vanished.

In pearl-white chemise and peignoir, Leah stood on the highest balcony of the hotel, breathing soft sea air. Tomorrow, she would meet Jess and Tova, and, God willing, they would make some long-range plans. Tonight... Tonight was for savoring nectars they had gathered from the Land, that kibbutz where they were welcomed in Hebrew tinged with Dutch, the place where roses bloomed and avocados grew. Herzliya, where David had told the Abramowiczes of his plan to set up in Ruth's name a memorial scholarship fund for the study of the Hebrew Scriptures, and they, knowing his beliefs, had blessed his "house." Haifa, where, as frightening as it might have been to know that terror reigned so near, on Beirut's airstrip, they two had felt the guarding hand of God. The vast green Valley of Jezreel, where someday, they both knew, Yeshua would end war forever with the sword of the Spirit, the word of his mouth. The Arabah, site of David's baptism, and his Lord's. Bayt Lahm, Bethlehem, birthplace of King David and in God's timing, of Yeshua, the Lion of Judah. Jerusalem, where the Lion had died as the Lamb and risen again, and Leah prayed for strength to follow him. Rishon le Zion, her ancestral home, with its productive vineyards and wineries, now home to more than 92,000....

Wine. At the close of his last Seder, Yeshua had taken the cup and told the twelve, "Drink of it, all of you; for this is my blood of the covenant, which is poured out for many for the forgiveness of sins. I tell you I shall not drink again of this fruit of the vine until that day when I drink it new with you in my Father's kingdom."

"In my Father's kingdom," Leah thought, at the wedding of the Lamb. You are beautiful, Lord, to ransom us with your spotless life so that we may be your body and your bride, one with you in mind and soul and spirit. We love you, Lord—and thank you for the analog of marriage way down here, on Earth.

The stars had lit the soft, clear night when Leah turned to let herself inside. She unclasped at the back of her neck a tiny pendant and held it in her hand. It was an objet d'art, an auroch in profile, its two horns as one—like a unicorn—ensign of her mother's tribe, of Joseph, and so, as David led her to recall, a symbol of Yeshua, too, in type. It had no wreath, David had said, because Ephraim could not yet stand to place the crown. But someday, God himself would see to it; every knee would bow, and Ephraim and Judah, the chosen Jews and their Messiah, would be one.

She laid the necklace on the dresser next to his, a delicate polished scepter through the six-sided star. He stood in white pajama bottoms, shaving; his structure, even slouching, made her smile. That he shaved at this hour pleased her. There is enough pain in our lives without our seeking it, she thought. She turned to watch the stars, to find familiar patterns in the sky.

Pain. She hardly recalled the first night's, but his words she would remember all her life: "Do you understand what it means to me that our marriage bed is undefiled? It's beyond price— the wedding gift no one else can give us or ever take from us." Sweet consummation of the law of Earth and Heaven; she was his and he was hers alone.

The room went dim and immediately the stars gave tender light. She felt his arm encircle her waist and draw her back against him; his fingers gently swept aside the hair above her ear, and desire pulsed through her. He kissed her neck and held her long, then turned her to himself. She saw the depth of love in those dark eyes and let her soul respond in love to his. He lifted her and kissed her, then paused before the window, clear, suspended. "*Adonai*," he said, low, into the heavens, "your children, *Abba*, have come home."

Acknowledgments

To my friends in the synagogue and in the church, I owe a word of sincere thanks. There would be nothing to say, were it not for the realities of their lives, their own stories. Some of these friends, both long-time and new, also kindly contributed information to my research.

My earnest and enduring interest in the grist out of which *Beloved Dissident* is milled would not have been enough without painstaking review of the manuscript by people of expertise in several fields, the cooperation and sensitivity of my editors, Alan Tannenbaum and Kathi Mills, and Kathi's creative and meticulous editing.

I thank Gene Whettstone for his careful reading of the segments regarding gymnastics and for doing me the honor of bonding with the protagonists in those segments. Mr. Whettstone's classic way of rewarding virtuosity on the gym floor is intentionally preserved in this novel despite its setting in the mid-1980s, a slightly later timeframe than his tenure as head coach at Penn State. Gene's continued involvement in PSU gymnastics has been of great benefit not only to gymnasts and fans in general, but to me, personally, as both a fan and a writer.

The staffs of Penn State's Speech and Hearing Clinic and Department of Speech Communication made me welcome as I researched therapeutic procedures for persons suffering disfluency, and I thank particularly Dan Tullos (whose role as a Ph.D. candidate in the mid-eighties mirrored Bill Hurland's) for his careful review.

I am grateful to Stanley Yoder, M.D., who thoughtfully explained to me the orthopedic conditions and treatments that were relevant to the injury described in this book; he also edited the written text pertaining to it.

M. Kathleen Bell reviewed the riding sequences and gave me good advice, as she always has.

I believe I owe my personal style to the candor with which Prof. Robert C. S. Downs critiqued my writing, and to his encouragement.

Steven Held, D.M.D., of State College, Pennsylvania, and David Decker of Tel Aviv, Israel, supplied answers to my hard questions. Shelley Feldman Haugh of Seattle, Washington, and Ilana Inspektor of Beersheva, Israel, reviewed the manuscript in its entirety, from quite disparate points of view. Their services were invaluable.

Marlene Stearns pointed me toward the right publisher. May God bless her.

To my son, Asst. Prof. Harry G. West, whose teaching interests encompass world affairs and cultural anthropology, I owe at least part of my diligence in research and the type of detail I chose to provide. He was as tough—and as encouraging—as Prof. Downs, and I needed them both.

My daughter, Anita West Kalajainen, true to her nursing profession, carried balm to my spirit during the production of this work by enjoying her "read," feeling friendship with my characters, and contributing helpful comments.

My husband, Harry H. West, a civil engineer and professor emeritus of the same at Penn State, provided the analytical mind that caught errors in my logistics and in the details of my settings, apart from "prosaic license." He was also the undergirder of my morale and my biggest fan, despite my distraction in favor of the book, as I wrote. I thank him, too, for adopting Leah Beaumont as his second daughter as he edited.

To God, who is the Author of all truth, to my family—including son-in-law Dennis Kalajainen and grandchildren Paul, Amy, and Mark, who love to read—and to the late Anna Light

Smith, without whose prompting I might not have begun writing fiction, I dedicate *Beloved Dissident*.

Laurel J. West
State College, Pennsylvania

References

Bibles

Leah's French Testament: *Le Livre*, Living Bibles Inerna't'l, Editions Farel, Fontenay-sous-Bois Cedex, France. Copyright 1980. All rights reserved. Quoted: John 5:39; also 5:39–47, literal translation by Laurel West.

The Bible of David, his rabbi, and the street singers: *The Holy Scriptures, Revised in Accordance with Jewish Tradition and Modern Biblical Scholarship*, Hebrew Publishing Co., New York. Copyright 1930, 1939. Quoted or excerpted: Joshua 23:10; Amos 9:11–15 (paraphrased); Judges 2:20, 22; Jeremiah 23:3, 4; Jeremiah 23:5, 6; Joshua 23:10–13b; Isaiah 32:4; Deuteronomy 6:4, 5; Isaiah 52:13–53:12; Jeremiah 32:31; Psalm 22:16c; Deuteronomy 18:15; Jeremiah 31:31–33; Zechariah 3:8c, 9c; Psalm 68:5; Hosea 9:13, 16; 2 Samuel 7:1–11 (paraphrased); Isaiah 11:13.

The Bible at the church and in Leah's and Evan's memory: *The Holy Bible, Authorized King James Version, Scofield Reference Edition*, edited by Rev. C. I. Scofield, D. D. Oxford University Press, New York. Copyright 1909, 1917; copyright renewed, 1937, 1945 by Oxford University Press, New York, Inc. All rights reserved. Quoted or excerpted: Jeremiah 16:14–16c; Luke 18:38–43; John 12:12–19; Luke 11:9, 10; Matthew 5:48 (paraphrased); Deuteronomy 32:21c; Genesis 49:17; Luke 12:32 Genesis 48:18, 19 (paraphrased); Jeremiah 31:9c; Matthew 16:25; John 16:33.

The Bible of the Good Friday program: *The Holy Bible, Revised Standard Version*, Thomas Nelson & Sons, New York, and Thomas Nelson & Sons, Limited, Toronto, Canada and Edinburgh, Scotland. Old Testament Section, Copyright 1952 by Division of Christian Education of the National Council of the Churches of Christ in the United States of America; New Testament Section, Copyright 1946 by the same. Quoted: Psalm 118:22. Allusion to: John 18:1–14, 18–25a, 27b–40; 19:1–19. Quoted: John 19:15–19.

Translations from Jesse's and Tova's Bibles, and Leah's homecoming passage. Jesse's: Ibid. Zechariah 12:10b (excerpted); Tova's: Ibid. John 2:19–21 (paraphrased); 1 Corinthians 3:16; 2 Corinthians 6:16; Leah's: Ibid. Matthew 26:27b–29.

The Bible at the Farrells' home: *The Holy Bible, New International Version ®, NIV ®.* Copyright 1973, 1978, 1984 by International Bible Society. Used by permission of Zondervan Publishing House, Grand Rapids, Michigan. All rights reserved. Quoted or excerpted: Revelation 7:5–8; Matthew 24:9; Matthew 24:29; Luke 21:25; Luke 21:33–35; Revelation 2:7b, 17b, 26; 3:11, 12; 21:22–24, 27; 22:5.

Source Book for Good Friday reading: *The Episcopal Book of Common Prayer (Psalter), 1977* edition, Charles Mortimer Guilbert, Custodian. Church Hymnal Corporation, New York. Quoted: Psalm 22:1, 7, 8, 14–18.

Leah's reference to Nancy Drew
The Nancy Drew Mystery Series, by Carolyn Keene (a collective pseudonym). Copyright 1930 to the present by various publishers, such as: Grosset & Dunlap, a subsidiary of Penguin Books, Putnam Publishing Group, Kirkwood, New York; Demco Media, Old Tappan, New Jersey; Simon & Schuster, Madison, Wisconsin.

Leah's gift book
Wanderings: Chaim Potok's History of the Jews. Copyright 1978 by Chaim Potok. Fawcett Crest Books, CBS Educational and Professional Publishing, a division of CBS Inc., by arrangement with Alfred A. Knopf, Inc., 1980.

DAVID'S PRAYER AT THE WAILING WALL
Prayer for restoration of the Jews from the Diaspora to Zion, traditional Jewish liturgy.

SONGS USED BY PERMISSION
Excerpted or paraphrased: "I Will Praise Thee" and "The Light of the World," Stuart Dauermann, composer. Copyright 1982.

DAVID'S ALLUSION TO *FIDDLER*
Fiddler on the Roof, a Norman Jewison Film, The Mirisch Production Company, screenplay by Joseph Stein, adapted for the screen by Tom Abbot; from the stories of Sholom Aleichem, by special arrangement with Arnold Perl. Copyright 1971, MGM/UA.

WEDDING CEREMONY
Adapted by permission from: *The Pastor's Handbook*. Copyright 1978, 1986 by Christian Publications, Camp Hill, Pennsylvania.